VALLEY OF THE TALL GODS
AND OTHER TALES FROM THE PULPS

VALLEY OF THE TALL GODS
AND OTHER TALES FROM THE PULPS

E. HOFFMANN PRICE

WILDSIDE PRESS

CONTENTS

VALLEY OF THE TALL GODS

I.

The Thibetan Scroll

M c TAVISH, the grey-haired Scot with the face like a grave digger's spade, sucked his curved pipe.

"Mr. Hamlin, even if this import business don't interest ye," he grumbled, "ye might pretend it's important. Now will ye get yersel' to worrk and check in those goods from Karachi?"

Red Hamlin chuckled good humoredly and shrugged. He did not blame McTavish; but the side alleys of Kabul were more fun than the Afghan American Trading Corporation ever could be.

"Don't worry, Mac. You can depend on me, I'll tend to it. Anyway, getting acquainted with the country is part of my job."

"And keeping an eye on Otto Kraft is part of your worrk!" The crusty old fellow spat noisily and hunched his bald head and broad shoulders back over his desk. "Didna someone tell ye *he's* in the import business, too?"

Red Hamlin's blitheness faded for a moment as he walked out. Kraft, with his *pince nez* spectacles and impressive manner, undeniably handsome and insolent face had fairly well monopolized Irene Gray, who seemed to fancy serious-minded men. But she'd wake up. He hoped she would.

Hamlin turned down a gloomy street where mangy dogs yapped at his heels and sullen camels, loaded with panniers that almost blocked the way, sent him scrambling for cover.

Tall Afghans and shifty-eyed Tadjiks regarded him with the contempt of true believers for any infidel.

Beggars, crouched in offal-heaped corners, whined in the name of Allah for a few *pice.* He tossed them coins, and knew that for thanks they cursed him, so God would forgive them for accepting an infidel's bounty. But Hamlin didn't blame the poor devils for cursing someone.

It was raw and sordid and it reeked to the stark blue sky just visible between the overhanging balconies which even at noon cut the light to a murky gloaming; yet Kabul had its glamour. Hamlin chuckled tolerantly, thinking of his father who had exiled him to this ancient city to acquire some common sense, and learn the export business under the guidance of hard-headed old Angus McTavish, the local manager. The joke was on dad!

He loitered in the rug bazaar, where glaring mockeries of the ancient weaves of Herat hung by their fringes. He detoured into the louse bazaar, where second-hand goods of all kinds were being hawked by sharp-eyed merchants.

"Antikas, huzoor!" they wheedled, having learned from Arab traders that these infidel pigs paid insane prices for a bit of broken pottery, or a corroded bronze coin.

Kabul was a heady town for a crack-brained chap whose broad shoulders and hard fists made him fearless wherever he went. The dry, racking cough of hasheesh smokers, the whining, nasal drone of a Pathan chanting to a *rebek;* the clamorous shouting of the slave that cleared the way for a woman whose great dark eyes smoldered through the slits of a veil that hid her face as effectually as her shapeless cloak hid her figure — what a town!

And it would be still more of a town if Irene Gray had not been thoroughly convinced that Hamlin was an amiable idiot. A sweet girl, Irene, even if a bit too serious-minded, sticking to that man-killing job and trying to help the one overworked doctor who was filling her late father's place at the government hospital until a surgeon could come from the outside.

In that murky tangle of bazaars, Hamlin was unaware of the day's waning. He had quite forgotten that time and duty existed when the ingratiating Hindu hailed him in English:

"Look, *sahib*. Extremely old and rare document from Buddhist monastery in Thibet. Very cheap, to you."

It was emblazoned on damask silk, cream-white with age, soiled yet splendid: a scroll wound about a rod with carved agate knobs. The script was strange; fine and black, with illumination in blue and scarlet and gilt. It must be Uighur, the father of modern Turkish, which is written in an alphabet borrowed from the Arabs, and distorted in the adaptation.

"Look, *sahib*," whispered the Hindu. "The popular robber who was only a few days ago blown from the mouth of a cannon brought this to Kabul. Very extremely precious, *sahib*."

Hamlin shuddered. It was gruesome, that old custom of tying a criminal to the muzzle of a cannon. Then he fingered the scroll; and that fascinating, illegible thing fairly begged him to take it. This was no fake. He could not read Uighur, but the chief surgeon, Dr. Henley, was a scholar. What an excuse to see Irene, and prove that he was really serious-minded — at times.

"Only a thousand *rupees, sahib*," smirked the Hindu.

"You're crazy!" snapped Hamlin. "Ten rupees."

They bargained. The red-headed American was learning rapidly. He spat, looked disgusted; the Hindu wailed and beat his breast, and came down a hundred. Hamlin came up five.

Then something pierced his intentness. He shivered involuntarily. Standing within a pace of him was a man strange even in Kabul. His feet were bare as his shaven head. One shoulder was exposed by the arrangement of his saffron-colored robe, and he held a small wooden bowl. A Buddhist pilgrim offering the world a chance to acquire mcrit by giving him alms.

Automatically, Hamlin tossed him a *rupee*. The monk smiled, and his flat Mongol face was endowed with dignity that accorded with the riddle of his slanting eyes. "No, friend," he said in stilted English. "Let me give to you, some advice, sir."

Hamlin blinked. "Advice?"

"Yes. That scroll brings no man any good."

Hamlin's stomach was uncomfortable. He had, without intent, witnessed the execution of the bandit. From the tail of his eye, he noticed a small, yellow-haired man with a face like the profile on a Grecian coin half crouching in the shadows of a vacant stall; his eyes glittered blue steel, his young face was tense. Without knowing why, Hamlin became stubborn.

"Sold!" he snapped at the Hindu, and flung him a wad of bills. Then he challengingly regarded the monk, but the yellow-haired man had vanished when Hamlin's glance again sought him.

"Let me buy from you," proposed the Buddhist. "I gave you a gift, and it was declined. Let me pay you to accept my blessing. I came all the way from Lhassa to recover that scroll."

"What's it good for?" demanded Hamlin. "Not that I'll sell it. I don't want a profit."

"It is good for —" The monk's eyes seemed to film, then brighten. They were startling, cryptic eyes, troubling and sharp. He came very close, and whispered: "You are wise and know what I am. You know I can not lie to you, or any man. I am Tsong Kapa, a person of no consequence. But I came to acquire merit by recovering that scroll. It has cost many lives, and it will cost many more. But the secret I will not tell — not the secret of the Tall Gods."

"I'm not scared!" Hamlin, however, was not too certain.

Tsong Kapa smiled. "There is not enough fear in you. Nor is there any greed in you. So you should let me take it." He became very earnest. "I beg of you, let me pay. I can. Poor as I am in person, I can get money for you."

"Sorry," said Hamlin, amiable but decisive.

"Peace to you, and to all living creatures!" Tsong Kapa's gesture made it a benediction. He turned to go, but paused and added: "We are all bound to the wheel, in this life and in the lives that follow. There is no evil but that which you draw upon yourself."

Hamlin tried for a superior smile, but failed. Then he hurried toward the customs house, where goods just shipped up from Karachi were waiting his attention.

The gates, however, were closed, and the sun was setting below the hills that rim the valley. Chill descended swiftly, and Hamlin hailed a rickety *tonga* to carry him to his quarters where hatchet-faced Yakub, his Afridi servant, would be cooking curry over a charcoal fire.

That evening Hamlin drove to the Government Hospital whose European architecture was incongruous against the squat, mud cubes of the surrounding houses. Irene's hours were all around the clock; but luckily, she was in her quarters, and Sita Deva, her shapely Hindu *ayah*, admitted him.

Business-like Otto Kraft's voice, however, told him that the evening was spoiled from the start. He was already on the job, and Hamlin grimaced as he followed the sleek-haired maid and her softly tinkling anklets.

"Why, Red — why aren't you out in disguise tonight?" Irene's mock surprise, and the brightening welcome of dark eyes slightly tinged with weariness almost neutralized Kraft's presence.

"I've been at it all afternoon," grinned Hamlin. Every time he saw Irene, he wondered anew how anyone could be quite so lovely. Neither her prim white uniform or the cap that all but concealed her soft black hair could keep her from being wholly sweet and alluring. Then, after he and Kraft had exchanged nods and mutual, silent contempt, he went on: "Dr. Henley busy?"

"Terribly," she answered. "I ought to be helping him, right now." A trace of weariness made the corners of her generous mouth droop; but only that, and the determined tilt of her chin hinted that she was shouldering half the woes of Kabul. Then, flashing the tall, blond German a more than friendly glance, she continued, "But Otto insisted I ought to steal enough time for a drive out on the plain."

That told Hamlin where he stood. She liked him, plenty; but only as an irresponsible kid, in spite of his being fully twenty-four, which was at least a year or two older than Irene.

"Mind giving this to the doc?" He offered her the scroll. "I mean, so he can tell you what it's all about. Picked it up in the bazaar, and not in disguise. Odd. Kind of fascinating —"

Then he fumbled, freezing from Kraft's superior stare.

"I hope," Kraft condescendingly cut in, "that you did not pay more than a few *rupees* for it. The markets are full of trash."

"That's not just a bazaar specialty!" snapped Hamlin. " 'Night, Irene."

And in a moment, he was back on street; one of the few wide enough for modern traffic. He frowned at the old red Mercedes that would soon be whirling Irene out into the moon glamour beyond the walls of Kabul, then decided to walk home instead of waiting for a *tonga*. It was not yet nine, so he would not need the lantern that law abiding pedestrians are required to carry as evidence of honest purpose when abroad at night.

But he had not gone far when he felt that lanterns should be required right after sunset. Someone was stalking him; he felt it as surely as any animal senses a beast of prey. He glanced back, and saw two vague, robed figures. In the half-gloom, they made him think of the newly dead seeking a place to haunt. He remembered the intent scrutiny of the yellow-haired Kafir in the market, that afternoon, and the monk's restrained eagerness.

That set him wondering as he approached the next side street. He was now considerably ahead of those ominous shapes in the rear, but someone was a short distance ahead of him, loitering. As he turned into the cross street, Hamlin caught a glimpse of the solitary prowler, doubling back with suspicious aimlessness, as though disguising his intent to follow.

FOR A MOMENT, Hamlin was lost in the shadows of over-hanging balconies. Before and behind him was a ribbon of moon silver in whose center was the narrow stream that gurgled down the street. No one entering the block could see him. He skirted the wall, and felt a cleft scarcely two feet wide. It led into a high smelling space between a pair of three-story buildings. Hamlin sidestepped, and waited.

Presently, feet were squashing in the muck. The man who had doubled back ploughed past him, unaware of Hamlin's presence. His hair was yellow, and the profile of his white face left no doubt that that was the Kafir from the bazaar.

Later, the other two came by, Silent and sinister. They must be the rear guard which, failing to pocket Hamlin, were cautiously carrying on, hoping to reset their trap. The American, finally venturing out of his hideout, grinned in anticipation of the joke.

But what happened was better than he had hoped. Someone cried out, wrathful and tense. Steel twinkled; mud sucked and squashed as men shifted for attack and defense. They were gasping, snarling; blades snicked and clashed.

"Sweet! They bushwhacked their blond buddy! Opened by mistake."

He relished that for a split second. Then he knew that the Kafir was being attacked. The error should by now have been exposed. Two to one was rotten, in any part of the world, and the little mountaineer's intent interest in Hamlin's purchase, that afternoon, made him more than just a man facing robbery and death. So on more scores than one, it was Hamlin's business. He stretched long legs down the street.

The fight was pretty while it lasted. The Kafir, like a cornered tomcat defying a pair of dogs, plied his own blade but his breath groaned and wheezed as he desperately fought. Then Hamlin landed with fists and feet. He stamped one assailant face down into the muck; a blade raked him, but he parried the thrust, and drove a heavy fist into a face that would never thereafter be the same.

Once the two lay groaning and twitching. Hamlin caught the Kafir, who gurgled, coughed, tried to talk. He was cut up, but very much alive. Hamlin said in Pushtu: "Easy, friend. Wait till I get you to the light."

The Kafir relaxed, and Hamlin carried him bodily to the Street. There he twisted a crude tourniquet to stop the dangerous bleeding at the fellow's elbow, told him to hold his hand to his temple to keep pressure on that artery. Then, Hamlin got the Kafir to a *tonga*, and hurried to the hospital.

Irene was not in when he arrived. An orderly took charge of the Kafir. And Hamlin, driving home, wondered how much was coincidence, and how much was design in that three-cornered tangle.

"That scroll. No damn doubt!" he told himself. "I wanted it. The monk wanted it. The Kafir had an eye on us all. He tailed me. Two others tailed him."

He sighed wearily, muttered a good night curse for Kraft, and waited for sleep to overcome the ache of his grazed ribs.

II.

Murder

THE NEXT morning, Hamlin ploughed into his desk and cleared it in record time. His paper work was completed shortly before noon. Then, bound for the customs house, he stopped at the hospital to see how the wounded Kafir was getting along. The sooner he got the answer to that riddle, the better.

Near the entrance was a broad-shouldered man in crimson uniform of European cut. He was on horse, and a mounted attendant held a gilded parasol over the dignitary's turbaned head. This was Dost Ali, high in the Amir's favor. He beamed, twisted his black mustache as he watched the soldiers who were marching a prisoner toward the city gate; and as the captive spat and cursed him, Dost Ali's smile broadened.

An orderly ushered Hamlin into the ward room. There Irene met him, forestalled his inquiry.

"His name is Jerjis," she said, "and he's from some outlandish spot way beyond the Chawak Pass. He was weak from loss of blood, and he spoke a mixture of Pushtu and some language none of us could understand. But he gave me this. He said it was for you. No, you can't see him. He's sleeping. But in a few days, he'll be ready for more brawls."

As Hamlin fingered the dirty little leather pouch Irene handed him, she went on: "Red, you might have been killed, interfering in that fight."

"Shucks, darling, I was just curious."

"That's just your trouble. You ought to be at work, and here you are, very much worried about Jerjis."

"You're all wrong," he protested. "It was a gorgeous chance to see you."

"You know more about riots and street fights in Kabul," she reproved, making a total failure of trying to be severe, "than you do about the Afghan-American Trading Company."

"Sure, I do," he admitted. "Love riots, fights, and — well, you, when you're not lecturing."

And then the leather pouch poured two golden coins into his palm. The bust of the king struck on them was very clear and sharp. They had the patina of ages, and it took no expert to know that for centuries no man's hand had touched them; not until Jerjis had dug into some buried hoard to finance his trip to Kabul.

"Oh — precious!" Irene exclaimed.

"Precious?" echoed Hamlin, voice trembling. "They're *staters*. I've seen pieces like that in museums. Alexander the Great might have spent them on his march to India. Good Lord! Don't keep that fellow full of morphine any longer than you have to."

A cannon shot shook the city, made the windows rattle. Irene gasped, and Hamlin instinctively whirled. The blast had come from the knoll just outside the walls. Something thumped to the roof, and then slid into the street, a floor below.

From where he stood, Hamlin could see all too clearly what had landed: a man's arm. Afghan justice had blown another criminal from the mouth of a cannon. He gulped, caught Irene's hand, but not in time to keep her from seeing. Her cream-colored skin went white as her skirt.

"I'm going back to work." He made conversation.

"Wait — I forgot —" She hurried to the desk and withdrew an envelope.

"Dr. Henley translated a bit of that scroll. But he's been terribly busy."

WHEN HE reached the street, he saw Dost Ali, splendid on his Turkoman horse, smiling as he lowered the pair of binoculars. The execution must have been entirely to his taste. Then the Afghan ceremoniously bowed and greeted in Oxford English. "Good afternoon, Mr. Hamlin. Charming day, what?"

"Yeah, great," grunted Hamlin. "Nice view, too."

Presently he was in the customs house courtyard, a walled enclosure jammed with bales and crates, camels and donkeys, uniformed officials, traders who cursed in a dozen languages. Dust thickened the air until the scurrying shapes were black silhouettes dancing among spices from India, silks from Turkestan, bundles of rawhide and dried apricots from Persia.

In the midst of the turmoil was a pyramid of packing cases from Karachi. Nearby stood an official, sweating and peevish. He clutched a sheaf of manifests and declarations awaiting the importer's signature. But a squint-eyed Hindu caught Hamlin's sleeve and whined: *"Sahib,* the kerosene. I have orders awaiting —"

"I'm sorry, Ram Lal," protested Hamlin, "but I'll have to take it into stock first before I can turn any over to you."

The official booted him to one side, but Ram Lal came back wailing. "But, *sahib,* see — I have begged the Presence to set my lot aside, ready for me to take as soon as you sign."

"How about it, Hussayn Mirza?" wondered Hamlin.

The Afghan official shrugged and offered him the declaration to sign. He said, *"Sahib,* certify that it is kerosene, and it is nothing to me."

Hamlin scribbled, yelled at Ram Lal, and watched his half dozen assistants shouldering the cases of fuel. One was leaking; doubtless the Hindu would put in a claim for two cans instead of one; but Hamlin was busy with his own employees.

And it was not until the three bearded officials and a chief inspector approached that Hamlin realized that something was wrong. Following them came a pair of soldiers, who were booting Ram Lal until he howled in Bengali. Two others had the case of kerosene, which they set down and pried open with bayonets.

"Sahib," thundered the chief inspector, "this is strange fuel you import. Smell it, please."

One whiff sufficed. The water-white liquid was *raki,* a blistering brandy, which like all alcoholic drinks was prohibited to True Believers; though its importation for sale to European residents was permitted.

"This entire consignment will be impounded," continued the outraged inspector, shouting down Hamlin's protests. "Smuggling, filing false declarations, and delivering that accursed stuff to a Hindu pig to tempt honest Moslems."

Hamlin was not under arrest; this mess involved the company. Nearby, a tall, blond man was wrangling with a group of officials: Otto Kraft, about to get an okay on his company's goods. Tuning in on the disturbance, the German chortled, *"Ach,* Mr. Hamlin, you should not confuse kerosene with *Schnapps,* eh?"

Mr. Hamlin grinned amiably, plucked Mr. Kraft's *pince nez* spectacles from his prominent nose, then knocked him end for end, leaving him beautifully centered in a ring of goatskin bags filled with rancid tallow.

The unexpected move had astounded Kraft.

"You damn' squarehead," stormed Hamlin, grin now gone, "if I could prove you monkeyed with that kerosene, I'd knock you borey-eyed!"

He stalked toward the compound gate; and it was not until he reached the street that he realized that in warning Kraft, he had robbed himself of any chance to prove his suspicions — which he'd have to do, or leave Kabul by request.

AT THE VERY best, a heavy fine would be levied against the company. The only other out was to have the influential Dost Ali intercede with the Amir; and that would be expensive.

Before telling McTavish of the disaster, Hamlin wanted to think it out at home.

He had little appetite for the pungent curry that Yakub, his tall, hatchet-faced Afridi servant prepared. Though convinced that he had been the victim of a conspiracy, Hamlin realized that his own position would be clear if he had paid strict attention to duty. He might even have noted that the leakage from the case of fuel had been *raki* and not kerosene. The glamour of Kabul and its fantastic streets now left a brown taste.

The rapacious Afghan officials would levy a fine heavy enough to allow graft for all, and still leave enough as a legitimate penalty to go to the Amir's treasury. If Kraft actually were involved, the Teuton would see that the demands were ruinous.

"No way," Hamlin finally concluded. "I can take the rap myself — it's addressed to the company."

HE HATED to face McTavish, but there was no way out. Thus, a few moments later, he was following Yakub, who carried the lantern. The Afridi's belt bristled with knives, and he carried a stout staff, but Hamlin was unarmed.

A foreigner had better be robbed than shoot a true believer in defense of his wallet.

The dour Afridi stalked on ahead. He had the mountaineer's swinging stride, so that Hamlin, despite his stature, had difficulty in keeping up. And Yakub, though he moved rapidly, probed the shifting shadows of the low archways that pierced the mud walls on either side of the narrow street. When he reached McTavish's door, in a more savory quarter of the city, he cat-footed to the massive panel, after a preliminary scrutiny of the archway.

He stood, tense and listening. The sudden out-thrust of his beard marked the tightening of his jaw. He shifted his staff to his left hand, caught Hamlin's wrist.

"All is not well — do not knock!" he warned.

From within came a vague stirring, and a muffled groan. Yakub gestured. The door, which should have been barred, was an inch ajar. From far back in the house came a man's wrathful exclamation. Hamlin shouldered past Yakub and flung the door open. The cautious Afridi followed, now that his master had recklessly taken the lead.

The sounds of a struggle guided Hamlin toward the Scot's living room at the end of the hall from the vestibule. He stumbled over a man who lay huddled on the tiles, and by the light of Yakub's lantern, caught a fleeting glimpse of McTavish's Hindu servant. His turban was unwound, and his face was bleeding.

The fellow was twitching and writhing — either dying, or recovering consciousness.

When Hamlin reached the living room he saw that McTavish and a red-bearded man were grappling for possession of the latter's knife.

"Hang on!" shouted Hamlin, lunging. But he slipped on the blood-splashed tiles, and instead of tackling the manager's assailant, he landed in a tangle of tramping feet, upsetting the pair.

McTavish yelled, snatched a decanter that had been knocked down in the struggle. The blow glanced, shattering against a chair and drenching Hamlin with brandy. Blinded, he could not see what followed.

McTavish groaned, and Hamlin lashed out, hoping to trip the assassin.

HE MADE IT. The fellow lurched across the doorway. Then came a triumphant yell, a sickening crunch, and the splintering of wood.

"*Wallah, sahib!*" shouted Yakub. "I got the dog!"

Hamlin, brushing the stinging liquor from his eyes, saw McTavish's assailant twitching on the floor. His skull was crushed, and blood trickled from his ears. McTavish, his grey face blood-splashed, collapsed as he tried to withdraw the blade that had sunk hilt deep into his chest. But he recognized his subordinate. He gasped: "Too late, Red. Carry on — until your father —"

That was all. McTavish was dead. Hamlin, deprived of the canny counsellor whose wrath he had anticipated, now had the entire burden on his shoulders. The Hindu servant came staggering in, blinking and groaning: "*Sahib*, I could not help it — he demanded to see the master — I did not —"

"Shut up, Hajara!" snapped Hamlin, still unnerved. "Call the watch. Run to the *kotwal*'s office and notify the police."

THE BURLY assassin might have been identified in a civilized country, but in Kabul it would be otherwise. After all, he had done no more than slay an infidel. It was improbable that he had come of his own accord. McTavish attended too strictly to business to have private enemies, but it would be dismissed as a fanatic outburst.

Hamlin, looking back at the afternoon's disaster, thought otherwise. In killing McTavish, some enemy had left the Afghan-American Trading Corporation in the hands of a youngster who had not distinguished himself with any particular ability for business; but Red Hamlin had aged years in that deadly succession of seconds.

Automatically, he moved McTavish into a more dignified posture. Then he stepped to the broad desk at which, even at home, the manager had pondered on the company's interests.

He had just signed a letter. Red's fist clenched as he glanced at it. It was to his father, and one sentence stood out like a line of fire:

"Your son is showing considerable ability. I am sure he will make good."

That bit deep, knowing that crusty old Mac had loyally kept his daily reproofs from his reports to New York. But it seemed too late now for Hamlin to justify the kindly false-hood.

II.

The Amir's Proposition

ONCE HE HAD rendered his report to the *kotwal*, Hamlin worked far into the night, checking over the files, studying the company's position and resources; but he was mainly concerned with the charges that would arise out of his error at the customs house.

His only chance of proving conspiracy would be by having Yakub go on the prowl about Kabul. Hamlin, though he was learning rapidly, was not well enough acquainted with local customs to hope to pry into the deadly and forbidden corners of the city — not, that is, until the grim-faced old Afridi gave him a lead.

In sheer weariness, he gulped a drink, then stared at the wall as he thought of the strange words of Tsong Kapa, the Buddhist monk: *"There is no evil but that which you draw upon yourself."*

"That's gospel!" he bitterly admitted. "And I've been hoo-dooed ever since I got that damned scroll! Just as he said!"

He fumbled for the envelope that Irene had given him, glanced at Dr. Henley's precisely illegible script. He had scarcely frowned his way through a few lines when he took his feet from the table and planted them on the floor.

"Crazy!" he scoffed; but he read on.

The Uighur manuscript told of the vast loot that Alexander the Great had buried in the Valley of Tall Gods northeast of the Chawak Pass. It described a crypt in an ancient Buddhist cliff-temple right on the age-old route that led from

Turkestan to India; the route of Alexander, and of Genghis Khan.

"Screwy," he muttered. Then he set the partial translation aside and began to wonder. Jerjis the Kafir had trailed him. The Buddhist monk had warned him. He dug up the two golden *staters*. They hinted that the Kafir must already have some source of ancient treasure.

But Hamlin was weary, and it was late. His immediate problem required a clear head. So he slept on his queries and suspicions; and by the following forenoon he was busy pulling strings to get an audience with the Amir.

The idea was to hit first, instead of waiting for the charges.

At four that afternoon, Hamlin called at the Ark, the sombre palace in which the Amir lived, and hid when popular uprisings made the city dangerous. The soldiers at the gates wore conspicuous silver medals, awarded for not having participated in the last mutiny. It was otherwise in the old days, when Abdurrahman Khan's iron hand had spread terror to the furthest corner of Afghanistan!

A glittering majordomo escorted Hamlin to an inner apartment. There a pair of chamberlains took charge. They were frigidly polite, but acted as though they smelled something peculiarly offensive. An Oxford education, Hamlin was learning, gives an Afghan nothing but an accent.

Finally he was ushered into a spacious chamber where ancient loot from India clashed with Louis Quinze chairs, gilt-framed mirrors, and a phonograph inlaid with mother of pearl.

The Amir, wearing a white turban and a grey tweed sport suit of English cut, sat cross-legged on a gilded day-bed. He did not like chairs, though he had them about as a modern touch. Several secretaries squatted on the floor at his feet. And at his right was Dost Ali, perched like a monstrous scarlet vulture in a lacquered, Chinese chair. Hamlin began to feel sick, seeing how things were lining up.

The formalities of presentation being over, Hamlin accepted the seat which the Amir offered. For a moment they eyed each other, the haggard, broad shouldered American and the stocky, under-sized ruler of the world's most hard-bitten country. The Amir's pudgy face was weary. He was not one of those men of blood and iron who had once ruled the land.

"I'm sure Your Highness heard of that deplorable mistake at the customs," began Hamlin, after an interminable exchange of compliments and inquiries about each other's health.

"Really unfortunate." The Amir nodded, amiable.

Hamlin bluntly went on. "That, followed by the murder of Angus McTavish, a few hours later, convinces me that there is a conspiracy to discredit my company, and leave me without the help of my Father's friend."

"Incredible!" murmured the Amir.

"But true. Perhaps I can induce Your Highness to postpone action until I can prove my point — at least, until the *kotwal* has completed his investigation?"

That was just an opener; no one fancied that the chief of police was even mildly interested.

"I regret," said the Amir, "that a fine will have to be levied. But if you can later prove your point, our treasurer will be happy to reimburse you. I can hardly believe that you or the esteemed late Mr. McTavish were guilty of attempted fraud, but it is your duty to be vigilant. Now, this fine —"

And then Dost Ali cut in. "Your Highness, we might dispense with that penalty."

The Amir was as amazed as Hamlin. *"What?"*

"Since the company's concession expires in three more months," Dost Ali explained very suavely, "why not cancel it at once?"

"Why not?" approved the Amir, brightening with pleasure.

He had at once caught the point: faced with cancellation, Hamlin would have to meet the bid of whoever was angling to get the concession. Little doubt now that Kraft was behind it all. And there was a chance that Dost Ali was playing the rivals against each other.

"Let us settle this on a more profitable basis," Hamlin demanded, resolved to risk it all at a single throw. "I have for some time had a clue to the treasure of Alexander the Great. If I find it, the state takes two-thirds, leaving me a third, and giving me a renewal of the concession."

The Amir laughed outright. "Every hasheesh eater in Kabul speaks of the hoard of Iskander Dhoulkarnayn! But your proposal is not as silly as it sounds, Mr. Hamlin. All you would have to do would be to keep on hunting, and indefinitely postpone the penalty."

"Look at these!" challenged Hamlin, producing the two golden *staters*. "They have not been circulated for centuries. They are Greek coins. A dying Kafir gave them to me, and —"

He paused, watching the Amir's change of expression as he scrutinized the antique beauty of the *staters*.

"You know where this came from?"

"Well, intensive search would be needed," evaded Hamlin.

"Do you realize that the chances are ten to one for your being murdered? The Kafir country has never recognized our rule; not even my grandfather entirely subdued them. You're either very brave — or desperate and ignorant."

"The last two, Your Highness!" chuckled Hamlin playing up his advantage. "You know how Alexander's treasure train went with him; how he left it in a pass of the Hindu Kush, guarded by a company of Macedonians, while he raided India. How he returned, stricken by fever and the heat, never again the man he had been. And those Kafirs are the sons of his treasure guard. So no man has ever conquered them, even as no man ever defeated Iskander! But — if that treasure is there, I'll get it!"

The Amir was now on his feet, black eyes agleam with borrowed enthusiasm. But Dost Ali interposed. "Why not a time limit? Give him thirty days. If this is a trick, you can still release the concession to a more reliable company, and get a good bid. Which will not be the case if the Afghan-American is shut down too long. Investors will be afraid."

The Amir's brows drooped, shading his eyes. "That is right, Dost Ali Mirza! Mr. Hamlin, you have heard the terms. The treasure of Iskander Dhoulkarnayn in thirty days, or your trading post is confiscated!"

Hamlin, escorted from the royal presence, was now convinced that he had been neatly outpointed. The score began to tally: Dost Ali, backing Kraft, had turned the gamble into a boomerang.

Hamlin saw Irene that evening, while Yakub was getting a crew of men and loading the equipment into the company's middle-aged Packard. Once it took them over the fairly passable first lap of the expedition, they would have to get mules and porters.

"Where's the rest of Doc Henley's translation?" he demanded. "And did that start turn out to be important?"

The grey-haired doctor at that moment emerged from his private office. His mustache accentuated the somber droop of his mouth. "Hamlin, I'm sorry — sorry as the devil — but you're not the only one who thought that manuscript was important."

Hamlin's knees felt like spaghetti. "What's that, Doe?"

The fragment which, with Jerjis's ancient coins, had inspired his brave bluff had been entirely too general for a treasure hunt that had a thirty-day time limit. The Valley of the Tall Gods was a vague spot in an indefinite region.

"It's gone. I missed it when I got back from attending to a couple of gun-shot cases. Gone, with my notes." He swallowed, then added: "I did my best, doing it over from memory. Here you are."

Hamlin forced a grin, pocketed the penned reconstruction, and said: "I'm betting on you, Doc. If someone went to the trouble of snitching it, it must be hot."

"It looked genuine." Just then an orderly came in, purred a mouthful of Persian. Henley extended his hand. "More grief. But good luck, Hamlin."

It was only then that Hamlin had a chance to explain the entire problem to Irene.

"Oh — Red!" She recoiled as she realized the significance of the loss. "And here I thought it was just some harebrained whim of yours. You *would* pick the most desperate way of settling your difficulty."

"They had me cornered," he soberly answered. "They, and particularly your little playmate, Mr. Kraft."

"How?" Sharply, eyes narrowed, chin up.

He blurted it out. She listened with growing incredulity, but her indignation faded.

"I know how you feel, Red," she sighed. "But you're wrong about Otto. I know he's tactless at times. But he's honest."

"Rats!" snapped Hamlin. "You would stick up for him!"

He turned, abruptly. Irene caught his hand. "Don't be

silly," she pleaded. "This grudge is just blinding you to your real enemy, Dost Ali. Can't you understand?"

"No. And neither do you. They're hand in hand."

He stalked out of the hospital. There was no telling what Irene might have let slip, being so assured that Kraft was on the level; she was entirely too much given to judging people by herself.

Halfway to his quarters, he remembered that he should have questioned Jerjis, who was rapidly improving. Those wild men were made of iron. But, piqued by Irene's attitude, he would not retrace his steps. Moreover, once Jerjis recovered from his wounds, he would consider that the two gold pieces had evened the score; there was more than half a chance that he'd be Oriental enough to knife his benefactor if doing so would regain the Uighur scroll.

Later, an official came to Hamlin's quarters with a sheaf of letters to the governors of the provinces along the march into Kafiristan. The Amir, however, was not giving him any soldiers. For the first part of the trip, they would not be necessary; thereafter, they would be useless.

IV.

Imprisoned

LONG BEFORE sunrise of the following morning, Hamlin checked up with Yakub and, found that the rugged old touring car contained all the equipment that they would need, including enough spare petrol to fuel it as far as the road permitted.

"One more item, Yakub. Where's that blasting powder?"

The old Afridi went back into the company's warehouse and emerged with a case of dynamite. In view of the frequent earthquakes that shake Afghanistan, Hamlin was preparing for the demolition of debris that might block the site.

It was still dark when they cleared the city gate. Yakub shared the front seat with Hamlin. Wedged in among the camp equipment in back was Shir Daoud, a tall Pathan; and beside him was Taimur, a deep-chested, thick-witted Uzbek with a flat nose and moon face. Since Yakub had recommended them, they would be trustworthy; but their courage or competence was another matter.

For half an hour they skirted the Kabul River, which foamed down from the foothills. The headlights were murky in the early gloom, and the rutted wagon track made every bolt in the venerable car protest. Then, as dawn thinned the mists, Hamlin's throttle foot sank. The stretch leading toward the mountain stream that fed the river was improving.

Fortunately he slowed down to feel out the rickety bridge that he knew was just ahead. As it was, he barely stopped short of the middle of the sway backed structure. The middle of the span was missing, and the treacherous trestle groaned as the brakes caught. It shuddered, sagged —

Hamlin whipped into reverse and jerked backward to the abutments just as the tortured timbers crumpled into the shallow torrent, thirty feet below. Alighting, he saw that the central timbers had been freshly sawed; and among the mule and camel tracks he noted fresh tire prints left by a car that could not have crossed long before his arrival.

He ploughed knee deep into the icy water and scrambled up the opposite bank. To repair the bridge would take a day. The nearest timber was a quarter of a mile away. And then he saw the heel prints in the earth! Heels are as scarce in Kabul as European residents! A man with large feet had been there, pacing about in the morning chill, supervising the setting of the bridge trap.

Wrath and a good guess spurred Hamlin to action. Whoever had expected him to pause for the bridge building had one error to his credit. "Yakub! Unload the luggage. Break out those ropes!"

Half an hour elapsed before Hamlin resumed the wheel and nosed the heavy car down the treacherous path to the water. There he hitched a one-inch rope to the front axle and snubbed it about a stump on the opposite bank. Engine roaring, hind end whipping and skidding, he ploughed in, praying that the ignition would not go out.

It SPUTTERED, missed, then caught again. And with Yakub, the tall Pathan, and burly Taimur snubbing the rope, he managed to work the machine up the further incline. Rubber fumes and the reek of hot lube blended with steam from the radiator, but finally he made it.

An hour later, they were on their way again. Hamlin went blasting into the hills and up the rocky imitation of a road that wound along the brink of ever deepening ravines as the trail led higher. Far ahead towered the mighty bulk of the Hindu Kush, whose gleaming snow caps peeped dazzlingly forth from rents in the mist.

They cleared a village without stopping.

"Grub, hell!" said Hamlin, "we're going on. Eat on the run!"

Yakub grinned and gnawed a chunk of bread. If the others grumbled, the thunder of the engine and scream of gears drowned it. But there was little speed once they passed the town. Hamlin, however, pushed on, and presently he caught a glimpse of a familiar red car: Kraft's old Mercedes.

No doubt that it was Kraft. It was the only machine of that make and color in Kabul; or all Afghanistan, for that matter. Red Hamlin, tramping on the gas, was now chewing the tires to pieces on the flinty rocks, but wrath did not quite discount skill. He was gaining.

Two of the crew were looking back, gesticulating. A third was relaying their reports to the driver, who was too busy wrestling with the wheel to look back. The big bus was loaded mountain high, but it had power. Hamlin groaned as Kraft aired her out on a fairly good stretch and literally walked away. Then he prayed for one of those tongues of rock in the camel trail to slice the oil pan, or rip the gas tank cross-wise when the springs yielded under the murderous impact of a cross wash.

Kraft was a master at the wheel, but he was more methodical, more prudent; and being in the lead, he had a chance to tempt Hamlin to over-reach himself and crack up. The American car, however, had bigger wheels than the Mercedes. Thus while Kraft at times had to pick his way, Hamlin poured in the power.

The road widened, suddenly. There was just a chance.

He backshifted to second, and his foot sank. The Packard roared forward. Kraft tried to swing in and block, but he was too late. Hamlin was inside; and what followed was the result of the American's having to cut in, abruptly, to avoid a boulder directly ahead. He hurled his wagon across the front wheels of the Mercedes. Fenders ripped and headlights splintered. The impact threw the heavier car out of control; and Hamlin's rear wheel, hurdling the boulder, flung him right and gave the leverage needed to tip Kraft over the edge.

The big car landed on its side, wedging among the upward reaching tongues of rock on the embankment below. The crew poured out in a tangle of baggage, but Kraft, clinging to the steering column, stuck and snapped off the ignition.

Hamlin had sheared the spokes of a rear wheel and blown out a tire. And while Yakub wrestled with a jack and made the change, Kraft and his men extricated themselves from the luggage the Mercedes had spilled. They were not a great deal the worse for the crash. Hamlin, resuming the wheel, hailed his fuming competitor: "Nice work on that bridge, Otto! Any message you want me to take?"

Kraft, set on foot some distance from the nearest village, would lose at least two days in rounding up a crew of porters; and in the meanwhile, there was a chance that local bandits would raid his equipment.

"*Wallah, sahib!*" beamed Yakub. "My liver turned to water. But that was skill."

"If you think I did that on purpose, you're crazy," declared Hamlin. "Not with a case of dynamite in the car."

But Yakub was not convinced. And he was still muttering in his beard when, late that day, the lights of Charikar winked at them from the darkness of the shadowed heights in front. They had won the first heat.

A guard of Uzbek lancers trotted forward to meet Hamlin. His approach had been noted many minutes earlier by the lookouts at Charikar, who kept an unfailing eye on the road that wound in and out and up into the hills. Thus, instead of parking in the *serai,* Hamlin's party was escorted to the governor's palace, a formidable fortress of sun-dried bricks.

Mahmud Khan, the governor, rode forward from his palace to greet the party. His half-Mongol blood was revealed by his faintly slanted eyes, and the prominent cheek bones cast into strong relief by the torchlight when he ceremoniously dismounted to glance at the American's credentials.

"My house belongs to the friend of the Amir. Welcome, *sahib*, and your men also."

THAT NIGHT many sheep were butchered. Yakub and his two aides stuffed to bursting, grunted and licked the grease from their fingers.

"Your car, *sahib*? By Allah, it is safe in the courtyard. It is on my head and eyes!" swore Mahmud Khan, leading the way to a somber room on the second floor.

There was a *charpoy* for Hamlin. The others spread out their sleeping mats. After a final florid burst of compliments, the governor left them to rest. He had scarcely gone when servants entered with a *sandali:* an oval brazier supported by three legs, and heaped with glowing charcoal. Over it a tabouret was placed, and on that a large, thin rug was spread, to confine the heat. Sharp gusts of mountain wind were searching the room, and the temperature was rapidly dropping.

"*Wallah!*" exclaimed Yakub, rousing himself. "Do it thus, *sahib*."

He moved his mat under the edge of the thin rug, which was spread tentwise, with the brazier serving as a tent-pole. The others followed suit, and then placed Hamlin's cot so that his feet, like those of his men, were pointed toward the fire at the center. Only their heads projected from the edges of the large rug.

Thus, with the slow burning of the charcoal, they would sleep warm for hours, unless the gusts that eddied in through the high, barred windows nipped exposed noses. Hamlin, not only well fed and comfortable, but also exultant at having stolen the first march on Kraft, relaxed and let the engine note that still thundered in his ears lull him to sleep.

His men were already snoring.

For a while his *charpoy* and the floor seemed to lurch and quiver, as though he were still in that road-racked car; but soon fatigue dulled the thrill of action finally directed toward a goal. He'd make good on poor old Mac's kindly falsehood.

It was a splitting headache that awoke Hamlin. Bound by Oriental courtesy to gorge himself on lamb and *pilau* and curry, he was not amazed at the excruciating throb of his temples. He rather envied his three men, who snored to rattle the tiles. They had been seasoned to alternate starvation and stuffing.

Bit by bit, however, Hamlin realized that his cheeks were lapped by hot air and not chilly draughts. He was so dizzy he could hardly raise his head. When he tried to stir, to sit up, he lurched from his cot. A shock of realization was what really awakened him.

For a moment he gasped, and tried to inhale fresh air to take the place of that he had gulped as he untangled himself from the edges of the rug which covered his cot. But the entire room, as well as the tent-like space of the *sandali* was charged with the deadly fumes of charcoal!

He was choking. The veins at his temples were at the bursting point. The ventilators near the ceiling were black, admitting not a glimpse of starlight. He staggered toward the door, fell, and for an interminable time lay gasping in the heavy fumes that blanketed the floor. But by sheer force of will, he drove himself on. A whiff of fresh air coming in under the door at the threshold revived him, and he managed to slip the bolt of the door.

Then he staggered back to his men. The torture in his head was increasing; his returning senses made him more conscious of it every instant.

"Yakub! Taimur!" He croaked, shaking them, slapping them. Finally, Shir Daoud muttered, and Hamlin dragged him from his mat. "Get out! Death is in this room. Grab thy comrade!"

Together, they booted and shook the other two. They were too groggy to carry them. And with little time to spare, the four half suffocated travelers slumped in the hall, just past the door.

Hamlin's three companions throttled their wrathful oaths when they finally understood the significance of the plugged ventilators. They went back for their boots, found their belts and side arms. Then they stealthily stole down the dark stairway, picked their way among the guests who lay snoring in the banquet hall.

*   *   *

THE CAR was in the courtyard. A pair of Uzbek lancers, patrolling on foot, were at the gate. It was massive; no less than two men were needed to move the heavy bar.

"That cut off one!" muttered Yakub. "By Allah — "

But Hamlin checked him as he drew his pistol to open fire on the sentries. "Easy, thou blockhead! We might fight our way out," he said in Pushtu. "But if the governor knows that we knew, he would hunt us down, so that we cannot tell the Amir. Do it this way, my sons."

They listened.

Taimur lurched drunkenly from the banquet hall, muttering and coughing as he held a wine-skin to his face. He choked, spat, let it drop to the flagstones. What remained of the contents gurgled out as he tried to regain his feet, all the while cursing and singing in Uzbek.

The lancers, who had whirled at the approach of the disturbance, lowered their long weapons. "Have a drink, little brothers," hooted Taimur.

"Bring it closer," invited one of the soldiers. "We can't leave our post, Allah curse the captain."

Taimur slumped in a heap as he reached the gate. Some coins tinkled to the stones. "Pigs, and fathers of pigs!" he coughed. "Trying to rob me?"

He lashed out with his pistol barrel. And Hamlin, who had crept closer under cover of the disturbance, silently felled the other lancer.

"Now, the gate, Taimur!"

Together, they eased the bar from its socket. Then, after releasing the brakes, they rolled the car backward. Scarcely three minutes had elapsed when the gate was again closed, and the heavy machine coasting down the incline, toward the *maidan*.

When the sentries recovered their wits, they would bar the gate and stick to their story. Everyone knew that starting a car made a terrific rumble. The only remaining answer would be, as Yakub put it: *"Wallah,* evil spirits whisked us away! And those dogs will be afraid."

Darkness and the grades favored them until they reached the edge of town. And when they could no longer push the heavily laden car, Hamlin stepped on the starter. They had expected to get porters at Charikar; but there was a chance of driving on to the next town, and pushing on from there before Mahmud Khan could pursue them.

Before the first ten miles were covered, Hamlin realized what odds he had assumed in driving beyond Charikar. They went down grades so steep that destruction was avoided only by felling some trees and tying them to the rear as drags; and the ascents, equally murderous, were achieved only by low gear and three men pulling on ropes snubbed to rocks ahead.

Porters and pack animals could have moved faster. Dawn found Hamlin's party sweating and exhausted. At noon, they were automatically driven by one man's will. But shortly before sunset, the trail widened, and grey walls and turrets of a town blocked the gaping cleft in the Hindu Kush. In sixteen hours, they had covered forty miles, and not much remained either of men or tires.

Hamlin wormed his way from the wheel as he pulled up before the sentries at the gate. They were grim-faced tribesmen, vassals of Afzal Khan, the overlord of that region. Wild men in shaggy sheepskins who fingered their sword hilts and rifle bolts as they speculated on the value of the loot; but Hamlin, confident that his letter from the Amir would pave the way, stepped forward with Yakub to demand immediate word with the captain of the guard.

The wolfish commander at once ushered them into the presence of Afzal Khan, a fat, crafty-eyed fellow with mustache that trailed to his collar bone.

Massive rings glistened on his pudgy hands. His face was oily as his manner, and his fingers made small, avaricious motions as he listened to Yakub's address. The local dialect was quite beyond Hamlin, which left him at a disadvantage.

"His Excellency says," interpreted Yakub, "that he is thy sacrifice. That the Amir's word is the law, and that he licks the dust from the Amir's threshold. He begs refreshment for his eyes, by seeing the hand and seal of his lord, the Amir."

"The oily louse," was Hamlin's thought. "Bargaining with him for porters and mules is going to cost me my hide." He reached into his sheepskin jacket to get the packet of letters.

They were gone. The cord which securely bound them to the lining had been clipped, doubtless as he slept in that gas poisoned chamber in Charikar.

"They're gone, Yakub," said Hamlin in English.

"So are our heads, *sahib*," answered the Afridi promptly. "And this father of a dog loves us not."

"Stall him off! Say that it is in the car."

But Hamlin had not a chance to get to the car. The Khan's mouth twisted, and he clapped his hands. The guard at the door closed in, rifles leveled.

"He says," growled Yakub, "that he must detain us. The Amir would require our heads of him, if he let us go on into this dangerous country and we were killed by bandits. Therefore since it is not expressly stated that we are to march on, he is guarding us from harm."

They were disarmed, then marched down a gloomy corridor, and thrust into a straw-littered cell. Though it was below the main floor level, its one window opened out over a chasm nearly two hundred feet deep. Far below, Hamlin looked once more at the impossible road up which they had toiled.

V.

Irene Pursues

HAMLIN chafed while two days passed, but the time was not yet ripe for escape by either stratagem or bribery. By craning his neck between the bars of the window, Hamlin saw that the car had not yet been looted. The khan, it seemed, was feeling his way along. It was not quite far enough from Kabul to be reckless.

"Look, *sahib*!" Yakub was at his master's side. "That son of a lewd mother is marching on foot. Kraft!"

"Where?" Hamlin, straining his eyes, could distinguish a *kafila* on the murderous trail, far to the southwest, and two thousand feet below. "How do you know it's Kraft?"

"My eyes are not what they once were," deplored the mountaineer, "but Iblis rip me open if that isn't an infidel dog. He is not bent with a pack. He is not driving a mule.

And his walk is clumsy, like all of his kind, saving your presence."

"If I had eyes like yours," grumbled Hamlin, "I'd see a way of getting out of here."

"We leave that to thy wisdom and Allah's," sighed the resigned Afridi.

"And He's taking a holiday!" was Hamlin's wry comment.

His men liked and trusted him, and thus they could not be concerned with problems his wisdom doubtless could solve. Wrathful, he gripped the crude, hand-forged bars; a futile gesture. They were anchored in lead poured into the solid masonry. The foundations of the castle were of stone, so that earthquakes could not shake it into the ravine below.

It was Kraft! Hamlin, straining his eyes, could no longer doubt.

Then, hearing sounds in the court, he shifted to the other side of the window. The Khan's men were boosting the loaded car into the enclosure. Ignorant of brakes and meshed gears, they were levering up the rear end and nosing it forward on sliding tires.

The look-outs in the watch tower had also seen Kraft; that was clear when bales, pack saddles, and rugs were heaped over the car, camouflaging it in a nondescript mountain in the angle of the wall. They were hiding all evidence of Hamlin's presence, so that the newcomers would not be alarmed.

It was midafternoon before Kraft's party toiled up the steep ascent. Men and animals were equally exhausted but the big German had taken his punishment like a veteran.

Hamlin, remembering his own exhaustion on arriving at this den of treachery, had to concede his rival a number of points. But he was hoping that Otto Kraft would be assigned to the same cell.

That hope, however, did not last long. Kraft, with some years' residence in Kabul, had done well with dialects. He addressed the Khan without using an interpreter. And as he spoke, he produced a packet wrapped in oiled silk and offered it to the lord of the castle.

The Khan, glancing right and left as if to note whether all were watching him, accepted the document, started as in awe of the seals that gleamed from its surface; then he touched it to his forehead and lips before he read. No spy from Kabul would tell the Amir that royal letters were not received with suitable reverence.

LATER, the bleating of sheep was abruptly cut off. They were being slaughtered for a banquet. Kraft, with credentials, was a guest of honor.

It was bitter cold that night. By dint of hammering on the door and yelling, Hamlin routed out one of the guards, and Yakub, offering the fellow several *rupees*, wheedled, "Bring us a *sandali*, O thou Father of Valor! *Wallah*, we are freezing. And also, a haunch of mutton. Even some bones from the khan's table."

The guard was agreeable, but wary. When he returned with the charcoal-laden brazier, a fellow soldier accompanied him, and with his rifle backed the captives to the further corner of the cell until the door again was locked.

"We have gained nothing but heat, *sahib*," deplored Yakub.

"Gnaw those ribs," said Hamlin, "and get away from that fire."

He muffled his hand with a handkerchief and lifted the brazier to the sill. With a mutton rib he carefully scooped the coals to the masonry, heaping them about a bar. The breeze fanned the red embers to a scarlet glow.

At times Hamlin stamped out the blaze as sparks set fire to the straw on the floor.

Yakub frowned, stroking his beard. "But still we can't bend the bars, *sahib*. They must be hot in the middle."

"Right you are," was the cheery answer. Then Hamlin carefully brushed the unconsumed coal back into the brazier and said, "Quick, water! And a rib!"

Yakub brightened when Hamlin used the end of the rib to ladle molten lead from the cavity in which the bar had been set. That done, he poured water into the hole. The gust of steam blew droplets of metal in every direction, and chips of rock cut his cheeks.

When the cloud cleared away, Hamlin knocked a sizable chunk of masonry from the sill. "Now we will bend the bar out. There is nothing holding the bottom. One more, and we can climb out. Even that ox of a Taimur!"

The big Uzbek grinned and squared his massive shoulders. He made short work of a wrought-iron bar held only at the top.

But it was slow work, and Hamlin had started late. A stirring in the courtyard made him rake the charcoal from the next bar, lest the glow arouse attention. Men were grumbling and muttering. Pack saddles creaked, tiny hoofs clattered, mules squealed and snorted, resenting the tightening of girths. They kicked and bit, and their drivers kicked and cursed.

Otto Kraft's hearty voice boomed above the confusion.

"Ya Allah!" explained Yakub, "that son of many fathers is on the march, and with fresh animals. *Sahib*, I have studied this thing. We can creep out, once these cut-off ones are on the march, and every one else is again snoring. There is a ledge —"

"That's what set me thinking," said Hamlin.

"By God, thou seest all things!" admired the old Afridi. "Then we will set out after them on foot — we will cut their throats — we will take their passports and their beasts."

Later, when the German's *kafila* was filing out the gate, Hamlin set to work on the next bar.

They could, perhaps, get the car out of the court; but it would be of no use on the advance. At the best, they could take no more than their spare weapons from the *tonneau*. Lacking pack animals, they would have to abandon all equipment and set out on foot to catch Kraft off guard.

The second bar yielded. Taimur's leg wrappings were twisted into an improvised cord. It was reinforced with Yakub's turban, which he had luckily refused to abandon in favor of a sheepskin cap. And presently, Hamlin led the way over the sill.

For a moment, his extended feet groped. He shivered, wondering if he had correctly estimated the distance to the ledge; but before he was fully stretched out, his toe found support. Then came a nightmare advance. Hamlin's bleeding fingers sank desperately into the joints of the ancient masonry. Its mortar pointing had long been worked out by frost and wind.

Grunts and gasps behind him told of the struggle of his men as they followed. It scarcely seemed possible that the barrel-chested Uzbek could cling close enough to keep his footing. But Taimur was there when Hamlin reached the crest of the wall that enclosed the court. Yakub grinned wolfishly and Shir Daoud crept up like a panther. He did not drop to the top of the heap that concealed the car; instead, he moved on, inch by inch, making a circuit of the court.

Hamlin, guiding his men by touch, worked them into the darkest shadows. He had planned to dig into the heap and find a jack handle, but Shir Daoud was not waiting for weapons. There was no recalling him; and Yakub, gripping Hamlin's forearm, whispered, "Allah is with madmen, *sahib*. It will be well."

It was well. There was but a single sentry walking post, and he never knew what flashed down upon him from the crest of the mud wall. The tall Pathan throttled his gasp, and the melon-plop of a head against the flagstones settled the matter of the guard permanently.

Shir Daoud cut across the court, and buckled a captured belt about his waist. Under his arm was the rifle which the sentry had set against the gate instead of shouldering it. But as he joined Hamlin at the buried car, they heard yells from far below, and the snorting of beasts, the tinkle of caravan bells. A warning shot rang out from the watch tower. Inside the fortress, men cursed and grumbled as they mustered under arms.

Hamlin and his men had barely plunged into the heap of odds and ends that concealed the car when the guard poured into the court. In the confusion of an alarm, no one noticed that the sentry was laid out. They assumed, doubtless, that he had quit his post to run toward the disturbance — bad discipline, but true hill-man soldiering.

Nor was there any interim in which the four skulkers could break out. The town was alive, alert, and excited. A night raid, so Hamlin gathered from scraps he could understand. But he and Yakub were wrong. A small *kafila*, closely guarded by the khan's men, was presently herded into the court; and by the red glare of flickering torches. Hamlin saw that the party included two women. One, mounted on a luxuriously caparisoned mule, was veiled; the other, riding at her side, was obviously a servant, whose station in life did not require the concealment of her face.

Hamlin, though he noted that one of the veiled woman's retainers was Jerjis, the Kafir, had no room left for surprise; not even when he realized that the Hindu girl was Sita Deva, Irene Gray's maid. She dismounted to support her mistress, whom fatigue made reel in the saddle. The veil shifted, and Hamlin had recognized Irene, weary but unafraid.

The girl from Kabul offered her travel permit to the captain and said: "We are the Amir's guests. Let us make camp in this court. And we need fresh animals at sunrise."

"That is but an hour," the captain inaccurately protested.

"No matter," she contended. "Now, what Feringhi travelers have passed through?"

The captain described Kraft.

"No others?" Irene was anxious; that was plain from her voice.

"On my head and eyes, assuredly no other." And he clenched it by swearing by his beard, and thrice by the name of Allah: a solemn perjury that convinced Irene, since few Moslems link falsehood with the "triple" oath. She did not know that this pious person was assuring himself that Hamlin, securely locked up, could not possibly have passed through.

Hamlin, listening from concealment, donned Shir Daoud's sheepskin coat and cap. He had to warn her; she had already expressed too much interest in him.

He boldly emerged from cover and shouldered his way among the soldiers. In that uncertain light they thought he was one of her men, and her followers mistook him for another of the Khan's officious crew. Thus he reached Irene's side and said in servant English: "Memsahib, this corner of court-enclosure are extremely superior for encampment."

She recognized his voice; and as he straightened up from his profound salaam, she caught a direct glimpse of the face that was almost hidden by the shaggy collar and hood. That overcame her incredulity; and Hamlin's presence, in the face of the captain's perjury, was ample warning. She answered: "Very well — Ranjeet. But first we need permission." Then, to the captain:

"Tell the Khan that I am waiting! He'll have you flogged if he hears that he did not get the Amir's letter as soon as it arrived!"

This playing the person of importance impressed the captain. He bowed, then hastened into the castle. The guard respectfully drew back.

"For heaven's sake, Red!" She swayed in the saddle, and he dared not steady her. "I nearly died, hearing your voice! What's happened — what's wrong?"

"Make a bluff of moving your outfit into that corner," he countered.

Irene spoke a few words to the Kafir, whose wounds had not kept him from riding. He whacked a pair of mules across the rump and herded them toward the corner. A Tadjik followed, and then the Pathan porters. During the confusion Hamlin continued: "I've got to duck before the Khan shows up."

Then, leading her mule after the others, he sketched the situation.

"Oh!" She was dismayed. "And I sent for the Khan! I couldn't have done worse!"

"No matter," Hamlin assured her. "I'll hide out. He won't know my men. He's too important to have noticed them, and this light is still tricky. Now — how did you get here? And why?"

"To warn you. Sita Deva has been picking up gossip. You know how native women know more about the inside doings than the Amir's secret police. It goes from harem to harem. Anyway, it's Dost Ali, out for your hide. To block you at all costs. He wants you out of Kabul —"

"You little idiot!" he reproved. "You faced capture by bandits ever since you left Charikar!"

"Not much, Red," she insisted. "I hoped to find you before you got into country where the Amir's letter wouldn't do any good. He thought a good deal of Father, so I was able to wheedle him out of a permit. I couldn't tell the Amir about Dost Ali. Lacking proof, an accusation would have kicked back. And there wasn't any other way of warning you."

"I'll be damned!" Hamlin was dazed. "This risk for me?"

She laughed it off. "I knew you were so dead set against Otto you were missing your real enemy."

Hamlin shrugged. Let Irene stick to her notions about Kraft. The chilly gloom had suddenly become warm and pleasant.

"Dost Ali," she went on, "is pulling wool over the Amir's eyes. But so far, his power is quite safe, and —"

She gasped as a flashlight blazed into the thinning gloom, and a suave voice said in Pushtu: "Welcome! I am dust beneath the Amir's feet, and my beard sweeps his threshold."

It was Afzal Khan, speaking a dialect of which he had previously pretended ignorance. His florid address ended in confusion when, by Hamlin's own flashlight, he recognized his late prisoner, free and beside the Amir's protected.

"This man," declared Irene, "is one of my party. He was sent in advance." But Afzal Khan snarled like a cornered wolf, and his soldiers crowded closer. Their chief, suddenly desperate, did not reach for the royal letter. This was no time for ceremonial. He now realized that he had made a fatal mistake in seizing Hamlin, and his best move was to make short work of the whole party, then trust to flight into the far hills into which no troops would venture.

He growled an order to his men and their rifles covered the group.

Sita Deva screamed. A bayonet backed Hamlin against the wall as Afzal Khan snatched Irene's veil from her face. The Kafir's long knife was knocked from his hand before it fairly left its scabbard, and the others were too surprised to offer resistance.

"There is trickery here!" declared the Khan, working himself into a high rage. "By Allah, who said that this was the Amir's letter?"

And then a tall, hatchet-faced man emerged from the heap that concealed the car — Yakub, with a rifle whose bolt click was as metallic as his voice.

"Back, sons of flat-nosed mothers! Or I'll blow the Khan's stomach into your faces!"

The muzzle of his rifle prodded the chieftain right above the belt. The Khan froze, and his oily face broke out in gleaming sweat. Not a soldier dared move. Yakub's face was twitching, and so was his trigger finger. He'd never killed a Khan, and that would be something his grandchildren would take pride in!

Afzal Khan's quavering command sent the soldiers well back. Hamlin stepped from the wall, and said: "Now that I've heard you speak Pushtu, we won't need an interpreter. Have your scavengers uncover my car. Yakub, don't kill him, or his men will make pests of themselves!"

Hamlin, waiting for the return of his captured arms, watched the soldiers roll the car clear of encumbrances. He guarded Yakub's back against attack from the rear. And presently, with Afzal Khan as a hostage, whose ribs were prodded by a pistol, Irene and Hamlin cleared the gate.

"You," HE SAID to his prisoner, "will go with me to guarantee good behavior of your people until we get out of your territory."

"By Allah, *sahib*, I see now that you are the Amir's friend! But this was not my fault. The tall man had a letter naming you. How could I know that it was stolen?"

"That's unfortunate, Afzal Khan. But you're going," Hamlin said. "And if your people love you, I won't have to shoot you."

Then, turning the captive over to Yakub, he stepped to Irene's side and urged her to hurry back to Kabul. She could take the car; and Yakub, who now knew the road, could accompany her to do the trick driving in the bad spots between there and Charikar. He concluded, "Now that I've got that louse under my thumb, you could walk back alone, and safely."

"I know that's the sensible thing to do, Red," she admitted, after a long moment of pondering, "and I'd be a terrible handicap when you cross the Chawak Pass." She laughed tremulously. "I don't know what ever possessed me to try to overtake you."

"I do," Red cut in. And he proved his knowledge by giving her the sound and hearty kiss he had been saving up for weeks; the one she'd consistently evaded in Kabul.

"Oh — Red, you idiot — right in front of these natives!" He laughed, drawing her closer.

So she returned it, then and there.

Yakub, hearing the orders, cursed in dialects the master could not understand; but he consented to accompany Irene back to Charikar, where she could get an escort to Kabul. And since Hamlin held the Khan as hostage, she would not need her natives. Jerjis and the others could reinforce Hamlin's party. With Afzal a prisoner, his men would have to help her over the rough spots.

"My wounds heal fast, *sahib*," said the Kafir. "I owe you my life. I will show you the quickest way to the Valley of the Tall Gods. It was for that purpose that I came with the doctor-lady."

And then the parties separated. Just as Irene nosed the unloaded car around the first downgrade curve, she risked a backward glance, and a wave of her hand. She was gone, but Hamlin, setting his own *kafila* in motion, was telling himself that he had already found something far more than Alexander's treasure.

VI.

Avalanche

JERJIS rode beside Hamlin as they advanced along the caravan track that led into the towering Hindu Kush. In addition to his own obscure dialect, he spoke a mongrel jargon of Pushtu and Persian. Hamlin, just able to get the main ideas, had to guess the details from the voice and gesture.

"Iskander," said the Kafir, speaking as though Alexander the Great had lived year before last instead of twenty-two centuries previous, "left the loot of Persia in the Valley of Tall Gods. My people, the sons of his treasure guard, never believed that he died, seeing that he was descended from the gods. So we kept faithful watch.

"But Genghis Khan came one day and the earth shook under his feet. There was a mighty slaying, and he took most of the treasure. But even he died, so our old men set to work teaching us how to restore the loot. Piece by piece, from

Kashgar — from Samarkand — from Herat. What one man buries, another digs up. Gold does not die."

"But that scroll?" demanded Hamlin.

"There was a story among stories," said the Kafir. "Of a monastery in Thibet. It told of a piece buried in the Valley of Tall Gods, and how to deceive the gods who guard it, so that they will not slay us. I went to steal the scroll, but I was too late. I followed the bandit to Kabul.

"Others followed me. You bought it. I watched you. But my enemies did not know that, so they nearly killed me. And since I can not now rob or kill you, I will guide you. Somewhat for the sake of the doctor-woman who healed my wounds."

That explained Jerjis and the monk, Tsong Kapa. And Hamlin already had the answer to other riddles. It was clear now that Kraft and Dost Ali, getting wind of the scroll Hamlin had given to Dr. Henley, had arranged to have it stolen. And Dost Ali must have incited Mahmud Khan to attempt to asphyxiate Hamlin's party and take his papers, so that Kraft would have credentials to take him on into Kafiristan.

This last, he reasoned, was to have served a double purpose: first, dispose of Hamlin; second, keep the Amir from knowing that Kraft was definitely against his American business competitor. Afzal Khan, despite his greed and trickery, might have told the truth; he might have seen Hamlin's papers in Kraft's possession. That at least explained the German's great haste to get fresh animals and move on before his imposture was exposed.

"By Allah, *sahib*!" swore the captive Khan, snatching at Hamlin's hints, "that was it! Mahmud Khan was close enough to Kabul to be corrupted by your enemies, and he is the son of several dogs, totally untrustworthy! Furthermore, the tall infidel did not know that I cannot read. I know only the Amir's seal when I see it."

HAMLIN laughed. That last did ring true. And since they were far from Afzal Khan's sphere of influence, it was safe to untie his ankles and wrists. He would not venture escape and flight, alone, through bandit-infested wilderness. And this proof of Hamlin's self-confidence impressed his men.

Haggard lines were etched about Hamlin's eyes, and not entirely from squinting at the dazzling snow of the Hindu Kush. He was scrutinizing every grey rock ahead and above. There was always the chance that Kraft might be lurking in ambush; in the forced march, they had in two days passed the remains of three of his campfires. Empty tins and heel prints left no doubt that he had taken that route.

The silence was eating into Hamlin's heart. The vast gulf swallowed up sound. The thin air forced men to husband their breath, and no one spoke.

They fought their way over the Chawak Pass. The struggle was as personal as wrestling, deadly as a duel with knives. A pack mule lost its footing, tumbled crazily for a thousand feet, became small as a fly before it faded in the hazes below. And only luck had kept Hamlin's shaggy Turkoman pony from plunging into a crevasse.

Then, clearing the Pass, Hamlin found live embers, deep in the ashes of Kraft's recent fire. He had carried fuel; there was no timber in this desolation. But as they picked their way down the trail, Jerjis said: "*Sahib*, there is a short-cut. Your enemy will expect you from the valley mouth. From this last camp, with the double-barreled eyes, he could have seen us climbing upward. Like those you use when you look ahead and say *damn-damn*, and tell us of the trouble that we cannot see until later."

THEY TOOK the short-cut. But Hamlin regretted that strategy. Jerjis took for granted what no one but a born mountaineer would have risked. Afzal Khan was groaning and cursing. Even Taimur and Shir Daoud muttered and prayed. However, at last, the Valley of Tall Gods opened out below them, and the battered *kafila* filed between the black palisades of a cleft that seemed the work of insane giants.

"See the steam rising from the hot springs, and the green grass, *sahib*," said Jerjis. "This is the path that Iskander closed behind him."

That was how the Kafirs explained the earthquakes that had blocked an ancient pass with debris. They scrambled on; the descent became easier. But sunset overtook them, and they made camp before reaching the valley floor.

Before a fire was started, Hamlin focused his binoculars on the moving spots on the further side. They were men; and towering above them were great, brooding figures with gilded faces, sculptured out of the cliffs.

The features were Asiatic; their long ear-lobes indicated Buddhist saints. The crypts cut into the black face of the cliffs indicated the cells that once had been occupied by monks. It reminded him of the caves of Bamian, but these were larger, and with few exceptions the monstrous figures that stood in the great arched niches had not been ruined by time and earthquakes. These were the Tall Gods, still guarding the Valley.

In the first flush of triumphant Buddhism, missionaries had come down from High Asia three centuries before Iskander set out to conquer the earth. This sacred site might have been deserted even in his time; and if not, he could have cleared it to serve his purpose.

Then, as the shifting of the sun sent long, red rays lancing for a moment across the green carpeted valley, Hamlin's glasses justified themselves. One man loomed head and shoulders above the others: Otto Kraft, stalking about the camp.

That night, before the valley was flooded by moonlight, Hamlin left the pack animals under guard and set out on foot. The distant glow of Kraft's fire guided him. When he was halfway to his objective, he sent Jerjis out as scout. As far as possible, he wanted to make it a complete surprise, swamping Kraft without firing a shot, or involving his men in a frcc-for-all.

Once Kraft was out of action, his men would lay down their arms. The surprise, however, was for Hamlin, and not his rival. Jerjis reported: "Sahib, the camp is deserted."

"They may be hiding in the tunnels cut into the cliff," warned Taimur.

"No," contended Jerjis. "I made sounds to tempt them to fire."

Ambush or no, Hamlin pressed on. Bit by bit the towering crags took shape in the gloom, and finally he could discern the blurred golden masks of the gigantic gods. Swerving to the left, he sent Taimur and Shir Daoud, widely spaced, to creep directly on, feigning the accidental noises of a not too clumsy advance.

There was no challenging fire, and no chance for him to slip up from the side as the scouts dug in and blasted at the lurkers. When he was certain there was no ambush, he finally risked a flashlight beam. The crude shelters were empty. There were no hobbled animals no pack saddles. He found only ashes, hoofprints, and the marks of Kraft's boots.

"*Wallah!*" growled Taimur. "The *kafila* marched by darkness to the mouth of this valley."

"They have not left long," Jerjis cut in. "There is no fresh dew on the trodden grass. The mists from the hot springs chill quickly."

"And look — four of the beasts are very heavily loaded," contended Shir Daoud. "Heavier than any inbound hoof tracks show."

The last unmistakable sign indicated that the hoard had been looted. From afar, a tinkling bell taunted Hamlin. The only resource was direct pursuit, and with tired beasts.

"Get the horses!" ordered Hamlin. "The pack train will camp here, and follow any way it can. Four of us will track him. We can ride faster than his *kafila* can march."

THE PROSPECT of overtaking four mules loaded with gold almost started a riot; everyone wanted to ride, no one wanted to bring up the rear with the pack animals. But Hamlin finally restored order. Then, with Jerjis at his side, he stepped into the great niche.

The back of the niche was pierced by a smaller arch, the mouth of a tunnel that reached into the heart of the cliff. Hamlin, however, did not cross the threshold. He stopped short at the lip of the hole that gaped from the paving. The tool marks were fresh. Kraft had uncovered a crypt.

"Looted it — and checked out!" was Hamlin's bitter conclusion. That clinched things; and as he awaited the approach of his horses, he paced up and down the niche, cursing Kraft's blind luck.

"Friend," said a familiar voice from the shadows, "a curse reflects back on him who speaks it."

Glancing up, he saw Tsong Kapa squatting cross-legged between the feet of the tallest god. In the glow of Hamlin's flashlight, the monk for an instant seemed to be their small brother; his bronzed face had that same cryptic calmness, that same gently mocking smile.

"How the devil —" exclaimed Hamlin.

"A Thibetan mountaineer," explained Tsong Kapa, "can cover space faster than the best horse. I came to prevent a looting that will release evil of greed in the world."

"Hell!" Hamlin spat. "You weren't fast enough."

"Mr. Kraft," asserted the monk, "did not find the loot. I advise you against seeking it, but if it is your destiny, you will do it."

More juggling of double-edged phrases. The monk's presence aroused Hamlin's suspicions. This pious rambling about acquiring merit was distinctly fishy. When the horses arrived, Hamlin quickly mounted.

"Greed and wrath lead to destruction," intoned the monk, but pounding hoofs swallowed that final counsel. Stealth was out of the question. The breathing of animals, the ring of hoofs, the clatter of dislodged stones would all too clearly herald Hamlin's advance once he ascended the trail that passed the mouth of the valley. So he charged on, leading the file into the pass.

He ignored Taimur's protests; but when the Uzbek suddenly yelled, the insistent note startled him. There was a rifle shot from the rear. He wheeled his beast, wondering for an instant whether the bullet zipping past him had come from carelessness or treachery.

The horse slipped, lurched heavily to the rocks. Hamlin, flung free, was pitched against the wall. He had barely scrambled to his feet when there was a low rumbling overhead. Earth and boulders poured down the steep slope, blocking the narrow spot from which his skittish animal had carried him with but a hair's margin.

Above him, men were yelling. Flame jetted from the upper slope. Taimur and his companions answered the fire. The skirmish developed so rapidly that Hamlin, jerking his rifle from the scabbard, had no time to wonder at that sudden cry of terror above him.

Something was rolling down the slope like a bundle of rags. Dislodged rocks clattered down, and the breeze was tinged with the nitrous reek of the blasting powder that had started the artificial avalanche of earth and snow. It was a man, battered and almost breathless from his swift descent.

Hamlin pounced on him. It was Kraft, muttering incoherently. The fire from overhead subsided. The lurkers were in full flight, now that their chief was out of action. First, the blast had been premature; then a rock, weakened by the shock, had given away, tumbling Kraft down the grade. Plenty to crack their nerve.

"Grab this fellow!" yelled Hamlin. "Cease firing! They're all scattered."

"I heard a sound overhead," gasped Taimur, bounding up. "Then a fuse was spitting fire. I yelled — I fired!"

"Pretty!" Hamlin surveyed the slide. "Can't get horses over this!"

But Jerjis and Shir Daoud were already clearing the crest of the obstacle. Their yells echoed, blending with the clatter of hoofs. Hamlin scrambled after them.

"The pack train, *sahib*"! they screeched.

So it was; Kraft's animals, abandoned by the flight of his panic-stricken men. But the prize was useless. Four of the beasts had packs that contained rock from the excavation, in addition to their usual burden. That exposed the trick; their deep hoofprints had drawn Hamlin on, and into an almost fatal ambush.

"It damn near looks as if Tsong Kapa was right about dirt kicking back at a fellow," he frowned some minutes later when Taimur lashed Kraft to one of the mules they had booted up the barrier of debris.

VII.

Iskander's Treasure

BACK at the cliff temple, Hamlin searched his captive and found that Kraft had the silk damask scroll; but that was no more help than Dr. Henley's reconstructed notes. The treasure was concealed somewhere in a vault at the end of the tunnel leading from the outer niche; but the cliff was honeycombed with chambers. Worst of all, Hamlin could not within his thirty-day limit return to Kabul for a closer translation.

Kraft, it now was apparent, had not been able himself to translate the Uighur scroll; and had not been willing to trust anyone else with the task. The ambush indicated that he had played for time in which to complete a long search, by trial and error.

"Thou father of a pig!" raged Afzal Khan, fingering the blade of his drawn *tulwar*. He was working up a high rage for Hamlin's benefit as well as the prisoner's. "Handing me a stolen letter, and tricking me into offending the Amir's friend!"

"Better not kill him until he shows us the treasure, *sahib*," suggested the practical Taimur, very thoughtfully honing a dagger.

"This man is in my face!" reproved Hamlin, using the phrase that indicated Kraft was under his protection. "Guard him, but do not harm him."

They muttered, all except Jerjis, who smiled and shrewdly eyed Hamlin and the captive. The little Kafir did not understand Moslem customs. No telling what he would do.

Tsong Kapa stood by, placidly telling the one hundred and eight beads of his rosary. But when Hamlin laid down the law the monk stepped forward and said, "For some past merit, this man was not permitted to kill you."

"Past merit?" echoed Hamlin. "What do you know about my past?"

Tsong Kapa smiled. "I was referring to his merits. In some previous life he did good. For him to have succeeded in that ambush would have set him back to labor through many incarnations before he again became a prosperous trader."

There was no use in trying to persuade the monk to help him with the Uighur script. Hamlin could think of not a single approach. And Tsong Kapa's next remark made less sense.

"Mr. Kraft — Mr. Hamlin — settle your differences, and forget this treasure. You will sooner prosper without it. Greed and anger recoil against you."

"Wait a minute!" Hamlin cut in, chuckling wryly. "If I don't find Iskander's treasure, I'll be failing my Father. Also, Kraft will complete a rotten piece of trickery. There ought to be some merit in my keeping him from succeeding in his plan."

Tsong Kapa's slanted eyes gleamed humorously. "So? A new way of acquiring merit?" A moment's Silence. "You think you are mocking me, but you are not. Get him alive to Kabul, and I will find the treasure for you."

"What?"

"There is merit in saving a life, even though death is nothing to the slain. I came from the roof of the world to find and destroy that scroll, but it was twice delivered into your hands; the last time, with the man you think is your enemy. So it must be your Karma to have it."

"The man I *think* is my enemy?" repeated Hamlin.

"Self is the only foe," the monk quoted. "Now give me the scroll and let me study it. If there is treasure here, I will find it."

Hamlin handed him the roll of silk damask. The monk gestured, and he followed, skirting the edge of the faked excavation.

TSONG KAPA advanced down a maze that ended in an elaborately sculptured vault. Its center was occupied by a pedestal on which four Buddhas sat cross-legged.

"These be the Buddhas of the four worlds," observed the monk. "And beyond them is the black torrent that symbolizes the gulf into which all worlds shall finally sink. Wealth is vain!"

He smiled at Hamlin's cautious approach to the cleft that split the floor. Apparently it was the scar left by an ancient earthquake. Far down at some immeasurable depth, water rushed savagely, on its way, perhaps, to crop out miles further on, from the face of some cliff.

"I will need no light but this candle stump," said Tsong Kapa; and that was Hamlin's dismissal.

For some time thereafter Hamlin occupied himself with supervising the encampment of his men. The pack animals arrived from across the valley, and he had to post lookouts, lest some unexpected valor on the part of Kraft's men climaxed in a raid. That done, he left his prisoner and the camp in charge of Taimur. Hamlin needed rest, and his brain was spinning with vain speculations concerning that incredible monk.

Two days passed. Tsong Kapa, oddly enough, did not once emerge from the darkness of the inner vault, though his candle stump could not have lasted more than a few hours. But when Hamlin finally came in with a flashlight and a fresh candle, he found the monk squatting there, scarcely breathing, and seemingly unaware of the intrusion.

Hamlin silently backed away from that uncanny presence. Tsong Kapa was in the attitude of meditation. The scroll was across his knees, and he apparently paid no more attention to it than he would to an earthquake or an explosion.

Outside, the men were gaming and wrangling. They were already spinning tales of how they would spend their share of the loot. Its discovery had been taken for granted; Tsong Kapa was plainly a madman, and thus his wits were with Allah, from whom wisdom came.

K RAFT, securely bound, continued to accept his imprisonment philosophically. Time was passing, and time was Hamlin's worst enemy. But at sunset of the second day Tsong Kapa, unnoted by any of the camp, slipped up beside Hamlin where he sat in the shadow of the niche.

"Come," he whispered.

Hamlin followed, and his hands trembled almost as much as his legs. He stood like a statue as he picked Tsong Kapa out of the gloom of the vault and watched him fingering the sculptured panels of the wall.

"Simple," said the monk. "Press the heart of this lotus bud, and seize the shoulder of this *asura*. Thus!"

A solid slab, too thick to respond to the tap of a hammer and so betray the cavity behind it, swung out and exposed a crypt. The dull surfaces of ancient gold reflected the candle's glow in Hamlin's eyes for some seconds before he could say: "Lord — there must be a ton of it!"

The heap of censers and flagons, salvers and bowls, was half obscured by a tangle of massive anklets and bracelets set with smoldering rubies and cool, unblinking sapphires polished in a fashion he had sometimes seen in the bazaars of Kabul, but utterly unlike the faceted gems of any modern lapidary. There were stones in that colorful confusion of wealth which he could scarcely name.

A tall mitre, its silver frame a skeleton from which trailed shreds of cloth once Tyrian purple; a peaked helmet, all inlaid with wrought gold; a Grecian casque whose verdigris was veined with silver which age had tarnished to a metallic dove-grey; and there were mouldering blades whereof only bronze and gems remained intact.

"This is well," said Tsong Kapa, utterly unmoved. "If you can make it serve instead of letting it master you. I came to bury its secret, but there is more merit in letting you achieve the duty you owe your father."

Hamlin said aloud: "I wonder if the Amir will melt this down for scrap gold."

But Tsong Kapa was not there to answer. Some far shadow had swallowed him. Hamlin swung the panel back into place, and with uncertain steps approached the camp fires where his men were plunging wrist deep into *pilau*. He wondered if they would knife him and make off with the loot; it was far too bulky for him to conceal in packs, and then pretend that he had abandoned the quest. He had not thought of that problem, having been too intent on discovery. He must think awhile before he acted.

So he planned; but Taimur, staring intently at him, licked the gravy from his fingers and approached, saying: "Allah has whispered to you, *sahib!* We knew you would find it!"

The others were on their feet before Hamlin could recover from the shock. Then he saw that their bronzed faces were loose with wonder, and their eyes were wide. They must have read his gait and his expression, since they had the intuition of animals and children and savages. And he realized that awe for the moment gripped them; so he boldly played his hand.

"IT WILL LOAD several mules," he announced, beckoning and turning toward the crypt. "Tomorrow we pack. This is the Amir's treasure, and it is on our heads. Come and see what Iskander Dhoulkarnayn buried!"

They followed, silently. Then a babbling in half a dozen languages as they crowded forward, watching the yellow flame of the flare bring ancient lights from the gold when he swung back the panel.

"*Wallah!* This was placed here by *afrits!* Thou fool, it belongs to Iskander of the Two Horns, and he will curse us for touching it! Nay, that will be on the Amir's head."

Several of the men eyed him furtively and edged away. Hamlin understood. He himself now shared the awe with which Alexander's name had been passed from lip to lip for twenty-two centuries. These men would cheerfully cut a throat for a *rupee* or a pair of shoes — but Iskander's treasure was as incomprehensible to them as a check for a billion dollars would have been to Hamlin. It was just a question of how long the spell of Iskander of the Two Horns would last.

He dismissed them with a gesture, then sat down to think it out. There was nothing to think, really; nothing but haul the loot to Kabul.

Hamlin did not know how much time elapsed before Taimur approached and announced: "*Sahib*, that accursed Feringhi is gone."

"What?"

"Yes. Kraft *sahib*. But there is no need to pursue. He could die a dozen times before he reaches the Chawak Pass being alone and having shoes that would make some mountaineer uncomfortable but quite proud."

"Does he know we have found the treasure?"

"Knowledge is with God," Taimur answered. "We will know when we run into an ambush somewhere on our march. Unless his throat, by Allah's mercy, be first cut."

Hamlin wondered if Kraft had won his liberty by strength and wit, or by a bribe of a few *rupees*. But there was no clue in the shelter which the prisoner had occupied. His pistol had been taken from Hamlin's tent, and a horse was missing. The cords that had bound him had been slashed.

Then one of the look-outs came bounding into the fire glow.

"Men are slipping down into the valley the way we came in, *sahib*. A horse neighed — a rock clattered! I heard."

"Douse the fire!" ordered Hamlin. "Run the animals into the niche! Taimur, break out the guns. Make no noise."

In a moment the camp was astir with silent activity. And presently Hamlin, creeping out into the gloom, could hear the vague sounds of an advancing *kafila*; the creak of pack saddles, the rattle of a dislodged stone. They were being caught flat-footed; this was no time to slip out. Hamlin's party, if it attempted to duplicate Kraft's trick, would be strung out, its flank fatally exposed to a raid. Worse than that, the valley mouth was blocked.

A ragged volley crackled from the farther side of the valley. Slugs smacked overhead, whined as they glanced from the cliffs. Taimur pumped lead at the flashes, until Hamlin checked him. But his blind shooting was better than his deliberate marksmanship.

A pack animal squealed, voices rumbled; and there was one yell, that could not be mistaken. Taimur patted his rifle and said: "One is dead. May Allah not be pleased with him!"

"Into the niche!" ordered Hamlin. "And no more shooting. Wait till they get closer."

They grumbled, but they obeyed him. And soon spurts of flame from the right and left indicated that the raiders were fanning out into a crescent. Their attacking fire was wild, but it converged on Hamlin's camp, effectively preventing anything like an organized departure.

Moonlight, later on, was deceptive, yet revealing. It halted the advance of the enemy. Hamlin roughly estimated their strength. He was outnumbered three to one. Thus, though he could not hope to break out by an open rush, neither could they charge in and overwhelm him.

"Anyway, we've got plenty of water," he said to himself, remembering the subterranean stream. He watched with Taimur, letting the others sleep. Tsong Kapa, just visible in the niche, had nothing to say. But he was awake. Hamlin heard the interminable soft clicking of his rosary.

Neither gold nor danger moved that strange man, and as the night wore on Tsong Kapa's inhuman calmness and utter indifference to the things that loomed large in a man's life began to make Hamlin wonder if the monk had not become somewhat like the Buddha that he served.

"Maybe he's right," muttered Hamlin, "after all."

Then he noted, abruptly, that through the eerie greyness of dawn stealthy figures were slowly advancing. He cursed softly, leveled his rifle.

Smack! Something dark jerked up, pitched forward, and then a yell tore the silence. Taimur's rifle spat lead. The men rolled from their sleeping mats, and the valley echoed with the spiteful crackling and the scream of lead. The invaders broke, took cover.

The flurry was over, but the siege was on. And Tsong Kapa, his nocturnal devotions over, had left his place at the feet of the Tall Gods. From somewhere within the crypts his voice echoed, sonorous and eerie:

"*Om, mani padmi hum!* Hail, dew drop gleaming in the Lotus Cup!"

VIII.

Treachery of Tsong Kapa

CUNNINGLY concealed in low-lying ground and out-croppings of rock at the further side of the valley, the camp of the besiegers was out of rifle shot.

They had high-powered rifles themselves. In their hands, however, no more accurate than the old-fashioned breech loaders that the tribesmen usually carried. Nevertheless, someone with good connections had supplied them with arms.

Whack! The fire increased, kicking up dirt and rock chips, or else spattering slugs high up on the face of the cliff behind Hamlin's party. The blinding spurts of powdered stone kept Hamlin from effective sniping, and as the shaggy Hazara tribesmen on the left peppered away, those on the right advanced to the outcroppings of rock a hundred yards closer to their goal.

They moved skilfully, each *echelon* in turn supporting the other's rushes. Though their advances had to be shortened as they closed in, their seemingly unlimited ammunition kept Hamlin's men from anything better than blind shooting.

"Lay off!" yelled Hamlin. "We'll be swamped if we run out of shells!"

And then, from the right, came a savage uproar. A file of raiders were pouring into camp. They were ducking in and out among the boulders at the foot of the cliff; and Hamlin, bounding to his feet, saw too late how they had gotten into position. There was a rope dangling down the face of the cliff. They had descended, thus, after skirting the wall of the valley. The last two of the flanking party were just letting go, dropping to shelter, when Hamlin's rifle smacked.

He scored. Man and gun pitched over instead of behind the protecting tongue of rock. In the meanwhile, the main attack had swept forward, firing and shooting. But they forgot that there were no more spurts of dust to spoil Hamlin's aim; forgot that one of the besieged would not go native under excitement.

One — two — three — four! Each recoil of Hamlin's rifle was followed by a split-second pause as he shifted, skipping two skirmishers, bearing down on the next. They wavered. Disciplined troops break when each third man drops, and these were no soldiers.

The center cracked as Hamlin jammed home a fresh clip. All hell was roaring at his right; knife and pistol and gun-butt were terribly tangled. His men were hard pressed, and from the corner of his eye he saw Taimur go down, red but slashing. Jerjis was flailing a curved sword, ducking a descending rifle barrel. Afzal Khan hurled an empty pistol into an attacker's face, then jerked a dagger.

Hamlin automatically slapped home the bolt of the Mauser. The riddled center was turning tail. But lead from the flanks swept past him as the howling tribesmen surged onward.

He felt the deadly breeze of wild shots. His helmet jerked from his head. Spatters of lead hit him, but he continued to fire, machinelike. At that range he could not miss. The whole line crumpled. They were bailing out.

Hamlin parried a sweeping yataghan, whipped up his emptied rifle in a butt-strike that doubled the swordsman. But before his pistol got fairly into action, the flanking party was in flight.

"Wallah, sahib!" panted Taimur, brushing the blood from his eyes, "if those dogs to the front had not run, we would now be dead men."

"Salvage the guns and ammunition before they pepper us!" shouted Hamlin, reloading.

H IS SNIPING kept the fugitives from reorganizing. And the Pathans, slipping forward, stripped the fallen raiders of belts and guns. Ammunition, nonetheless, was painfully scarce. Half of Hamlin's party were wounded; two were beyond doctoring, Tsong Kapa told him.

The long, grim hours of the ensuing stalemate dragged on. Hamlin could not escape nor counter-attack; the enemy dared not rush his position. His men, cooling down from their futile victory, were becoming sullen and despondent. Waiting kills an Afghan. But Jerjis, bland and amiable, came to Hamlin. "This land is my home," he said, "and it is good for me to die here. But your men are sick because they will not be buried among their own people. I know a path out of here, on foot."

"On foot?" Hamlin queried.

"The treasure is not worth their lives, Hamlin *sahib*. It belongs to Iskander of the Two Horns, and they are afraid."

"I will consider what you say," Hamlin dismissed him.

Long shadows were marching across the valley when a look-out's challenge brought Hamlin to his feet. He dashed to the southern end of the camp. The cause of the disturbance was Yakub, his Afridi servant, who should have been in Kabul with Irene Gray.

"Sahib, I could not get here any sooner. I have been on foot, and they were riding. Dost Ali — "

"What happened to her — Miss Gray?" Hamlin cut in, suddenly chilled by misgivings. Yakub could not have gone all the way to Kabul, and then returned.

"My face is blackened," groaned the leathery old fellow. "We met Dost Ali just past Charikar. We had not a chance. But I escaped, so I came to find you."

H<small>E</small> WAS worn out from exhaustion and lack of food. He had no arms except his long knife.

"Eat first," said Hamlin, helping him toward the shelter where fires were being kindled. So it was Dost Ali who was attacking him!

Rations as well as cartridges were dwindling. And as he pondered on Irene's plight, all that remained of Hamlin's courage was his grim exterior. Dost Ali could have made such revealing moves but for one reason: to keep all news of his treachery from ever getting back to Kabul. Now he was bent on utter extermination of the red-headed American's party.

"A messenger is coming from the enemy's camp, *sahib*," Taimur reported, gesturing out toward the plain.

Hamlin wearily arose to parley. But before he set out, he gathered his men about him. "Tonight we leave," he said. "Jerjis will show us the way. It will be difficult, but how often have you been stoop-shouldered with gold?"

There was no tremor in his crisp voice. He stood tall and straight among tall men. That the enemy elected to parley, instead of attacking, heartened his men. He sensed that, and played it up. "They are weakening. They will not press us hard when we have all the hills for a battle. Dost Ali is afraid, so he sends a mule driver."

"*Wallah*, that is true," agreed one. Others echoed: "There is a chance. By Allah, we can roll rocks on them from ambush!"

That was enough. Hamlin strode out in the slanting shadows to the gilded plain beyond. A turbaned tribesman, still beyond accurate rifle range, was advancing, extended arms holding a gun over his head. After a few more yards, during which Hamlin watched him through his glasses, the bearded Hazara laid his weapon on the ground, and continued, empty-handed, but wearing side arms.

Hamlin followed suit. The encounter was about halfway between the two camps.

"I am Yusuf Khan," announced the envoy, his shrewd eyes

uneasily shifting to Hamlin's pistol. "And I will let your party go unharmed, if you surrender Iskander's treasure."

"You're also a liar," countered Hamlin. "You're Dost Ali's servant, and he is afraid to meet me."

"God, by God, by the One True God!" swore Yusuf. "I am indeed —"

"Satan loves those who swear falsely," reproved Hamlin coldly. Then, winking: "Listen, friend, why pick gold for Dost Ali to seize? Join me and leave him sitting where he is. That is better than losing more of your men."

That was Afghan technique. Yusuf's eyes gleamed avariciously under their shaggy brows. Then he shook his head and countered haughtily. "We have the means of getting all. If we share it with Dost Ali, that is our business, not yours."

"But first, I am here to tell you that Dost Ali will deliver the Feringhi woman into your hands if you will abandon the treasure. It is known that you love her. Dost Ali is very wise, bringing her with him. Now, what answer shall I take back?"

THIS WAS what Hamlin had feared, ever since Yakub's return. Now that it faced him, he saw that there was a right as well as a wrong way to make the most of defeat.

"Tell Dost Ali that I will send the treasure to him, loaded on five mules. He will then send the Feringhi woman to my camp. If he tricks me and keeps her, my men will know that he intends for none of us to reach Kabul alive, so they will attack, and too many of you will die for it to be a bargain."

That was bluff. Hamlin was counting on the effect of all that treasure delivered to Dost Ali and his avaricious cutthroats. It would intoxicate them. There might be quarreling.

Yusuf recited the terms. Hamlin nodded, and the Hazara concluded: "So be it, then. Tonight — five mules, and their drivers bearing torches. And the Feringhi woman's life answers if there is any trickery."

When Hamlin returned to camp, he learned how fugitive was the courage he had stirred up in his men. Taimur was the center of a sullen group. Yakub and Jerjis stood apart, with Afzal Khan.

"*Sahib*," began Taimur, "we feared treachery, so two of us followed at some distance, to protect you."

Hamlin knew what that meant. They had overheard the

bargain, and mutiny was simmering. He would lose face if he backed away, made any move to compel obedience. Yet they were all armed, and he was too close to have any chance to defend himself.

"For such loyalty," he observed, "Allah will reward you."

Taimur fidgeted, fumbled for a moment, then said: "All this which has happened has been for the sake of the treasure. We can not hope to get alive to Kabul with it. But we kiss the dust beneath your feet. We will be thy sacrifice."

"That's fine," he approved, outwardly.

"Once that loot is taken from here your enemy will no longer seek you. Instead, he will pursue us."

"And we will therefore go with it into Turkestan," Shir Daoud cut in. "We will save you. You are our father and our grandfather."

Then, glance shifting, he saw that the three who stood apart had been disarmed. From the shadows at his right, a bolt clicked, and a voice warned, "*Sahib*, do not oppose us. Do as we say, and it will be well for thee. Since Dost Ali will risk the curse on this loot, so will we, being better men than he."

The rifle was no more than a yard away, muzzle reaching over a heap of baggage. No chance of cutting that man down, even if the others were not ready and desperate.

He had learned much about Afghans since the march began, and particularly about these who fought shoulder to shoulder with him. The knowledge was bitter. He was glad that Yakub and Jerjis had been disarmed; they at least were still for him. And he wondered about Afzal Khan, who had once been his captor. Why had that moon-faced trickster not joined with the mutineers?

"Have at it, then," he agreed. "But leave me five mules."

He turned and strode toward the blackly looming niche in which the tall gods mocked the vermin at their feet.

Men with torches followed him and the unarmed trio trailed along.

Once in the vault, Hamlin opened the treasure crypt; but the torch flames did not play on ancient gold. There was nothing save a sheet of paper. In the silence that followed, Hamlin picked it up. It was written on with a charred stick, in English and in Pushtu.

"Which of you can read?" he demanded bitterly, and as he spoke, he wondered why his voice did not shake. Everything was crashing into chaos about him — mutiny among his own followers, treachery here, and no chance to barter for Irene.

Taimur stared at the sheet. Then he howled: "Find that accursed infidel! Where is that idol worshiper? He has robbed us!"

They forgot Hamlin in their wrath. The outburst proved that Taimur could read. Without doubt the Pushtu lines meant the same as those in English. Hamlin slowly read the English version:

> *Observing that there is no help for you either against Dost Ali or the avarice of your own men, I have disposed of the loot for which too many men have died. I have gained merit, for, with the treasure gone, there is no need for any man to slay you. Peace to you, and to all living creatures.*
>
> *Tsong Kapa, the least of created things.*

X.

Speaking of Treasures —

Slowly Hamlin followed the howling men outside. Almost listlessly he watched them turn the camp inside out, raging and cursing all the while. But no trace of the Thibetan monk was found.

No pack animals were missing, nor any weapons. Nothing was gone, except Tsong Kapa and enough loot to burden a mule caravan. Their rage became choked as this magical significance was borne in on them. How could Tsong Kapa have gone? Awed surmise made their mutter, peer sharply over their shoulders.

"*Ya Allah*, this was a devil — an *afrit*. No man would have done it — vanish thus, with more than a pack train could carry. By Allah, it is useless to hunt him — he would slay us. Always he was muttering strange words —"

Hamlin felt like agreeing with the men. How the devil had Tsong Kapa pulled such a trick? Unfortunately, an American could not blame it on evil spirits; that went against the grain, though it seemed by far the simplest solution!

And all the while, misery left him numb. Slim chance of convincing Dost Ali that the loot had vanished; hence, none of liberating Irene. Dost Ali could not afford to have her return to Kabul and gain the Amir's ear. There would be an "accident" on the road.

Logically Hamlin's fate would be linked with Irene's. Things had happened too swiftly, he had been under too severe a strain to realize all the possibilities; but now he saw that even if Tsong Kapa had not taken a turn at playing destiny, the goal would in the end have been the same.

"Taimur!" he shouted, voice ringing like a bugle. "Before you go, let us have vengeance on Kraft *Sahib*. Had he not tried to trap us, we would even now have had the treasure and been on our way."

"How, *sahib*?" There was a chorus of shouts. Those who heard clamored after Taimur.

"He is in Dost Ali's camp," said Hamlin, "but we can get him."

That was not so appealing. One of the Pathans suspiciously demanded: "*Sahib*, who brought thee news of this thing? Some of us overheard the messenger's speech, and he said nothing of that infidel pig!"

"Blockhead!" laughed Hamlin as the troublemaker snapped at the bait. "How does Dost Ali know that we found the treasure? Only Kraft could have told him. And unless Dost Ali *knew beyond guessing*, would his men have rushed us until we shot half of them down?"

"Allah! Wisdom drips from his mouth!" There were bursts of approval, and Hamlin knew that he had won.

"I have forgiven you," he went on, "for your disobedience. Now I will save your heads. Listen — when Dost Ali fails to get the loot tonight, he will hunt you down to the last man, torture you into telling a secret you do not know. Which of you could make him believe that the treasure flew into the night?"

They muttered, stroked their beards. Who, indeed?

"There is no help for it unless you do as I say. But I know the way. It is easy."

This was one man unshaken by magic. They chorused: "Thou art our father and our grandfather! Tell us, *sahib!* Tell us!"

He answered: "We will send five mules as we agreed. They will not carry gold, but men. As for me, I shall flank attack, and those three you disarmed will go with me." He paused, sharply eyed Taimur, then said to him: "And you, also, for we shall have the most dangerous work."

THE BROAD-FACED Uzbek grinned, and his deep chest expanded. "Get busy, O sons of flat-nosed mothers!" he shouted at his followers.

He herded them to their work, leaving Hamlin busy with what had suddenly become an important resource — the box of blasting powder and the fuses.

Later, at the appointed time, they moved out. Since there could be no exchange of signals, Hamlin's only hope was that those who were to go forward with mules bearing armed men instead of treasure would not jump the gun. He had to be behind and above Dost Ali's camp by the time the approach of flaring torches distracted the Afghan's attention.

Jerjis led a perilous course into the gloom. He was nimble, surefooted, and seemed to climb by instinct along the path his keen eyes had picked during those hours when it had threatened to become every man for himself. Hamlin trailed along, bringing up the rear. Each man carried a portion of the low grade blasting gelatin. Capped, fused, and exploded in the open air, it would do comparatively little damage, but Hamlin was counting on the surprise effect.

Finally, they were rounding the rim of the valley. Hamlin paused, almost directly over the encampment, nearly a quarter of a mile below. Men were squatting about a smoldering fire.

The tents and shelters were buried in shadows, except when outlined by a breeze momentarily brightening a fire. But one shelter near the center of the encampment was steadily silhouetted by an unwavering glow from within. That would be Dost Ali's tent, or possibly Irene's prison.

And then Jerjis led the way down the sheer wall to the cleft through which they themselves had descended, only a few days ago. Thanks to the thin cord that the Kafir had brought, Hamlin and the others could follow. They were trembling and sweat-drenched when they finally reached the steeply sloping, narrow trail.

THEY WAITED. Half an hour went by. God alone knew whether a strange quirk might have turned their comrades to attempt flight.

"They are giving us plenty of time," Jerjis assured him. "Once armed men are found in the treasure packs, they will be dead unless you are ready to strike."

Reasonable, after all. But Hamlin had seen too much of native fickleness the past few days. Yet, he had to move, to act, blindly trusting the other contingent.

"I'm going to get a closer look," he said. "And remember — when you touch matches to the fuses, heave quick. They're cut short."

He crawled forward, until he was crouching in the shadow of a rocky buttress only a few yards from the lighted pavilion. A woman was speaking in Hindustani. When he heard another woman answer, his heart rose and choked him. It was Irene, replying to her maid.

"It isn't so hopeless, Sita Deva. He'll get us back to Kabul, somehow. Yes, I know you are sure we would be ambushed, but I have no fear."

Hamlin fingered the haft of his knife, tempted to slit the tent wall, get Irene, and end the suspense! But two women could not follow him in that dangerous retreat up the face of the cliff; not until Dost Ali was disorganized.

Then, far off into the blackness of the valley, he saw torches moving slowly. Dost Ali's men perceived it; their voices rose, harshly guttural and tense. They were moving forward.

What kept him from slitting the wall of Irene's quarter of the tent now was Kraft's voice, coming from the front. The German was saying: "I might have expected this —"

"You fool!" laughed Dost Ali. "You fled from the treasure site. You would have been murdered by your own men. They look down on a bungler. So you have no claim on the loot, now."

"But we're in this together!" protested Kraft.

"We are not," suavely corrected Dost Ali. "Not in *this*. I sent you here. You failed. I had to come because Irene Gray suddenly left town to warn Hamlin. She's now my guest, but no thanks to you. And her presence, not yours, is getting that loot from Hamlin."

"But —" Kraft choked, and his accent became thick. "But this is all part of the original plan. I told you of the chart —"

"Helpful!" This, with smooth irony. "As though I was not there when he told the Amir about it."

"The Amir!" growled Kraft. "And if *he* ever heard of your schemes, you'd be leaning against the muzzle of a cannon."

"Don't threaten me," warned the Afghan, his voice a blend of silk and iron. "You cannot hurt me without hurting yourself. Being a protected foreigner goes just so far. Perhaps you could stir something up by exposing our agreement to freeze Hamlin out of the trading business. Regardless of what might happen to me, there are others — others you don't know, *Herr* Kraft — who'd become panic stricken and — but you know what happened to McTavish."

"But you can't give her to Hamlin." Kraft's voice shook. *"She'll die with him."*

"Our only safety, my friend," soothed the Afghan. "Her father stood high in the Amir's favor, because of a bit of surgery. But you're a grown man, Kraft. She's seen too much, thanks to your bungling."

"Ach — but you can't!" groaned Kraft. "By God, I will tell the Amir everything. I'll face the music unless she goes back with me."

"I don't think you'll do anything of the kind," contradicted Dost Ali in his precise Oxford accent.

Kraft made helpless, incoherent sounds. His concern for

Irene made him seem very much like the man who had caught the tiger by the tail, daring neither to go on nor to let go.

THE AFGHAN's men were challenging the approaching pack train. Hamlin could now clearly see the wavering torches, the plodding beasts, and a tall, robed figure with a white turban reddened by the flame.

"The loot is here!" Dost Ali's voice rang triumphantly. Then he shouted to one of his men: "Bring forth the *memsahib* quickly — so those fellows won't try a surprise move."

That had to be stopped before Irene got too far from the pavilion. Hamlin drew his pistol, hoping his men could gain a few more paces; but the choice was taken from him.

A pistol smacked. Dost Ali groaned. Kraft roared wrathfully. The servant yelled. Irene's outcry was muffled by two more shots. The camp became a howling confusion. Hamlin bounded into the open. And then, from his right rear, came a long, ripping rumble of the bombs, the squeal of stampeding mules, and the shouts of the three who had waited in the rear.

Animals crashed through the shelters. Men drawing knives and pistols charged toward the pavilion. Kraft, fuming weapon in hand, was outlined by the light from within the tent as he cleared the threshold. His face was white, and his eyes blazed desperately. Kraft, having riddled Dost Ali, was running amuck.

Hamlin had no chance to cut him down. Gun-flame dazzled him, and his own shot went wild. Then they crashed head-long, the German still firing blindly. Hamlin, scorched and stunned, lashed out with his boot as he groped to regain the pistol that had been knocked from his grasp. But that kick was sufficient. Kraft, smacking back against a tent peg, was knocked out, his scalp furrowed by the hard wood.

It happened in split seconds. Hamlin caught a glimpse of the treasure train; the mules no longer had packs. Five men were rushing the camp, firing as they ran. The enemy's panic maddened them, and vengeance made them reckless.

And then Irene and her maid came piling out of the pavilion.

"Get out — get back — that way!" shouted Hamlin.

She stared, bewildered. His face was dirt and blood-blotted, unrecognizable as his voice.

"It's me, Irene — Red! Go back that way!"

"Oh, Red!" Instead of obeying, she came toward him.

And then a voice, low yet clear above the murderous tumult, interposed: "Do as he says, and I will go with you."

It was Tsong Kapa, bland and unruffled as the Tall Gods who were looking across the valley at the flames that now leaped from the burning shelters. Hamlin was swept up in the rush. Knives raked him. His last shot blasted away the frenzied clinch of Yusuf, with whom he had parleyed that day.

They both went down, and Hamlin jerked the *tulwar* haft from the Hazara's limp fingers. Before Hamlin could gain his feet, the rout swept beyond the reach of the crackling flames. Bolts were slapping home; reloaded guns were rattling aimlessly, being fired on the run, but driving the defenders into the open valley.

Hamlin did not follow. Irene now was his concern.

"Irene — it's over! Where are you?" The wind had shifted, and the unfanned flames no longer crackled. His voice boomed in the sudden silence.

"I heard you, darling!" Her laugh was shaky. "You needn't shout so."

SHE emerged from cover only a few yards from where he had first slipped into camp. Sita Deva clung to her. Tsong Kapa strode some paces to the right, and a little to the rear. With the emergency over, it was not fitting that any female creature be needlessly near his sanctified person.

"You idiot!" Hamlin, being neither Buddhist nor monk, knew that two arms could not get her at all close enough. "I told you to get out."

"I knew that it would be over swiftly," interposed Tsong Kapa. "And that rock would stop stray bullets."

"Where," demanded Hamlin of him, "is Iskander's loot? How the devil did you get it away? It weighed a ton!"

"It did," sighed the monk. "Never more weight for less worth."

But Hamlin had no time to listen now. Startled by "the return of his triumphant men, he thrust Irene from him and bounded toward Kraft. He was just in time to strike aside Yakub's dripping *tulwar.*

"*Sahib!*" reproached the old Afridi, "his life is forfeited."

"No. It is valuable. All the more so since we are alive to bear witness that he shot Dost Ali treacherously in the back."

"That is right," approved Tsong Kapa. "You heard the conspiracy, even as I did. Dost Ali and Mr. Kraft were to put your company out of business. Then, with Dost Ali's influence, the rival company, bribing customs officials, could bring goods into Kabul without duty."

"But the loot, Tsong Kapa?" Hamlin returned to the treasure. "Where is it? Getting it back to Kabul will be deadly work."

"I came to Kabul to recover the scroll, lest greed would lead to many deaths. So I dropped it into the subterranean river, whose great depths and relentless current have swallowed it beyond the reach of any man. It can cause no more strife, nor any greed. You may now go to Kabul without any man whetting his knife."

He paused and there was no sound except the sighing of the wind. Hamlin's men did not understand a word, but they stood gaping, gripped by that deep voice. Then Kraft groaned, and tried to rise. Irene was regarding the monk with wide eyes. She nodded very slowly, whispered at last: "He's right, Red."

Hamlin blinked, and started as though hot iron had touched him. Then he said: "You knew that if we'd surrendered it, she and I and my men would never have reached Kabul alive?"

"No man knows anything certainly," answered Tsong Kapa. "With the love that led Miss Gray into peril for you, and brought you to make this sacrifice for her, you could scarcely have failed. But this way is best, and Dost Ali died by a grasping hand — not by yours."

Hamlin nodded, gesturing toward Kraft. He said to the prisoner: "You will defend yourself against a charge of murdering the Amir's tricky favorite. By telling all your story, you can doubtless save your head — and save my trading concession."

"Peace to all living things," beamed Tsong Kapa, raising one hand in a gesture of benediction. He bowed, and began fingering his one hundred and eight beads. *"Om, mani padme, hum!"*

"Red," whispered Irene, "for a loafer, you've done famously —" She was rudely interrupted. But the curve of her upturned lips and the glow of her eyes as her lashes dropped had something to do with the sudden interruption. She wriggled clear of his arms, a bit breathless, and reproved him. "Red — don't — you'll horrify Tsong Kapa!"

"Hell," grumbled Hamlin, "you're not going to kiss *him*, and even a Buddhist monk can stand a look."

He half turned; but Tsong Kapa was no longer in sight.

"He would do that, just that way," chuckled Hamlin. "Yakub — Taimur! Start packing! I've got the treasure here in my arms."

LIVE BAIT

Davis P. BARRETT's mother, who had died when he was six, doubtless thought that he was a beautiful child; but then, she was his mother, and something like thirty odd years may have changed little Davis. Mrs. Barrett's youngest son's face was now the Rock of Gibraltar done in that shade of bronze which comes from long exposure to the breath of blistering deserts and tropical jungles. His broad mouth was a thin, straight line no wider than the edge of an officer's dress-sword, and somewhat harder. His blue eyes glowed with ominous, volcanic mirth as they watched two perfectly barbered, tailored, and manicured gentlemen whose tables were at the corner of the tiny dance floor, and to Barrett's left.

The two racketeers were inseparable friends. They had assumed — somewhat erroneously, as it later developed — that their being at Club Martinique was pure coincidence, and they had agreed to combine their tables when their feminine companions arrived.

A waiter was bringing a note to the gentleman whose table was nearest Barrett: Guido Pichetti. Barrett's shaggy, reddish brows rose just perceptibly. His chin, which he fingered abstractedly, was thrust forward. There was something tense and expectant about Barrett, as though he were a panther about to spring. His interest seemed centered on the note, rather than on the perceptible bulge of the left breasts of the nicely fitted dinner jackets of Messieurs Pichetti and Spud Malone.

Club Martinique was a mirthful madhouse of blatant music, alcoholic laughter, and tinkle of ice against the sides of many tall glasses. White arms and shoulders, and whiter shirt fronts stared spectrally through the bluish glare of the spotlight that made the shifting bands of smoke seem like phantom serpents writhing in the warmth of a ghostly sun.

The reek of gin, perfume, cosmetics, and unextinguished cigarette butts was the odor of gaiety to most of those assembled: but to Davis Barrett it was the exhalation of death, and the end of a story. . . .

Guido Pichetti had opened the note. His swarthy features flushed with rage, then bleached sallow as he leaped from his table. What he said to Malone, and what Malone replied was not audible above the blare of the music; but Barrett's expectancy was not in vain. There was an almost simultaneous flashing of hands to shoulder holsters —

Barrett's lips relaxed enough to reveal a glimpse of his teeth as two pistols blazed into the satanic bluish moonlight, and their roar, almost a single, prolonged report, bellowed above the brazen clang of the orchestra. Barrett ignored the ensuing uproar and confusion as a glance, before the crowd became too dense about the fallen, assured him that the heretofore bosom friends had killed each other. He sighed deeply, slouched against the back of his chair, and for the first time realized how highly keyed he had been for the past half hour.

Justice that was beyond the power of the law.

Vengeance . . . and the end of the story. . . .

A burly, red-faced, grim mouthed man emerged from the gaping, babbling, hysterical crowd that pushed in as close as it could to the double X's that marked the respective spots where Guido Pichetti and Spud Malone had become public benefactors. In his hands he had a letter and an envelope, both of which he thrust before Barrett.

"Dave," he demanded, "what do you know about this? One look tells me it's fishy as kippered herring — even if Damon and Pythias were too dumb to realize it."

Barrett regarded first the envelope, then the letter, then John Healy, Chief of the Detective Bureau, who was beginning to understand why he had received a tip to be present, though unseen, at Club Martinique.

"End of the story, John. It's been a strain, figuring out ways of making these rats kill each other."

Healy grunted, nodded, then said, "Pretty good, Dave. Only, it's not the end of the story by a big damn sight! You've not finished something, you've started something. Watch your step."

Mrs. Barrett *might* have been right, some thirty years ago. Her lean, broad shouldered son, while far from handsome, in his lighter moments had a pleasant smile, and an engaging friendly manner.

"Thanks, John," he said quite affably as he rose from his seat. "Come out to the house some night soon. I have some mighty interesting jig-saw puzzles."

And a few moments later, Barrett was at the wheel of his Issotta, driving up Saint Charles Avenue toward Audoubon Place. He was smiling to himself at the gullibility of two dear friends whose lurking suspicion of each other had been detonated by the note Barrett had prepared and planted.

Two DAYS later — thirty-six hours, to be accurate — Barrett's smile vanished. What he had called the end of a story had become the beginning of a longer and grimmer tale. His blue eyes were hard as sword points as he paced up and down the wine-red Boukhara rug in his library.

"Marie," he demanded abruptly as he halted and faced the girl who sat buried in the depths of an over-stuffed chair, "are you sure Lee hasn't just left town suddenly on urgent business?"

Marie Simpson shook her blonde head and dabbed her tear-reddened eyes. She had never learned the art of effective weeping.

"No, Dave. He'd have wired or phoned me by this time." She swallowed a sob, then said pointedly, "And I don't think you believe he's left on a business trip, either."

Barrett's features tensed. Vengeance was bearing bitter fruit.

"Suppose you run along home," he suggested with a gentleness that seemed out of keeping with his rugged features and the usually incisive snap of his voice. "You know I'd go through hell and high water for Lee. And if there's anything off color about his being missing for the past twelve hours, I'll tear the roof off."

As he spoke, he helped Marie Simpson with her coat.

"Dave, do you think —"

"I'm not thinking anything," he evaded. "But I'm going to see. Now run along, and pull yourself together."

As the door clicked closed behind Marie Simpson, Barrett's eyes flashed to the half opened desk drawer. During the brief interview he had feared that his very effort not to think of what the drawer contained, not to let his eyes stray toward it would betray him to Marie's intuition. His hand halted midway as it reached for the envelope.

"Jackass!" he said aloud. "Healy was right."

Barrett's bitter thoughts were interrupted by the arrival of John Healy. He indicated the chair that Marie Simpson had left but a few moments ago — or how long had it been that he had stared at that desk drawer?

"What's new and good, John?"

"About Lee Simpson, and it's not good," said Healy as he selected a cigar from Barrett's humidor and jammed his bulk into the spacious chair. "You're his number one friend. Where is he?"

"God knows," replied Barrett. "And I will if I live long enough. Has his wife —"

"Uhuh. Run me ragged," interrupted Healy. "But no sign of him."

"Where do I come in?"

"Simpson's not got two nickels to click together," answered Healy. "And no enemies. The way I got it doped out, someone is getting at you for that job you pulled at Club Martinique. Somebody took a tumble."

Barrett flinched as at the thrust of a red hot iron.

"Right, John. I'd rather face a machine gun than this."

"Don't worry. You probably will, before it's over. Have you gotten any demands for ransom or the like?"

Barrett shook his head.

"You're a damn liar," declared Healy with the license of friendship.

"Have it your own way. And if you've any dope, pass it along. I'm on the job myself."

"No good, Dave," said Healy with a peremptory gesture. "That's the trouble. You've been on the job too much. You smoked out so many of these rats — and now they're pulling your teeth by snatching Simpson."

"My teeth," countered Barrett with an ominous glitter in his eyes, "aren't pulled yet. I want you to keep your hands off. None of your men following me around when I take the warpath. Will you give me a break? Stand clear?"

Healy saw Barrett's glance shift and linger on a rack of firearms that made the library look very much like an arsenal.

"Sold."

"Thanks, John. And remember, I've got my reasons for playing a lone hand."

Upon Healy's departure, Barrett re-read for the twentieth time the letter he had received that morning:

> **Bring $20,000 in new, unmarked hundred dollar bills to the main entrance of the Crescent Compress Company at midnight. If there is any sign of police interference, or if my men do not report by one A.M., we'll ship Simpson's head to join his finger. Come alone and unarmed.**

There was no signature. None was needed. Jake Moroni had made a final counterattack that would not fail as the others had. A small parcel which had accompanied the letter bore witness that the enemy meant business. It contained the fourth finger of Simpson. The blackened nail, recently crushed by a hammer tap, identified it beyond any doubt.

Barrett knew that the demand for the ransom was camouflage. Moroni had based his *coup* on the friendship of Simpson and Barrett. He knew that Barrett would willingly and knowingly walk into an ambuscade for the sake of Simpson.

"The Hell you say!" muttered Barrett as he thrust the letter back into his desk. "Using live bait . . ."

He grinned sourly, and added, "I'll do the same."

At ABOUT the same hour of that same morning, Jake Moroni was holding high court in his armored office in an otherwise deserted warehouse near the river front. Moroni's swivel chair was a throne, and his well-tailored suit of imported worsteds was the imperial purple that had slipped from the shoulders of his predecessor when the muzzle of a .25-3000 reached through a loophole in a brick wall and snapped a tiny slug through a pistol-proof vest.

In front of Moroni was a mahogany desk entirely suitable to an executive whose payrolls were as great as those of the city, and whose revenues were greater. At his left was a gaudy Japanese screen that added to the grotesquerie of the crude office. The screen, however, was no evidence of the house beautiful; it served a useful purpose. The center of one of its painted chrysanthemums had been neatly cut out with a knife.

Moroni's swarthy features smiled unpleasantly as his dark eyes bored coldly into the pudgy, evil faced ruffian before him.

"Orders are orders," he declared with ominous evenness of tone.

"I don't give a damn!" exclaimed Moroni's lieutenant, and commander in chief of the Praetorian guard of hop heads, and assorted assassins. "Tinkering with Barrett is like boxing with a tiger. Shaking him down for twenty grand to save Simpson's hide is one thing. That's easy. But trying to grab Barrett when he delivers the jack is plain foolishness."

"Mmm . . . hmmm," breathed Moroni. His snake eyes flickered to the right. He seemed for an instant to be peering through and past the thugs who sat on a bench along the wall. "Carver! Are *you* man enough?"

A tall, rangy fellow whose bony features wore a warped, perpetual grin, fidgeted for a moment with the brim of his hat. His glance switched from Moroni to the lieutenant on the carpet, and back to Moroni again.

"Jeez, that ain't a fair question," he protested. "I'm workin' for you, but I'm directly under Schwartz. Ya know —"

He made a gesture of resignation.

"Mmm . . . discipline," murmured Moroni. "Yes. Discipline is splendid." Then he snapped a question: "How about you other punks?" The other two on the bench started, frowned ponderously, nodding and rubbing their chins as though a portentous decision was on the verge of birth. The atmosphere of the tiny, soundproof office became electric from the tension.

"Yellow from your back bone to your belly!" crackled Moroni. "Just like this slob."

The slob on the carpet flushed.

"Who's yellow, you —"

His hand made a swift gesture; but it was not fast enough. A spurt of flame poured from the loophole of the chrysanthemum. As the pudgy lieutenant reeled crazily and collapsed, a pistol appeared in Moroni's hand. The three along the wall kept their hands rigidly motionless.

"You bastards gimme a headache," said Moroni pleasantly. "Mike — Otto! Get the hell outa here while I talk to Carver."

As the pair left the office, audibly sighing their relief at dismissal, Moroni beckoned to Sam Carver.

"I been fed up with him for a long time. You got guts enough to take this job?"

Carver swallowed just once.

"Sure thing. Only I'd like to know just what you want done."

"That's the talk," approved Moroni as he replaced his pistol. "When Barrett shows up tonight, I want you birds to nab him, tie him, and bring him to the *Carlotta*. And I don't want you to croak him —"

Sam Carver frowned perplexedly.

"Jeez, that's a contract. He's a fighting fool, and —" He saw Moroni's eyes shifting speculatively toward the man who lay on the floor. "But I'll make it — but it won't hurt to tap him on the nut just to keep him quiet, without really *hurtin'* him?"

Moroni nodded and smiled thinly.

"Just remember that a dead man can't sign an order for fifty grand. But *after* we get the dough . . ."

Carver grinned.

"Sorta double play, eh, Mr. Moroni?"

"Right. And just a bit of advice, Sam. You been getting too friendly with my secretary."

His voice was low, confidential, and alarming.

"Honest, I ain't done — I mean, I didn't mean a thing. Just bein' friendly to Nor — Miss Arradonda."

Moroni stroked his bluish jaw and smiled affably.

"I understand that, Sam. But it just don't look right. She's nothing to me at all, only . . ."

"I got ya, Mr. Moroni," Carver hastened to assure his chief.

"Okay. And no slips tonight. I'm counting on you. Twenty grand, and Barrett in shape to sign an order for fifty more, and then we'll have no more phoney letters and civil war."

Despite his chief's warning, Sam Carver phoned Norma Arradonda, and after being assured that the coast was clear, called at her apartment. He came to the point at once.

"You and me are strangers from now on. Positively farewell appearance."

Norma was dark and shapely, and lived up to the exotic ear pendants she affected. Her full lips were red as a saber slash against the transparent, creamy pallor of her skin.

"Matter, Sam?" Her delicately penciled brows rose in Moorish arches.

"Moroni's set on rubbing me out," Carver explained somberly. "That Barrett job —"

"You have been buying me too many drinks at Club Martinique," mused Norma.

"So I heard. And here I am."

"Still," resumed Norma, "I think you're heated up about nothing."

Carver shook his head.

"Barrett has been on the spot half a dozen times — and each time he's beaten it, with a surprise party of his own. And when he pulls a dumb one, his luck saves him."

"I'm scared of that guy's luck. He's a hoodoo. And he's filled a private graveyard with mugs that tried to get him. Snatching his best friend is like spitting in a tiger's eye."

Norma shook her head.

"Wrong, Sam. Him and Simpson are old buddies. And if you don't return by a certain time, it's Simpson's head. He knows it. That's going to make a boy scout out of Barrett."

"I don't care if it's supposed to make a good Christian of him," countered Carver dolefully. "I'm bein' framed — just like Dutch —"

Carver checked himself abruptly, swallowed, said nothing.

"Yes?" murmured Norma.

"Nothing!" snapped Sam. "I'm doing this job, and then

I'm going to the country to raise chickens. There's no percentage."

He reached for his hat. Norma stopped him at the door.

"Since you're not going to see me any more," she said, "you might at least kiss me good bye — you're a good egg, Sam, and I hope you get the breaks . . . oh, just a minute. . . ."

He paused as she scribbled an address and a telephone number on a slip of paper.

"Call me here, once in a while — *but disguise your voice.* Someone might be listening in on an extension. Don't say too much. Just enough so I'll know you're thinking of me. He's got his guts, trying to keep you from even being friendly in a nice way. . . . 'Bye, Sam."

Norma was part of the dictator's intricate web of evasion and espionage. While terming her a secretary was perhaps a shade too figurative, hers was an important part in Moroni's system of seeming to be in several places at once, and proving it by answering, from one point, calls to half a dozen offices. Norma was much of the brain of the organization — but Norma was, after all human. . . .

THAT NIGHT Barrett dressed very deliberately, as though for a dinner engagement instead of a rendezvous with kidnappers.

"Damn your black hide, Amos," he said reproachfully, as he regarded the tie that his white-haired old colored handyman had laid out. "Do you think that goes with this suit?"

"Yas suh, Mistah Dave! Ah thinks it's jes go'geous," the old man insisted with a nod and a grin. Then he turned to the rack to replace his favorite among Barrett's array.

Barrett was content with the amendment submitted by Amos. As he adjusted it, he fondly regarded the Colt .45 that lay in his dresser drawer, and regretfully shook his head.

"That black scarf, Amos," he said abstractedly, as he detached a gold penknife from his chain. He took the scarf, snapped it several times, whip-like; and all the while, one eye half closed, he pondered as though considering a hitherto unweighed element of the evening's dangerous work. Barrett finally knotted the penknife into a corner of the scarf, then stuffed several packets of hundred dollar bills into his pockets.

"Amos," he said, "here is the key to the Ford. In case I don't come back, you can have it."

The old man's eyes widened, and his black face lengthened.

"Whhhh-y, Mistah Dave," he sputtered.

"Stick around and watch the phone," said Barrett. "And you don't know where I've gone — not even if the President calls!"

"Yas, suh, Mistah Dave. An' ain't nuthin' goin' a happen to you."

"I wish," reflected Barrett as he took the wheel of the heavy sedan that was next to the Ford coupé, "that I could be sure Amos is right."

Barrett parked near the corner of Munn and Tchoupitoulas Streets. Even by daylight, the vicinity seemed to have been blighted by a lurching vengeance that had doomed to failure the warehouses and ship's chandleries that line the river front.

"Munn Street . . . one block long — but it may take me the rest of my life to reach the end of it," was Barrett's thought as he sought to accustom his eyes to the blackness. The moon was still so low that the shadows of the buildings on the right blended with black bulk of those on the left. He shivered as the penetrating wind bit like a bayonet. Barrett drew his top coat about him. His fingers, grasping the lapels, touched the hard silk of his scarf.

"One concealed weapon, anyway . . ."

A gold penknife. If he had brought a pistol, he might be tempted to use it, and thus surely kill Lee Simpson as well as the one who received his fire.

"God, but it's dark. . . ."

Barrett was used to the haunted blacknesses of Asiatic jungles, vibrant with the silent slinking of the eater in search of the eaten; yet Munn Street, which led to the river, was shrouded by an obscurity more malignant than any he had ever penetrated. Barrett shivered again, but this time, not from cold. He smiled, and his gait became fluent as that of the hunter.

Barrett forced himself to consider the moment at hand

rather than the other life which hung in the balance. It was his fault that Simpson was in danger, and his duty to extricate him, regardless of the cost.

Twenty paces into the darkness. Then someone emerged from a doorway and said in a low, decisive voice, "Stick 'em up, Jack."

But it was the muzzle of a pistol that someone else jammed into the small of his back that gave force to the command. Barrett's hands rose.

"Now back into this doorway — Mike, frisk him, right now!"

Deft fingers went through his pockets. There was a mutter of satisfaction as Mike drew out four packets of bills. For an instant the beam of a tiny fountain pen flashlight winked at the numerals that marked the denomination. The reflected glow, however, revealed more than the direct light: Barrett noted that his captors were not masked. It seemed to make no difference to them that Barrett had in that moment's illumination seen enough to identify them.

There was an unavoidable conclusion that Barrett had to draw — unless he could convince himself that his captors had been careless, and had not realized that Barrett would ever afterwards recognize them.

"All right, fellows," said Barrett pleasantly. "You've got your money — now where's Simpson?"

"Ain't that a hot one, Sam?" chuckled the one who had searched Barrett.

"Simpson is in a safe place," came the reply. "And you're coming with us. Think we're going to turn you loose before this money's been checked to see nothing's phoney?"

"Reasonable," admitted Barrett. "I'll sort of be taking Simpson's place, so you can turn him loose right away."

"Uhuh," grunted Sam, apparently pleased by the prisoner's ready acquiescence. But to Barrett the arrangement was confirmation of his first suspicions.

"Mike, tie this bird," commanded Sam. "Lower your arms, you — but don't try any funny work."

"How is he going to climb down to the boat if his hands are tied?" wondered Mike. "And that Jacob's ladder up the *Car—*"

"Shut up, you boob!" snapped Sam Carver. "Grab that cord!"

"Aw what if he does —" countered Mike, then checked himself.

But that slip sufficed to assure Barrett that he was destined to board one of the many abandoned ships, wartime built merchant marine, moored along the opposite bank of the river. The secreted penknife might enable him to cut his bonds; but a doubt had risen in Barrett's mind: would Simpson be released, now that the ransom had been delivered, or would he be executed as part of the reprisal?

Barrett's captors were indifferent to future identification; and that could betoken but one thing other than gross carelessness.

A desperate scheme crystallized; and in an instant Barrett made his decision.

Sam, pistol in hand, was a blur in the darkness a yard ahead. Mike was fumbling in the gloom at Barrett's left, seeking a coil of rope. Surprise can work wonders. Barrett felt the enemy's assurance, and hoped that they did not sense his own.

Barrett's fingers closed on the end of the scarf about his neck and dragged it clear. They thought that he was unarmed; yet that folded square of silk was a silent, instantly fatal weapon which was invisible in the darkness.

As Mike rose and turned, Barrett moved with that catlike swiftness which had so often served him — and saved him. The silken scarf, weighted with the knife, whipped about Mike's throat. There was no warning in its touch. It seemed to be but the trick of a gust of wind; and in the obscurity of the doorway the gesture did not register.

The weighted end passed over Mike's shoulder as Barrett side-stepped, seized the enfolded penknife with his left hand and at the same time put all his weight behind his right, which grasped the free end of the scarf.

"Wh—"

Cut off before it was spoken; and the sharp cracking sound meant nothing to Sam Carver, least of all that Mike's neck had been broken.

All in one flashing instant; one fluent, continuous, deadly

swift gesture. Had there been a blow, a shot, an outcry, Carver would have acted at once. He sensed that something deadly and inexplicable had happened before his eyes; but he had also to reconcile his intuition with the knowledge that Barrett's plays had always been accompanied by the flash of steel, the jetting flame of pistols, the impact of hard driving fists.

He lost an instant before he clubbed his pistol so that in accordance with orders he would not kill the fifty-thousand-dollar prisoner. And that instant sufficed for Mike's body to catapult out of the darkness, drive Carver crashing back against the wall.

Then savage fingers closed about his throat as the first blow of his pistol butt struck Mike's limp body to the ground. Carver writhed and struggled, smote blindly at the enemy within his guard. His feet were tramping on a man's body. . . .

"Mike," he contrived to gasp hoarsely before his breath was utterly cut off.

Barrett's fingers sank relentlessly home. Lee Simpson's severed finger lent a murderous fury to Barrett's constricting grasp. He followed Carver to the paving. The blows of the pistol butt had ceased . . . *hours* ago, it seemed. . . . Finally he relaxed his grip, drew a deep breath, realized for the first time that glancing, misdirected blows had battered his head and shoulders. Barrett stretched out on the cold paving, dazed by his exertions and the slaying frenzy and the destructive nervous tension of his lightning assault.

In a moment, however, he recovered. He was trembling violently, seeking to reassemble the elements of the suddenly devised scheme. Then it all came back to him; but before going about what he intended to do, he paused to search the two who lay on the floor of the deep doorway recess.

Dead, not merely out.

He scrutinized the contents of their pockets, piece by piece.

"Here's the touch!" he exclaimed as by the light of the fountain-pen flash lamp, fortunately undamaged, he read the notation on a slip of paper, in feminine script:

Norma — Main 7771 — blind listed, so learn it and then destroy this.

That Sam Carver was a fair approximation of Barrett as to stature and conformation had already entered the plan; but this brief note suggested an interesting amendment, despite the fact that the open implication of an undercover friendship *might* be misleading. Yet, from his observation of Moroni's organization, he could at least be certain that the note was written by Norma Arradonda, and not by some obscure namesake.

Barrett's eyes glittered with that same fierce mirth of two nights ago, at Club Martinique. Then he remembered Lee Simpson's peril, and his mirth became exceedingly bitter. Barrett strode swiftly toward the ferry landing, a block further upstream, saw that the aged ticket taker was nodding at his post, and stepped into the telephone booth. He called Amos and gave the old Negro two simple orders. This done, Barrett returned to the doorway on Munn Street and set to work exchanging clothing with the late Sam Carver.

In a few minutes the first move against the enemy was completed. With the flashlight Barrett checked his work to see that he had made no slips in the dark.

"If this don't work . . . good God, but it's *got* to work! It can't flop!" he told himself as he repressed a shudder at the thought of the dead man's apparel that now clothed him.

He heard the sound of a car pulling to the curbing. Old Amos . . . nevertheless Barrett advanced with drawn pistol until he was close enough to identify his servant.

"Go back home, Amos," he directed. "Leave the Ford here."

Barrett dashed back to the doorway of death, shouldered Sam Carver's body, and placed it at the wheel of the sedan. Mike was then stowed in the Ford coupé which Amos still had an excellent chance of inheriting. From the coupé Barrett took a double-barreled, ten gauge shotgun. He lowered the window of the sedan. . . .

A sheet of flame, a roar, the splintering of glass — Barrett knew that his work had been good, but he did not care to verify the fact by close inspection. He disconnected a gas line, let the ground beneath the car become drenched, then struck and tossed a match. As the flames rose in a lurid column, he turned toward the Ford coupé, to drive down town.

"It's got to work," he reiterated as he banished, by sheer force of will, the panic that assailed him at the thought of failure.

Barrett, hard bitten, and seasoned as he was by the World War, was shaken by the gruesome work of the past few minutes — and then he remembered Lee Simpson's severed finger, and Moroni's characteristic duplicity as revealed by the two who did not know that a silken scarf was a deadly weapon.

"Live bait, eh?" he muttered grimly.

Barrett drew up to the curbing some ten blocks short of Canal Street. He dragged Mike from the coupé, supporting him as though he were hopelessly drunk. The vicinity, though bustling during the day with trucks approaching and leaving the establishments of the produce dealers and commission merchants, was utterly deserted at night. Nevertheless, Barrett played his part by muttering incoherently as though he were as intoxicated as his burden was supposed to be.

Barrett knew that there was a telephone pay-station in the entrance that led to the second floor of the building. He maneuvered Mike into position, supported him with his elbow, then called Norma Arradonda. Barrett made an effort to disguise his voice to resemble the husky rasp of Mike.

"Norma.... This is Mike," he began hurriedly. "You know — Sam's buddy —"

"Yes?" came the voice of Norma, with a peculiar, rising inflection that sent chills creeping up his spine. Warning? Anxiety? Dawning suspicion? A host of fatal possibilities trooped home in an instant. Lee Simpson's life was at stake. And then —

"Sam croaked Barrett and took the twenty grand —"

Barrett distinctly caught Norma's gasp of amazement and consternation. But what else? Concern for Sam's fate when Moroni learned of the trickery — *perhaps.*

"We're checkin' out. Meet us at Ponchartrain Junction! Quick! Yeah, hurry like —"

Barrett dropped the receiver, drew a pistol, and at the

same time broke off his conversation to cry out in terror, "Sam — fer Chris' sake."

The crackle of the pistol cut short the shriek. Over the wire, the deception must have been perfect.

"That, and Mike full of lead," was Barrett's thought as he leaped to the coupé, "ought to convince them I'm dead and Sam's skipped with the ransom. Now let's see what they'll have at Ponchartrain Junction."

Barrett headed for the first city station beyond the main L & N depot.

Simpson, in view of Barrett's supposed death, would have no further vengeance-appeal for Moroni. But if Moroni suspected that it was not Barrett who was at the wheel of the flame warped sedan —!

Barrett was grateful that he knew of several readily accessible public phones which were inconspicuous. There was one on Decatur Street, across from the French Market coffee stall. Made to order! He called John Healy at his residence.

"I've been bumped off. You'll find my body at Munn and Tchoupitoulas Streets," he informed the Chief of Detectives. "Land on Moroni and his boys for killing me. Right now, and for God's sake, shake it up! Stick to that story. It's foolproof. And it's Simpson's head if it flops."

Barrett smacked the receiver into place and drove on.

"That'll keep 'em off of Lee, wherever he is."

Barrett, whose successful campaigning had in the past been largely dependent on the proper interpretation of underworld whispers, had heard of Sam Carver's interest in Norma. Garrulity is the most fatal affliction of the racketeer. Thus, though Barrett inferred that Carver's interest had blossomed beyond mildness, he was not certain enough to predict her attitude toward Carver's supposed proposition. She might be loyal to Moroni — in which case there would be a reception committee awaiting Carver as represented by Davis P. Barrett; but that was a chance that could not be avoided.

Barrett parked in a side street, and taking full advantage of the darkness along the L & N tracks, made a careful reconnaissance. His wearing Carver's gray suit made him a good target; and Barrett was still uncertain as to what and who would meet him.

He saw a cab pull up across the tracks, heard the door slam, and watched its tail light disappear.

The passenger was a woman, and she was approaching the deserted station. The waiting room was in darkness save for a single feeble globe. By its dim glow he recognized the shapely figure; exotic coiffure; and graceful, confident gait of Norma Arradonda as she crossed the threshold.

Bait . . . live bait . . . who else might be there. . . .

"Live bait it is," he told himself as he advanced. *"But which of us?"*

The girl, who had been watching his approach, emerged to meet him. She barely suppressed a cry of alarm as she realized that Sam Carver's gray suit did not contain Sam Carver. But Barrett's smile reassured her to a degree, so that she was perplexed rather than alarmed, Barrett, whatever he was, was not a woman killer.

"Sam didn't kill me," he explained. "That was just a handy stall. We made a bargain. Moroni thinks I'm dead. You know where Simpson is. Here's the twenty grand I'm giving you, from Sam, if you'll tell me where my buddy is held a prisoner."

It caught Norma off guard, but she quickly assimilated it.

"This money," she said, "is your security against Sam, and Simpson's our —"

"Right," said Barrett. "Now you get on that phone and get things going. The minute I know that Simpson is in the clear, you get the money. And don't worry about Sam — Moroni can't touch him."

"Dirty trick," was Barrett's thought as he caught a significant light in Norma's eyes. "She likes Carver . . . plenty."

But the memory of Simpson's severed finger stilled his qualms, and steeled him to carry on with his playing on the girl's obvious affection for Carver.

"But he'll know you're not dead," she objected.

"No. Mike's doubling for me — Sam didn't trust him, so —"

He made a gesture of finality. Norma understood. Despite her connection with the racket, she was for a moment taken aback by the grimness of Sam Carver's subterfuge.

As she paused for words, Barrett suddenly realized that he

had been off guard for a moment, that his keen attention had relaxed. He glanced over his shoulder, caught a metallic glint. And before Norma could utter the words that were on her lips, Barrett's hand shot forward — not to his holster, but to the girl, striking her to the floor as Barrett himself plunged forward.

He made it with a split second to spare: a drumming fusillade rattled through the silence, and sent the panes beyond them splintering and tinkling to the floor.

"Wiggle clear!" hissed Barrett as he whipped his prone body to cover and flashed his pistol into line. The gunner was momentarily off guard, and certain that his volley had dropped Barrett and Norma. But the smack of Barrett's pistol sent him pitching backward. Another, coming from cover, returned Barrett's fire, spattering him with wood splinters, but doing no damage.

"Come out and take it, Carver," said a voice. "Or we'll chop the dump down and the Jane'll get it too."

"Smack!"

And a grunt of pain.

"Spill it!" urged Barrett in a low voice. "Don't be fussy about ratting! Can't you see somebody tapped your line, and Moroni's out for you and Sam?"

A siren screamed in the distance.

Barrett's pistol fire, now more accurate, halted the charge before it got a fair start.

"Here's the note you gave Sam. That proves I'm on the level."

He emptied his pistol, and drew the other salvaged weapon. Help was close; but the enemy could stick to the last second and still make a getaway. Some of them were slipping around to attack from the rear.

"Come across!" he barked above the deadly chatter of the automatic and the splintering of glass and wood. "You can't get away with this. You've got to leave town. And twenty grand — *crack-crack* — 's a good stake."

"The *Carlotta*. Opposite Jackson ferry," she replied.

"Phone the police!" commanded Barrett as he jammed home a fresh clip, wondering as he did so whether he could hold the rush.

But the arrival of the police patrol spared Barrett the test.

As the melee subsided, John Healy entered the station, alone.

"You jackass!" he demanded, "why didn't you tell me you were throwing a party here?"

"Cops hanging around would've crabbed the works. Send some men to the *Carlotta*. Get Simpson. And tell your outfit Sam Carver is here, dead. Don't let *anyone* get wise!"

Healy was perplexed, but he asked no questions.

"Duval! MacCarthy!" he bellowed. "Get this, and hop to it!"

He repeated Barrett's instructions, then added, "Don't lose a second — I'll hold this down — to hell with what's in here, hurry, damn it!"

As the patrol car took off with a roar and a clash of gears, Healy turned to Barrett.

"Lord, Dave," he said, seeing Barrett's drawn, white features — white as his tropic tan allowed. "Did they get —"

"No. Didn't plug me, much — but if anything's slipped — Lee Simpson —"

Healy's eyes opened wide as Farrell explained a few things.

"But I don't quite understand," he protested.

"You're dumb!" snapped Barrett, giving him a hard glance. And then, "Norma, you don't have to wait here until Lee's in the clear — here's the dough. We'll drive to the airport and get you out of town right now!"

"But we found Mike Tomaso's body in a *phone booth*," Healy persisted, ignoring Barrett's murderous glance. "Not in your burned up car. Who —"

Norma's slender form jerked as from an electric shock. Her features twitched from the horror of sudden understanding. Then her hand flashed forward. Four packets of bills caught Barrett full in the face.

"You dirty son of a bitch!" she said with a deliberation that made the words even deadlier than their coming from a woman's lips.

Barrett nodded. Healy seized her wrists.

"I feel like one, Norma," he said solemnly. "But Lee Simpson was my friend. Had to do it. Now you get out of town, and take this dough — call it insurance money — anything you please."

"You big sap, are you giving her that jack?" demanded Healy.

His voice boomed above Norma's low, terribly calm reiterations of hatred, and contempt, and grief, grotesquely mingled.

Barrett started to answer, then changed his mind. He hardly expected the detective to understand his feelings regarding the evening's strategy.

"I hope they've killed him!" shrieked Norma, her calmness breaking.

The telephone in the closest booth rang. Healy, who had given his men the number, snatched the receiver. He listened for a moment; and during that moment Barrett felt strangely empty, and futile. He poised himself on the balls of both feet . . . his fists were clenching painfully tight . . . he forced himself not to think of anything. . . .

"All clear, Dave!" roared Healy's voice after several age-long seconds. "Simpson's okay!"

Barrett slowly exhaled the breath he had been holding. He listened again to Norma's invective, once more low-voiced. Then he smiled, shook his head.

"John, drive her out to the airport and see she gets out of town — charter a plane if necessary, but get her out, or her life's not worth a dime."

He hitched his belt, redistributed the weight of the emptied pistols, and shrugged as he heard the grief stricken girl's final appraisal of him.

"*C'est la guerre!* — or something like that. They oughtn't have used live bait. . . ."

MUMMIES TO ORDER

THE OVERHEAD LIGHTS beat down on the mummy stretched out on the broad table, and picked the premature gray from Murray Deane's averted head. His deep-set eyes glowed, and his tanned face was set in squarish angles. A frown of concentration puckered his forehead as he bent over the dried flesh and the leathery skin stretched over ancient bones.

Deftly, he plucked the crisp, brown linen from the throat of the mummy, exposing a carnelian amulet, engraved with sacred symbols. Deane nodded, rolled his camera tripod into place, and switched on the flood lights. Their heat brought sweat to his forehead, and it trickled down his cheeks. But he did not notice the glare, nor the bitter dust that settled on his lips.

Slowly, patiently, he was unveiling the secrets of old Egypt. An American museum trusted his judgment and his skill, and had sent him to Cairo as director of operations.

Deane muttered wrathfully when he heard the persistent tapping at the laboratory door. Hassan, his Arab servant, was at the threshold.

"*Effendi,* two gentlemen wish to speak to you. It is urgent."

Deane irritably smote the mummy dust from his hand.

"Who are they?"

"That red-faced Crawford, *Effendi,* and the fish-eyed grave robber."

"Heyl?" Deane grimaced. He had met the two, and he disliked them both. One was a loudmouthed amateur collector; the other, Gunther Heyl, a dealer in outright fakes, as well as genuine antiques illicitly purchased from native tomb looters. "All right, send them in!"

Both wore white tropicals. Heyl, who followed the red-faced man into the laboratory, had a receding chin and protruding blue eyes. Apparently he never saw enough of the Egyptian sun to become tanned. Crawford mopped his forehead, and spent a moment glancing about the room.

There were mummy cases, their gilded masks staring inscrutably at the visitors. Embalmed cats filled a cabinet. Several shelves were cluttered with human skulls and withered limbs. These human relics testified to the violence of grave looters who had dismembered the dead, seeking jewels and amulets.

Crawford shivered. He did not like the fixed stare of that woman's head. The artificial eyes were uncanny, and the luxuriant black hair made the flattened nose, the sunken cheeks with their scraps of adhering wrappings all the more gruesome. Deane chuckled, then said:

"Hullo, Heyl. Do you think you can do as well as the old-time Arab vandals? What's on your mind?"

Crawford stood there, a pudgy hand vainly extended. Heyl, however, was too smooth to take offense at Deane's insinuations.

"You've met Mr. Crawford, I think."

"I have. And I told him that everything I discovered was subject to the Egyptian government's orders, and my museum's. Nothing for sale."

"But we don't want to buy," Crawford cut in. "Not this time. As I told you, I've made a hobby of Egyptology. Ever since I retired from plumbing supplies."

Deane spat. Curio hunters, not students.

"And finally," Heyl resumed, "I found something choice on my own account. The mummy of Bint Anath, the Eighteenth Dynasty princess who married —"

"And you had to find her! Or is this another fake?"

"I wouldn't ask you to convince Mr. Crawford that the stuff is genuine Eighteenth Dynasty, unless it were real. I couldn't risk it, could I?"

"Won't he take your word?"

Heyl shrugged. "There are so many frauds, I can't blame him for being wary."

"It isn't that, Mr. Deane," Crawford added. "It is just that you're the foremost living authority on that period. Anyone else might make a mistake. And I'm paying a stiff price for the mummy, the furnishings, the tomb frescoes —" He winked, and his face looked like a wrinkled harvest moon. "Delivered in New York."

"One thousand dollars, Deane," Heyl said, edging closer. "For your opinion on the genuineness."

"Get out! I'm not here to help any tomb dredger cheat the Egyptian government. Look at all this stuff I have here, working on it, making records. My museum gets only a small portion, the government takes the rest. Do you think I'd help you rob them and science in general?"

"Now, Mr. Deane — er, Doctor Deane, rather — I'm handling the actual smuggling. You won't be responsible."

Deane raised his voice. "Hassan! These gentlemen are leaving at once. Call a cab for them."

Crawford became redder.

"See here," he sputtered, and shook his fist. "I know how you get tips from the natives! How that helps you make all your discoveries. It you think you're going to find Bint Anath's tomb yourself —"

Then Hassan approached. *"Effendi,* the cab is outside."

They left, cursing and muttering.

"Follow those fellows," Deane said to Hassan. "That's your job from now on. Find out what natives Heyl is working with."

Hassan bowed until his white turban was almost level with his waist.

"On my head and eyes, *Effendi!*"

THE NATIVE quarter of Cairo was an old story to Deane, and to Hassan also. Gossip and rumor would uncover the back trail of the grave looter and his customer. More than mere loyalty to the museum and the Egyptian government moved Deane. Illicit pillaging and curio hunting had hopelessly ruined many a precious find, had obscured many secrets of the past.

It was not for any personal advantage that he was trying to uncover Heyl's supposed find. It might be genuine, and priceless.

Deane went back to his work. He turned on the X-ray machine, which enabled him to photograph the skeleton and internal structure of the mummy, without disturbing the wrappings. When inscriptions were obliterated, when mummies had been moved from one tomb to another, thirty centuries ago, Deane could identify their true period from the kind of amulets, the way the body had been prepared, the way it had been bandaged.

Deane grinned a little and said to himself:

"Maybe I scared Crawford out. In which case, Heyl has to find another customer."

A WEEK later, Hassan's investigations brought results. The wrinkled servant handed Deane a slip of paper, all written in spidery Arabic script.

"*Effendi*, this is from Nefeyda, the Coptic girl who dances at Quasim's coffee house."

Deane had heard of Nefeyda, and seen her. She had a good act, and it drew crowds of tourists to the cafe.

"How does she fit into this?"

"She would not say, except that she knew something of interest to you."

He glanced at the note. The message was as vague as the report. As Deane removed his stained smock, Hassan said:

"*Effendi*, better take your pistol. I saw Heyl and Crawford at Quasim's, once or twice, before I got a chance to talk to Nefeyda."

Deane laughed. "Heyl's not dangerous. He doesn't want to be conspicuous. Not Heyl, and not with what the authorities think of him. He was probably showing Crawford the sights and trying to sell him something just as good!"

"Allah is the knower," Hassan said, noncommittally.

Half an hour later, Deane parked his car on the Muski, and went on foot, for the streets of the native quarter were too narrow for vehicles.

Not far from the spice bazaar was the yellow horseshoe of light that marked the entrance of Quasim's place. The second floors of the houses overhung the narrow street, so that they almost met in the center. It was a tunnel whose farther end opened into a shadow kingdom, and the robed figures that stirred vaguely in its depths reminded Deane of the dead who had lost their way.

Egypt's ancient dead were serene and orderly, in their homes west of the Nile, and Murray Deane was at ease among them. But living Egypt, that night, made him feel as though he walked among those who should be buried. The reeking alleys, the heaped offal, the sickening sweetishness of cassia and olibanum and musk exalted by the shuttered bazaars made him think of corruption that had not quite been embalmed.

Not even the flare of yellow light gave him any sense of reality. The plucked strings of an *oudh* and the mutter of a little drum lent no more than eerie animation to Quasim's coffee house. Deane shivered, and stepped into the arched doorway. He stood there for a moment, then shrugged. This was all prosaic enough. Quasim, greasy and wearing a top-heavy turban, was explaining to some tourists that cream is not served with "Turkish" coffee.

He seated himself on one of the upholstered benches that lined the wall. He liked his coffee bitter, so he said to the proprietor's son:

"Wahad murreh."

A blonde tourist laughed nervously and said to her companion:

"Why did we come here? That fiddle squeaking makes me think of ghosts gibbering!"

"Wait till you see Nefeyda. The guide said she wears . . ."

They went into a huddle about that. Deane was certain they would be shocked, but not in the way they anticipated. As he sat there, skillfully sipping the foam-topped coffee without scalding his lips, he watched the blue curtain at the farther end of the paneled room, and listened for the first tinkle of Nefeyda's heavy anklets. He wondered if she would know him.

Then the drum muttered, and she glided from behind the curtain.

Nefeyda's face made Deane think of the high-bridged nose and piquant cheek bones of an alabaster statuette he had found in a tomb at Biban ul Mulouk. There was more to the illusion than the slow pace and statuesque postures of her dance.

The jangling notes of the *sistrum* in her hand were echoes from some long-buried temple, and she herself seemed something that had stepped from a painted fresco. She had tightly curled hair, and her frail gown gave her the antique silhouette.

The tourists leaned forward, eagerly watching every gesture. But when the music ceased, and Deane went toward the blue curtain that separated the coffee room from the rest of the house, he saw that they were eyeing him, nudging each other, and whispering.

"If they only knew what the date is about," he said to himself, "they'd not be so thrilled!"

Nefeyda was following him, anklets jingling.

Deane turned as the curtain rippled into place after her.

"My servant said you had word for me," he said, and dug the crumpled note from his pocket. "But he didn't tell me any more than that."

Nefeyda looked up with mysterious, almond-shaped eyes. "I wasn't sure how far I could trust him."

"I'd trust him with my life."

Nefeyda shrugged. "One hears things whispered about. There is more buried than has ever been dug out."

The Copts, who were descended from the ancient Egyptians, often had bits of lore from the old days, but they were usually wary about telling what they knew. Though Christians, many of them still feared the vengeance of the dead gods.

Deane watched Nefeyda flash a furtive glance over her shapely shoulder, and toward the blue curtain. During that moment of silence, he fancied that something had come out of a tomb to speak to him. He stepped nearer, and his voice shook a little when he repeated:

"Your message. You had some word for me."

"I've heard of you," Nefeyda whispered. "You've always been kind to our people when they worked for you, digging. But that fish-eyed man wasn't. So I'm telling you —"

"Heyl? Gunther Heyl?"

She nodded.

"How do you know? How much do you want?"

She reached for a black cape and flung it about her olive-tinted shoulders. Arms folded under the trailing garment, she stood there, studying his tanned face.

The scrutiny was mutual. As he returned it, he was more

certain than ever that she was of that ancient race, undefiled by any foreign blood. With her small hands and feet, those almond-shaped eyes with lashes so closely spaced that the lids seemed smudged with black, she was old Egypt, living again. And all that made her answer seem natural:

"Whatever you say is fair. Rather than have Heyl desecrate the bones of our ancestors, I'll tell you. I'll go now. My act is over."

Deane drove to the Nile, and crossed the Abbas II bridge. The moon rose and silvered the flat expanse that the river inundated every season. Miles ahead, rocky bulwarks rose from the Libyan Desert. Nefeyda said not a word as he swung south to skirt the outer canal. The twenty mile trip ended near the village of Saqaara, where cubical houses were half hidden by tall palms.

Somewhere in the desert, a jackal howled, eerily. Just beyond the huts of the Fellahin was one of the cities of the dead. The wind wandered over the sand, making it whisper and hiss. The hollowness of hidden tombs enticed the breeze, and the underground emptiness muttered. The dust blown to Deane's lips was bitter from the dead that tainted the everlasting dryness.

When he pulled up, under a cluster of palms that were some distance beyond the village, Nefeyda shivered, and pointed toward the nearby house.

"Many of our people believe it is sacrilege to desecrate tombs. I'm almost afraid to go on. Sooner or later, a curse destroys robbers. I'm betraying a secret to you. You'll take the things which Heyl hasn't moved. It'll be on my head."

There was something in her voice that made Deane share her qualms for a moment. Then he forced a chuckle.

"As long as none of Heyl's gang is hanging around, I'll risk curses!"

She recoiled a little at his words. Her almond-shaped eyes reproved him for blasphemy. Then she said:

"That house over there. They were digging a well, and cut down into a tomb. One of the passages is just beneath the house. I know where the key is hidden."

He went with her to the gate, and watched her lift a flat rock from the sand. She took out a key, and opened the way to the courtyard. Then Deane remembered the headlights of his car.

"I'd better turn them off," he said. "Someone in the village might wake up and see them."

"Give me your matches. I'll light a candle inside."

It was not more than fifty yards back to the palms and the car. But on his return, Deane was strangely uneasy. He was certain that someone was watching him. The same sense that makes animals restless before a storm or earthquake now warned him. He ran toward the courtyard. Whitewash mirrored the moonlight. Inside, a yellow light flickered. Without knowing why, he croaked:

"Come out of there, Nefeyda! Someone's snooping."

There was no answer. All he heard was a cry of dismay, suddenly choked and ending in a cough. There was a sound as of furniture legs shifting over the floor; a thump, a whispering rustle, a wheezing gasp. Deane was bounding forward when this happened. Even before he rounded the end of the passage, he knew what to expect. Death, the presence he had so strongly felt, must have struck.

A curious odor now tainted the air. The smell was like quince blossoms, and bitter almonds. Nefeyda lay crumpled on the hard-packed earth floor, but there was no sign of any vial from which poison could have come.

Her olive-tinted limbs still twitched. Her eyes stared horribly, and her lips were drawn back in a frozen grin that made a mockery of her beauty. The candle flame wavered enough to make the profile of a mummy case dance on the bare white wall. There was a fine white film of dust on the floor, and only Nefeyda's feet had disturbed it.

Deane, standing there, noticed all those things as he told himself:

"This curse business. It's crazy. There isn't any such thing."

But there she was, rigid and staring. It was not until the liberation of those strange sweet fumes that she had fallen, choking. Dizziness made the candle flame dance before Deane's eyes.

He went toward the girl, having convinced himself that she had fainted. But there was no heart beat when he knelt and bent over, laying his ear against her breast; nor could his fingers at her wrist detect any sign of life. Her fingers were clawed, as though she had fought for an instant against an uncanny assailant.

The candle winked out, suddenly, as though snuffed by invisible fingers. Deane leaped to his feet, a hoarse cry on his lips. He bounded toward the hall which opened into the room.

There was a whispering creak of metal. The invading patch of moonlight became narrower. The door closed before he could reach it. He hurled himself against it, pounded until his fists were bruised. But there was no opening the door.

At first too shocked for thought, he slumped back against the panel, waiting for his sagging knees to let him slide to the floor. Then he recovered a little, and found his box of matches. After several fumbling attempts, he struck one without breaking it. However the door was secured, it was not from the inside. He went back to the candle on the stand, near the mummy case.

He had some difficulty in getting the wick to light. Finally it sputtered, crackled, and a feeble flame rose. Deane paced up and down the dirt floor and tried to think it out. He was drenched with sweat. His lips were dry, his mouth was dust, and his knees shook.

A sudden rush of unreasoning terror made him hurl himself at the door, clawing, pounding, kicking. He did not feel the impacts that battered his body and exhausted his strength. He knew that he could not run away. He knew that he must finally tell a story that would brand him as a madman whose brain had been touched by too much tomb dredging. But he had to get out of that accursed house.

The subtle odor of death and decay which had at first made him uneasy now became stronger. His efforts kicked up dust, choking and bitter — the finely powdered myrrh and olibanum and the linen from long-dried corpses.

The candle, for some moments unwavering, now flickered violently. It winked out, and the darkness that stifled Deane became alive with presences. He was no longer alone with the girl whom invisible death had struck. The newcomers muttered and chirped and mocked him in a strange tongue.

He understood words that were identical in Coptic and in ancient Egyptian. They were cursing him, and Nefeyda. His sobbing breath could not quite blot out the eerie whispers, nor the soft padding of bare feet.

A hinge creaked as he lunged again at the door. It was yielding a little. He made another desperate effort to knock the bolt from its socket before those gibbering presences materialized enough to throttle him. But his own exertion overcame him. He sank, battered and half conscious. Cold hands caught his wrists and ankles. Stifling folds of cloth cut off his breath, and tomb dust choked him.

When he recovered enough to renew his struggles, he knew that any effort would be useless. Broad-shouldered men with narrow hips and sloping foreheads stood about him, arms folded. All but one wore the tight-fitting kilt of ancient time. That one had a flowing robe, and his shaven skull indicated that he was a priest.

The room was one of several connected by passageways whose darkness gave no hint of the extent of the maze. The walls were painted in hieroglyphics. In one corner was a stone slab. On a trestle was a mummy case. Near it, on a table, was a mummy, wound with countless yards of time-yellowed linen.

Bit by bit Deane recognized the purpose of the implements and the urns and the vat which was in the shadows. This chamber of the tomb had been converted into an embalmer's workshop, and the obsidian knife that lay on the slab was used for making the first incision in a corpse.

The man with the shaven skull spoke, very slowly, so that Deane could understand:

"I am Anu the Priest, and I lived in this land before the first pyramid was built. I have come back, and reclaimed my body, having spent the required time in Amenti, that dim land where all men must go to atone for their evil, or be rewarded for their good. I have seen Osiris and his forty-two judges. They sent me back, and these others have come with me."

The kilted men said nothing, but as one, they nodded.

Anu spoke rapidly to them, and four of the six left the room. Deane could not answer. All were emaciated, as though their newly revived bodies had not yet eaten enough to fill out the desiccation of the grave. And each had the scar of a knife on his side.

"There are hundreds who should be with us," Anu went on, "but they cannot come, since their bodies have been destroyed by robbers and looters. They wander and cry in the dark, being only living shadows."

Deane could neither disbelieve nor accept. Coming after that succession of shocks, Anu's words made a final and numbing impact. He sat up and croaked:

"Why am I here?"

The priest stared blankly. Deane repeated the question in Egyptian, and pronounced the dead language as best he could.

"You will see, in a moment," Anu answered. "There is a way in which you can atone for sacrilege."

That noncommittal reply sickened Deane almost as much as the odor of death and the grave. He had opened many a tomb, he had scoffed at curses. But now he shuddered at the implication of the embalmer's implements.

"By our old magic," Anu went on, "we can let a substitute body serve as a new home for one who is released from Amenti's shadows. We will have such a corpse, presently."

Deane yelled. His cry of horror did not make the three from the grave change expression. But as he flung himself to the slab and snatched the obsidian knife, they closed in, and it was not necessary for the priest to lend a hand.

"There is no use struggling," he said.

They did not disarm Deane. Somehow, his fingers remained locked about the ragged blade of chipped flint, though there was no strength left elsewhere in his body.

"You can't carve me up! I'll —"

They ignored him. His incoherent defiance was mockingly echoed from the passages of the maze. Their icy hands had him secure. The odor of the tomb stifled him. Then Anu called to the others.

They came out, and for a moment Deane thought that they had arrived to bear him to the slab and use the knife. Then he saw that they were carrying Nefeyda on a litter. They rolled her from it, and to the stone that had supported so many of the ancient dead.

Anu smiled. "Your conscience was more vengeful than we are. It is not lawful for us to take life. But she is dead, so we need you."

When the shock of reprieve dimmed enough, Deane found his tongue.

"Why?" he demanded.

"None of us," Anu explained, "is a *paraschiste*, so we are not suited for the duty of making the first incision in a corpse. Neither are we embalmers. But you understand these things, and what you do not know, I can tell you — about the prayers and the ritual."

He gestured, and one of the men tore Nefeyda's gown to the waist. Another took a crayon of red earth and marked where the incision was to be made.

"She has died for her blasphemy," Anu resumed. "Being of the ancient race, and betraying the tomb of her ancestors, the gods damned her. There is no resurrection. Anubis must eat her accursed soul. But if the sacred ritual of embalming is performed, one whose body was destroyed by looters like yourself can come back and find a new home."

Deane was sickened from contemplating the lovely form that he would have to mutilate. Examining the work of an embalmer, reading in old papyri how the work was done was one thing; the doing was another. When they let his hands go, he stood there, swaying dizzily.

Anu smiled. "You understand, and there is the mark. And there is the jar into which you will place her heart. There are the tongs with which you will extract the brain, through the nostrils, according to custom."

"Shut up!" Deane gasped, choking.

"And here are those who wait with stones which they will hurl at you as you run from your work," the priest went on. "They will curse you, as they cursed the *paraschiste*, ages ago."

"I won't!" Deane turned. "You can't make me!"

For a moment he faced the living dead who stood there, each holding a pebble, each ready to hurl it, and to cry out the prescribed curses. The long-sustained tension, the terror of Nefeyda's weird death, the struggle for escape had all shaken him so that what was before him became more horrible than death itself.

"I won't!" he croaked, and lunged at the priest, slashing.

Anu laughed, and the men caught him from every side, just as he stumbled in his attack. They crushed him to the floor. Their hands were claws that closed about his throat, cutting off his gasps of air that reeked of corpse dust, and linen wrappings pulverized in the struggle. The choking vault blackened, and red spots danced in the foul darkness. He heard Anu say:

"Leave him here. He does not eat or drink until he obeys."

As he lay there, panting, bare feet padded in the gloom, and somewhere a door closed. He was locked up with the woman whom a strange doom had stricken.

LATER, DEANE sat up and fumbled for his matches. From what he had seen of the masonry, he judged that the embalming equipment had been installed in a tomb. And while no two homes of the dead were ever identical, they followed a pattern that he could picture with his eyes closed. Somewhere in the maze, there must be an outlet that was not closed.

His matches had been lost in the scuffle. His watch did not have a luminous dial, and he had no idea of the passage of time. Time ended in this vault which reeked of the long dead, and the musty spices which told of perfumed corruption. Slowly, Deane crept toward a wall, and followed it. He skirted a sarcophagus, which he recognized from its sculptured sides; a massive stone coffin, and not the vat he had noted during the moments of illumination.

Deane rounded its corner, and got back to the wall. There was an opening, and the floor dipped slightly down. As nearly as he could judge, he was at the mouth of a passage about two feet wide. As he advanced, the air became dense and musty. Dust rose from the paving and choked him. It was so fine that its touch to his palms was almost greasy. This was ancient dust, settled out of air long unstirred, and unlike the sand particles in the vault he had left.

Then debris began to block his path. He crept under a slab that had fallen from the ceiling. The paving was cracked, perhaps by a long-forgotten earthquake. And finally, Deane felt a breath of clean, cold air. Somewhere, there was an opening that led to the desert's surface. In a few moments of increasingly difficult progress, he reached heaped-up sand

and chunks of rock. Overhead, he caught a leakage of moonlight.

Eagerly, he clawed at the crevice, ignoring the chance that a sudden slide might bury him. But the flinty debris tore his hands, broke his nails, and in a few moments, his fingers were raw and bleeding. The thing to do was to go back and get the embalmer's knife. By patient combing of the floor, he might find the weapon he had dropped during the struggle.

When he reached the starting point, Deane began his slow, blind search. Up and down, he worked his way from end to end. Once, finding the door through which the resurrected dead had gone, he spent some time tugging and clawing at it, but it resisted his efforts.

Finally, he forced himself to calmness.

"Take it easy!" he repeated, and licked the dust from his lips, wiped the stinging sweat from his eyes. "Hang on. The dead can't come back. Those curses don't work. It wasn't the old gods that killed Nefeyda. Whatever it was, it's no curse!"

Muttering self-assurance that he could not entirely believe, Deane resumed his slow search, patting the floor as he crawled, sweeping it with strokes of his palms. Nefeyda's perfume, distinct in the musty darkness, made him shudder. Her dead presence shook him. In whatever uncanny manner she had died, they could do the same to him.

At last he found his matches. Seeking them had kept him from going mad in that oppressive gloom and silence. But for that one slender hope, Anu's prediction would have come true — Deane would have cracked.

He struck a match and found some bits of age-yellowed sycamore from a coffin. He tore some scraps from the mummy's wrappings. They were coated with bitumen, which burned with a smoky flame. By the light of this short-lived torch, he found the flint knife. It lay near the slab.

He turned his eyes away, to avoid seeing Nefeyda's frozen face. Perhaps the old gods had less power over him than over one of her ancient race. But he cried out with relief when he snatched the knife and scrambled away, to take more scraps of resin and bitumen-soaked linen to tie to the torch.

Deane hurried down the passageway. He did not know how he would account for Nefeyda's death when he escaped. His story would brand him as a madman. Her disappearance would make questioning inevitable. Horror left him not a chance of reasoning.

Once at the end of the passage, Deane thrust the improvised taper into a crevice, and set to work. The haft of the flint knife cut his hands and he had to be careful lest the brittle blade snap and leave him helpless. Sweat drenched, he dug at sand, until he got enough cleared away to give him a hold on one of the rocks that reached down. Then he put the knife into his pocket and began to tug and twist. But the leverage was not enough.

Finally he got a foothold, and arched his back so that his shoulder bore against the key to the crevice. Straining until red spots danced before his eyes, he endured the cutting of the rock through his coat. Sand trickled down, and fresh air followed it.

His feet slipped when the keystone yielded. He fell from his narrow perch, and rolled into a corner, just as an avalanche poured down. He was half buried, and the approach to the surface was blocked by yards of sand. There was no more light. He had only succeeded in imprisoning himself more securely. It would take hours for him to claw away the debris.

And then he thought of getting one of the Canopic urns, knocking off the neck and making a scoop. That would hasten his progress. But he had scarcely returned to the vault when the door opened, and the priest and his men came in. Anu noted Deane's torn coat and trousers, and said:

"You waste your time trying to escape. Do your duty, and you will go free."

Deane staggered forward a pace.

"I won't! You couldn't trick me with your talk about living dead. You're alive! I can see where your corpse skin is cracking. From fighting with me."

Anu's bronzed face twisted a little.

"It doesn't make much difference, after all. Someone will find the note this girl wrote you. Your car is outside. Sooner or later, the police will find you here, with a corpse floating in a bath of natron. Suppose one of us did the work — do you think that any story you can tell will help you?" He extended his hand, displaying the note.

They had him cornered. That much was clear. The reason behind it all was something that did not enter into the gruesome situation.

"Go ahead! You killed her!" he croaked. His voice cracked, and he reeled. "Go ahead and see if they can prove me guilty!"

This sounded like desperate defiance, and Anu smiled indulgently. He did not suspect that Deane was pulling himself together, prodding the masqueraders into revealing more of their plans.

"That'll be easy, Mr. Deane," he said. "We'll just lock you up with the dead. You'll stay here until we want you to be discovered."

Deane's shoulders slumped. "If I do the work —"

"We'll turn you loose. There is still time for your car to be taken away, and the wind will wipe out the tire tracks. You won't be discovered. But you must embalm this woman according to the old rites. As you have guessed, we are alive, but there is very much about old Egypt that you do not know. Least of all why we want this done. The old beliefs are not dead. This proves their life."

Deane tottered forward a little. "Give me the knife."

The priest nodded contentedly. Another robed figure entered the room, and stood in the shadows, somewhat apart.

"Where's the knife?" Anu asked. His helpers muttered and glanced about. "Find it, you fools!"

Deane actually had the flint blade in his pocket, but he had to catch the ghouls off guard before he could risk using it. Bit by bit, the ghastly situation made sense. As he stalled for a breathing spell, he pieced his guesses together.

Hassan's investigations must have aroused suspicion, and thus the tomb looters had been prepared for Nefeyda's treachery. They had killed her and at the same time trapped Deane.

Heyl, he reasoned, must be behind all this. It was his illicitly concealed discovery that she had exposed, either for spite or for a reward. This was an Eighteenth Dynasty tomb; that mummy could be Bint Anath's.

But however that might be, the looters had Deane cornered. Nefeyda's corpse, embalmed and concealed, would be a club over his head. He would have to assure Crawford that the treasures were genuine. And from then on, Deane would have to authenticate all Heyl's offerings to gullible collectors, whether faked or real.

Deane now realized how useful he was to the looters. That gave him courage. They would have to protect him with perjured evidence, once Nefeyda's disappearance was traced to him, as it would be, for some of Quasim's customers had seen him leave with the girl. Also, these ghouls would not want to hurt him, unless in self-defense.

As they obeyed Anu, and sank to their hands and knees to find the missing knife, Deane muttered:

"I want to smoke. God, it makes me sick." He fumbled and found his pack of cigarettes. "Give me a light."

Anu graciously handed him the taper. He had taken it, and was holding it up so that his assistants could peer into the dim corners. Deane touched light to his smoke, and then he flung the taper at the mummy on the table. The flammable linen burst into smoky flame. Anu yelled, and just then, Deane's hand came out of his pocket, armed with the flint knife.

The squatting helpers heard the cry, and saw the flame. They leaped toward the mummy to extinguish it. They did not know that Anu's cry was prolonged by anything but wrath. But a flint blade had ripped him, and he fell, clutching his stomach.

Deane launched himself at the men who were falling over each other in their scramble to smother the flames. He slashed, long, deadly strokes with the glass-hard blade. Taken utterly by surprise, they got in each other's way. Before they could realize what was happening, two of them were drenched with blood.

The flames rose, red and smoky. Choking black fumes thickened the air. The man who stood to one side closed in, but Deane whirled, butting him in the stomach with his shoulder.

Some had recovered, and were belaboring him, booting and kicking and choking as he slashed their legs. Someone was coughing:

"Don't kill him, you fools! Grab him — and hold him!"

This was a European's voice — the voice, now undisguised, of Gunther Heyl. Deane stabbed upward but the brittle blade snapped on a rib. He was unarmed, and the survivors were on him. Their weight bore him down, and the dense fumes, searing Deane's lungs, weakened him. His desperate outburst had taken his last remnant of strength.

"Open the door," one of the Copts gasped. "Open — we're choking."

A bit of fresh air thinned the smoke. Deane caught a glimpse of dawn from outside. Then that was cut off. They were lifting him to his feet. He had lost his chance. One had found a steel knife, and was approaching Nefeyda.

But that blow was not struck. There was a yell from the tunnel which had collapsed during Deane's vain attempt at escape. Hassan came in with several Egyptian police. Crawford, red-faced and puffing, followed them. His cheeks and forehead were slashed and battered.

That ended the show. Deane and the survivors were hustled up the stairs, and into the barren room. Two men carried Gunther Heyl outdoors. His macabre makeup was drenched with blood. He was groaning and half conscious. The flint blade, though breaking, had torn him.

There were two cars in front, but Deane's was not in sight.

Later, when the choking fumes of the burning mummy had thinned, Deane demanded:

"The girl! Is she really dead?"

"Beyond all hope, *Effendi*," the police official answered. "And we found you because your servant and Mr. Crawford helped us."

"*Effendi*, you remember I warned you," Hassan explained. "When you did not listen, I hid in the trunk of your car. All looked well, when we came here, so I did not come out. Then the girl screamed, and the door closed. There was nothing I could do. By Allah, I cannot drive a car, so I ran. All the way to the Sugar Factory police station. They would not believe me. I was frightened, and they thought I was crazy."

"So," said the official, "when he told us about Heyl and Crawford, we drove into Cairo and looked for both. We found only Crawford, and your servant nearly killed him before we could stop him. Then he told us of Heyl and we believed your servant and came out."

"The house was empty," Crawford interposed. "We went

around in circles until we found a hole in the sand. As if an underground passage had collapsed."

"That was where I was trying to dig out," Deane explained.

"Then we heard the yelling below," Hassan interrupted. "We dug in from the top, easily."

"But how did they kill her?" Deane demanded, shivering.

"Now that it is daylight, we can see what you missed," the police official said. "Those fine bits of glass on the floor. The surgeon perhaps can tell us what the little bottle contained before it broke. Perhaps a gas. Something like cyanogen, though I do not understand these things."

Deane shook his head. "But if I had followed her, I'd have been killed, and they wanted me alive."

"*Effendi*," said the official, "they seized you after she was dead. Now, had you gone with her into the house, they could have seized you first and taken you away, then poisoned her. But what I do not understand is, why did they do these things?"

"You can ask Heyl, if he's able to talk. Or his fake corpses. But I've got a good idea, already."

The official laughed. "A flogging will make them talk! But let me hear what you think."

Deane explained his suspicions: how Nefeyda had died for exposing the clique of looters, how Heyl had planned to blackmail him into helping sell illicit finds and outright fakes.

"Once I had embalmed Nefeyda," he concluded, "his possession of that made-to-order mummy could at any time frame me as a madman and a murderer. But as long as I played his crooked game for him, he would of course protect me as a valuable ally. You see, he'd already started, by taking my car away. And his crowd would all swear that I'd never left Cairo with Nefeyda."

Quasim's presence among the conspirators clinched that. Deane had scarcely paused when there was a howling and yelling and cursing outside. The police official stroked his mustaches and smiled.

"My men seem to have gotten the prisoners into a confidential mood, Mr. Deane. Let us go out and have them confirm your opinions." He winked. "If they did roll your car into the Nile, doubtless they already wish they had followed it."

Deane went out. When he reached the door, he saw that the police were beating the prisoners' feet with batons. They were all trying to speak at once, Heyl loudest of all.

"And they claim we have a third degree back home!" Deane said to Crawford. "Now, if there's anything I can tell you about Egyptian antiques, drop in some time."

Crawford shuddered. "I'm through! I'm looking for a safer hobby."

For a moment Deane would have agreed with him. That was when they put Nefeyda's body into the police car. Then he remembered his unfinished work, and the laboratory that demanded his presence.

There were still secrets of the past for him to unveil.

THE BURNING CLUE

"DO YOU MEAN to say," demanded Claire Dennison of her newly widowed sister, Martha Jarvis, "that the insurance company refuses to pay off, simply because you can't prove that Jarvis died before 12 noon instead of some time after that hour?"

"That's exactly it," said Martha, sighing wearily. "You see, the premium hadn't been paid for some time. The extension expired at 12 noon of the very day that his latest playmate called with her pearl-handled light-housekeeping pistol and demanded a showdown. With no insurance, and the house mortgaged to the last shingle, I'm left absolutely broke."

"If that red-headed good-for-nothing hadn't become penitent a minute after she did the first good deed of her life, and then shot herself, we might prove that Jarvis died before noon," thought Claire; but she said to her sister, "Can't you find *anyone* who heard the shots?"

"Not a soul. There's so much shrubbery around the house, and it's so far from the street — and, you know, a .25 automatic is hardly louder than the snapping of a stick. Claire, there's just no use!"

"But we've got to figure it out, Mart!" insisted Claire. "Let's see — old Aunt Julia says she left the house about half past eleven that morning. How did you know the time?"

"The radio was announcing a domestic science lecture, and Jarvis said, 'Shut the damned thing off!' They checked the broadcasting station, and got the time. She also remembered she had just loaded his pipe. That's it, over there."

Claire followed her sister's gesture, and saw a Turkish water-pipe with its brass fittings, and flexible stem, nearly two yards long, coiled about the neck of the glass water jar.

"She told the coroner all about loading the pipe," resumed Martha. "And how she came back, finding them both 'all daid,' and the pipe turned over, and a hole burned in the rug."

Claire noted the clean-cut, square hole burned through to the warp of the old Persian rug.

"How did that happen?" she wondered.

"When that woman shot him," explained Martha, "he had the pipe stem coiled about his wrist, like he always did. They'd been quarreling before Aunt Julia left. Anyway, she opened fire. And it didn't take much of a move on his part to pull the pipe off the table. The cake of charcoal that keeps the tobacco burning just ate its way into the rug."

Claire's fingernails were turning from rose to dark brown from the smoke of her disregarded cigarette.

"Mart," she said, finally, "call Aunt Julia. I want to talk to her."

For several days Claire pondered on the elusive problem, but in vain.

"Good Lord!" she exclaimed a dozen times over, "why couldn't one shot have stopped his watch, like in a story mystery? All those details, and not one thing to prove he died before noon!"

The deep brand of that last pipe stared up at her from the rug, and mocked her. There was a record of the crime; but it was as vain as the fleeting, spiteful crack of that tiny, deadly pistol which no one had heard. But how to use it?

Claire questioned old Aunt Julia over and over again; but the old woman recollected only irrelevant details. But finally, out of the confusion, Claire picked a bit of hope. She phoned her sister's lawyer.

"Mr. Cartwright," she said, "bring the insurance adjuster, and a copy of the testimony of the coroner's inquest — yes, I have something up my sleeve. . . . Please try, anyway. . . . Thank you."

They called the following morning: Cartwright, politely humoring a woman's whim, and utterly hopeless of deriving any benefit from it; and Bartlett, the adjuster, courteous, suave, and determined that his company would not pay

$50,000 on any policy that had expired, even if only by five minutes.

"Mr. Cartwright," began Claire, "when did Aunt Julia turn off the radio, the day Mr. Jarvis died?"

The lawyer consulted his file of testimony.

"At 11:32 A.M.," he answered. And then, to Bartlett, "Here it is."

The adjuster nodded. "I'll accept that. It's official."

"And according to the testimony," resumed Claire, "she set his pipe before him at practically the same time."

"Right," admitted Cartwright.

"But I don't see," protested the adjuster.

"Just have patience, Mr. Bartlett," said Claire, sweetly. "Oh, yes, I forgot something. How long could Mr. Jarvis have lived after the shots were fired?"

"Death was practically instantaneous. According to our doctors, he couldn't have lived over a minute, if that long," replied the adjuster. "But —"

"That's fine. Now, Aunt Julia," continued Claire, turning to the old Negress, who had entered in response to her ring. "Prepare that pipe, just as you always did."

"This is irrelevant," protested Bartlett. "We're not interested —"

"Oh, but you will be!" enthused Claire, as she smiled at his disgust. "Do step into the kitchen and watch."

Bartlett swallowed his impatience. They all watched Aunt Julia put a square cake of charcoal on the gas burner, then shred a golden brown leaf of Persian tobacco, soak it in water, and wring it dry. She molded it into a heap, and placed it in the bowl of the pipe. Then with the brass tongs she picked up the glowing charcoal and laid it on the tobacco.

"Take it out in front," directed Claire. "Just where Mr. Jarvis was sitting."

"Really interesting," began Bartlett, ironically. "Still —"

"Might as well see it through," suggested the lawyer.

They sat there, watching the film of white ash accumulate on the surface of the charcoal. Claire put the mouthpiece to her lips, and drew deeply. The pipe gurgled, and bubbled, and a tiny wisp of smoke left her lips. As the charcoal burned, the outer coating of ash fell away.

"Do try it," invited Claire, offering the pipe stem.

Both men hastily refused.

Claire's glance shifted to the clock on the wall. She drew again. Another tiny wisp of smoke. She coiled the flexible stem around her wrist.

"The way they do in Cairo," she explained, with a triumphant glint in her eye. "Like Mr. Jarvis did."

"Mrs. Dennison," protested the impatient adjuster, "I can't see that this is getting us anywhere!"

He rose as if to leave.

"Oh, you don't? Well, Mr. Bartlett, it's about time to show you!"

She also rose to her feet.

"Look out!" the men cried in warning. But too late. The flexible stem about her wrist dragged the pipe from the table. The glowing charcoal lay like a great, living ruby on the Persian rug. They smelled the stench of burning wool.

"Let it alone!" commanded Claire, sharply, as Cartwright seized the brass tongs.

They glanced at her, and at each other, and at Claire's sister, and shook their heads significantly.

"Look!" she insisted, ignoring their meaning glances.

She saw them wince as the square of red hot, living fire perceptibly settled as the nap beneath it was consumed. The wanton destruction of that antique fabric had an almost horrible fascination for them. They saw the black, oily distillate from the wool rise up along the edge of the coal. Then the coal shifted again, sinking deeper.

"Mrs. Dennison, are you in your right mind?" demanded Bartlett. "That rug is worth hundreds —"

"Not hundreds," retorted Claire. "Exactly $50,000!"

The adjuster stared, speechless.

Claire seized the brass tongs. There was a perceptible sigh of relief as she picked the hungry destroyer from that rich, old rug. And then silence as they regarded the caked blackness that marked the burn.

"Mr. Bartlett," began Claire, breaking the silence, "compare that burn with the one made when Mr. Jarvis was shot. As you may have noted, I smoked the pipe about ten minutes before I overturned it. The size of the hole I burned will convince you that Jarvis could not have been smoking much longer when he overturned his pipe.

"The cake of charcoal diminishes about a quarter of an inch every ten minutes. Try it.

"And," she concluded, "you see, this rug is worth $50,000!"

"Guess you pay off, Bartlett!" exulted the lawyer .

"You win," admitted the adjuster, as he reached for his pen, and a sheaf of papers.

THE DEVIL'S CRYPT

I.

Satan's Footprints

GUIDEBOOK tourists to Southern France concentrate on Biarritz; but those who love unspoiled antiquity prefer Bayonne, that gray-walled city that basks in the warmth of the Pyrenees and guards the road to Spain. The moat that girdles the citadel is dry, and the drawbridges are no longer serviceable; but at sunrise, when the Lachepaillet Wall and the cathedral spires seem floating on banks of low-lying river mists from the Nive and the Adour, Bayonne is a hashish dream rather than a city.

France and Spain, England and Navarre, have contended for possession of that fortress; and before them, the Moors occupied that old city which was once the encampment of Roman legions; but it is only at night that one remembers the crypts and passages that undermine the citadel, and senses that the soil, which for centuries has drunk the blood of defender and invader alike, is still thirsty.

Bayonne is an old gray sphinx, somnolently smiling through the veils of her mystery.

Two men emerged from the Lachepaillet Gate as the cathedral clock struck eleven. They were bareheaded, and in full evening dress. Davis Barrett, the younger, was tall, bronzed, and rugged as the massive masonry of the walls. The elder was grizzled, with fine, stern features and bristling, close-cropped hair, which gleamed white in the moonlight. It was no promenade to continue a private discussion that would have been disturbed by the laughter and music and tingling glasses in José Guevara Millamediana's luxurious apartment; they walked with expectant, searching alertness; and the elder was perturbed, as though he feared to find what they sought.

"Why," demanded Barrett, "do you think you'll find Louise here, of all places?"

"Her apartment, just a block from Don José's, must have been her destination, but she's not there. And since she left without her cloak, she must have intended to return in a few minutes. As it is —"

D'Artois shrugged, regarded his friend. Barrett glanced up toward the parapet along which ran rue Lachepaillet.

"She could have slipped," he admitted.

"Precisely, my friend," replied Pierre d'Artois. "With a bit too much of Don José's wine — a moment of dizziness, a misstep in the mist — there's no guard rail up there."

Barrett agreed. It was logical; yet he sensed that his companion had withheld more than he had expressed. He shivered in anticipation of the end of what had started as a casual courtesy to allay the misgivings of Yvonne Marigny concerning the unduly prolonged absence of her sister, Louise.

They bounded the swelling curve of the bastion that marks the turn of the wall toward the Gate of Spain. Barrett's heart and breath for a moment stopped as he abruptly halted, frozen by the horror that confronted them.

The gray sphinx had lifted her veil, and revealed not her seduction, but her terror and darkness.

A woman lay on the sandy bottom of the dry moat. Fright had so hideously transfigured her face that it was her scarlet gown and blue-black hair and silver *lamé* slippers rather than the olive-tinted features which Barrett recognized. He saw how Louise Marigny had died, and tried to convince himself that it was illusion, and the fantasy of a moon-haunted night.

"Pierre — look at her throat! Look at —" His voice cracked, and for a moment failed. Louise Marigny's throat had been terribly mangled, as by a beast of prey. Barrett resolutely denied the thoughts that followed his first impression.

D'Artois, his seamed features pale and drawn, nodded.

"My friend, look again. You have seen but half of it."

Barrett wondered what further horror there could be; but his gray eyes followed the old man's commanding gesture and saw the footprints of that which had roamed by moonlight.

Man, beast, or devil, its feet were webbed; yet for all the resemblance of the tracks to those of some monstrous aquatic fowl of aeons past, there was that which suggested a hybrid combining the feet of an anthropoid with those of a web-footed bird, or bird-like reptile.

"And the prints end after a few paces," muttered d'Artois.

"It might have jumped to the bank," countered Barrett, making a final effort to lend a touch of sanity to the outrageous implications of the suddenly ending trail.

D'Artois shook his head.

"Impossible. Facing the way its tracks indicate, it would have had to clear the moat by leaping crabwise. It must have flown away."

"Good Lord! A bird with feet that large! Or a winged reptile — couldn't possibly be!" Barrett was thinking of the *pterodactyl*, that flying, reptilian slayer which has been extinct for uncounted thousands of years.

D'Artois for a moment studied the uncanny trail.

"Something worse than any honest reptile," he muttered somberly. Then, to Barrett: "Let's notify the *Sûreté*. At once."

Barrett was glad to leave that sinister spot; but as d'Artois turned: "Pierre, one of us should watch here until the police arrive."

"There is no time to waste in courtesies to the dead," he countered. "And I may need your assistance. *Allons!*"

And presently, passing the Lachepaillet Gate, they ascended the slope, skirted the parapet, then turned down rue Tour de Sault, near whose end was the 13th-Century ruin which d'Artois had restored and modernized, making of it a town house wherein he was not only comfortable, but content in being in the heart of the old city he loved so well.

D'Artois led the way to his study on the second floor, stepped to the telephone, and called the Prefect of Police. The machine gun sputter of d'Artois's French was too much for Barrett, but he caught a phrase from time to time, and the incredulous horror of the Prefect's voice as it filtered faintly from the receiver.

"He will make plaster casts of the footprints; he will measure the stride; he will look for bits of hair, thread, lint," d'Artois enumerated as he replaced the instrument. Then, with an expansive gesture, "but he will find nothing!"

Barrett set down the decanter of *Vieux Armagnac,* whose level he had appreciably pulled down while listening to d'Artois remarks. The fiery liquor burned out the chills that had raced up and down his spine.

"You haven't much respect for the Prefect," he said with something approaching a smile. D'Artois's extensive studies in criminology and psychology at times made him critical of the *Sûreté.*

"This is something which transcends scientific crime detection," the old man countered. "It is not a case of an assassin disguising his feet with something which will leave an outlandish footprint. Yet that is what *Monsieur le Préfet* will attempt to prove, and he will fail.

"But I will approach from another angle."

As he spoke, d'Artois, with swift gesture, swept his desk clear of its accumulated debris. Then he laid out a sheet of paper and with a compass drew a circle which he divided into twelve equal sectors. That done, he took from a bookcase a thin volume whose pages were divided into columns. It was an ephemeris.

"Mon ami," explained d'Artois in response to Barrett's exclamation, "astronomical tables are not exclusively used for navigation. An ephemeris, you recollect, is also used by astrologers."

"I am inquiring into the planetary aspects. In the meantime, do you swill the rest of my brandy. Your stomach doubtless needs settling."

Barrett selected a cigar from d'Artois's humidor; then, his curiosity overcoming him, he peered over the old man's shoulder, watching him enter astrological symbols in the twelve sectors of the circle. The cigar had accumulated less than an inch of ash when d'Artois thrust back his chair.

"I see more than murder and mutilation," he declared. "I see a sinister configuration that cries out of an old and malignant magic. Neptune, in the Eighth House, indicates death by *strange spiritual causes.* And look at the position of Saturn, the lord of those who follow *subterranean pursuits;* Uranus, the sovereign of thaumaturgists and black magicians; and over all is the evil aspect of the moon, the mother of sorcery."

"Still and all, Pierre," interjected Barrett, perplexed by the astrological jargon, "you've only repeated what we already know. We saw it was uncanny and horrible. Anyway, this astrology business —"

"Has been degraded by charlatans, I grant," snapped d'Artois. "But it is none the less a true science, and only limited by the intelligence of the investigator.

"I am looking into the background of this monstrous crime. And the first move is to seek *underground,* a black magician working in some of the hidden vaults beneath the city. Check up on all those known or suspected of having occult connections. Thus we have already eliminated all common criminals, *n'est-ce pas?*"

Barrett, impressed by his friend's solemnity, conceded the point, outrageous as it was to hear a sane, hard-bitten old soldier and scholar to speak of black magic as an actual menace; but d'Artois's ensuing assertion left Barrett too astonished even to protest.

"And the first of these devil mongers and dabblers in the occult that I will investigate is our charming host of the evening, Don José. He is the head of a clique that has gathered in Bayonne. On the surface, they seem to be harmless cranks who babble of telepathy, mysticism, and the like; but tonight's tragedy confirms my contention that modern Bayonne is living up to its ancient reputation for being a nest of malignant occultists and necromancers!"

"Good God, Pierre!" Barrett finally contrived to ejaculate. "Why — that's utterly impossible —"

"So was the gruesome tragedy in the moat," retorted d'Artois, his blue eyes cold and glittering as sword points by moonlight. "And wait till I tell you the rest: *Yvonne and Louise are twins.* If there is one iota of truth in astrology, Yvonne will succumb, or at the best, narrowly escape the doom that overtook her sister.

"Their horoscopes, while, of course, not identical, would be so similar that both would be susceptible to the occult evil that is stalking tonight. The stars have warned us. You watch the living while I set out to trip up the monster responsible for that ghastly crime. Hurry — before it's too late!"

Barrett's last remnant of skepticism melted before his friend's unwavering conviction. He followed d'Artois to the street, and through the river mists that billowed from the Nive and marched up rue Tour de Sault like a phantom army.

II.

The Beast from the Crypt

D'ARTOIS's car was parked near Don José's house. "I will not only need it tonight," explained d'Artois as they hurried along rue Lachepaillet, "but we must also get Mademoiselle Yvonne — get her away from that party. That Spaniard —"

"But I don't see how he could be connected with it," contended Barrett. "He was there, all the time, among his guests. Yvonne just stepped out for a moment for a breath of air, or —"

"*Imbécile!*" snorted d'Artois. "That's just the point: Don José being always in sight of his guests gives him a perfect but deceptive alibi."

"But that doesn't prove —"

"Of course it proves nothing. But if you'd read that fellow's book on Tibetan magic, and heard the rumors of his doings near the roof of the world, you would think twice, *pardieu!*

"Alone, I am handicapped. But fortunately there is in Bayonne an occultist who can help me. A profound scholar whose researches can perhaps save the day: Sidi Abdurrahman, an Oriental mystic and *Chêla*, a disciple of an occult Adept."

Barrett shuddered as they passed the bastion of the Lachepaillet wall and heard the detectives, already on the case, and the crisp, incisive voice of the Prefect who had appeared to take charge in person. And then, presently, they heard music, and laughter, the mirth of Don José's guests. Barrett nerved himself to ascend the stairs and enter the glow of lights and the mocking presence of gaiety.

Yvonne, they learned, had left Don José's house only a few minutes after d'Artois and Barrett had gone in search of Louise.

"*Por Dios, Señor,*" said the courtly Spaniard, "she fancied her sister was ill and went home to join her. I trust that you will present my compliments and regrets to the lovely Louise. I am indeed sorry that she had to leave so early. Is it possible that she may return for her wrap?"

Don José was mocking them; and Barrett, remembering d'Artois dreadful surmises, sought to deny the thought that Yvonne, like her sister, had gone out into the mist and the moonlight to meet a horrible death; nor was he reassured by the fierce glitter in d'Artois's eyes and the twitch of his waxed moustache as he paused a moment before replying, "I will take her wrap, and leave it on my way past their apartment."

D'Artois and the Spaniard regarded each other as though they had crossed swords instead of glances; and during the exchange Barrett sensed a sudden tension, a current of deadly animosity, like a dagger biting through a shroud of silk. He saw Don José's cheeks for an instant lose their olive tint; and the dark eyes, troubled by the frosty, unwavering stare of d'Artois, seemed eager to shift.

"*Sacré salaud!* hissed d'Artois, "you know she will never need her wrap. I am busy this evening — *and you know why.* But I will meet you, with sword or pistol. Soon."

Don José recoiled before the insult and the vague accusation. Then he shrugged, smiled blandly, twisted his black moustache.

"*Señor,* I have not the least idea why you insult me, or what you are implying. Neither am I interested. But if you live long enough, and your courage is equal to the occasion, I will be happy to meet you with any weapons you may prefer."

The stilted, formal speech would have seemed absurd to Barrett had he not sensed the deadly, blazing hatred that flashed for an instant from Don José's eyes.

"*Mordieu, cordieu, pardieu!*" retorted d'Artois, advancing

a pace. "If anything happens to Mademoiselle Yvonne, I will not meet you with weapons — I will dismember you by hand."

They exchanged bows with punctilious formality; and then d'Artois turned and led the way to the Mercedes.

"I am more than ever convinced that in some way he's responsible. He, or one of his devil mongering clique," declared d'Artois as he took the wheel.

"But how could he? It's utterly incredible —"

"Science scoffs at sorcery, glibly explains its manifestations as *hysterical hypnosis*," countered d'Artois. "But that does not make it any the less magic. Remember what you saw in the moat and how the horoscope confirmed our first impressions. Certainly I am at loss, but Sidi Abdurrahman's years of study will solve the riddle."

"Maybe," conceded Barrett, "you're right. Oddly enough, your remarks didn't puzzle him as they should have."

"By no means strange," retorted d'Artois as they drew up before the apartment of the two sisters. "He knew that I knew."

A sturdy, white-haired Basque maid admitted them. Yvonne Marigny received them in the living room. Her olive skin was deadly pale, and her dark eyes burned with an unnatural light.

"Yes. The *Sûreté* notified me, just a few minutes after I arrived," she said with a calmness that was more devastating than any outburst of grief. "I had a premonition of evil when Louise slipped out for a breath of air. And when I sent you to look for her — *mon Dieu!* It was too late."

"But why did you leave before we returned?"

Yvonne shook her head.

"I don't know. Just an irresistible urge to get away. To go home. Like the instinct that urges an animal to creep off to its den and die."

She shuddered, made a perplexed, despairing gesture.

"So . . . you were almost driven from there," said d'Artois, speaking very slowly, and glancing meaningly at Barrett. Then his eyes flashed toward the windows and their closely spaced wrought-iron bars. He nodded approvingly; and Barrett caught the unspoken thought.

"*Mon vieux*, do you stay here with Mademoiselle Yvonne.

I am going to get Sidi Abdurrahman. He lives out beyond the Mousserole Wall, not far off the river road."

Then, as Barrett accompanied him to the door, he continued in a whisper, "The same strange, unreasoning compulsion that sent Louise to her death may send Yvonne wandering by moonlight. Don't let her out of the house. Hold her. Tie her, if necessary!"

The door clicked closed behind d'Artois; and a moment later they heard the soft whir of gears.

The proximity of tragedy depressed Barrett. He resolutely directed his eyes away from the barred window, and the moon-drenched mists beyond, and sought to banish the memory of what he had seen in the moat; but a strange fascination forced him to gaze into the ghastly glamour of the night. Barrett shivered, rose from his chair, intending to draw the shades to screen that ill-omened view. Yvonne nodded, sensing his motive, and smiled wanly through the tears that glistened in her dark eyes.

"Monsieur Barrett," said Yvonne, "this is all so terribly unreal . . . it is like an awful nightmare. It seems as though all the evil that has ever existed is concentrating about us."

Thus she described the feeling that Barrett had vainly sought to dispel. He had assured himself that it was but natural for Yvonne, grief-stricken and horrified as she was, to infect him with her own emotions; and yet, that reassurance by no means convinced him.

He noted that the lights were dimming. He frowned perplexedly, and resumed his seat, instead of drawing the shade.

"Bum voltage regulation," he insisted; but Barrett's intuition told him that the trouble was not electrical. Then he saw that wisps of mist were swirling and drifting in through the window.

Yvonne stared into the coals of the grate, whose ardent glow had suddenly cooled. The girl herself had become lethargic, as though her spirit had left her. For a moment Barrett felt utterly alone. It was as though Yvonne were a lovely simulacrum and not a woman who shrank shuddering into the depths of her spacious chair.

Gray vapors swirled and surged through the room. A chilling breeze urged the mist whorl into sweeping spirals; mists that came neither from the Nive nor the Adour, nor any earthly river. Barrett thought again of d'Artois's solemn declaration, *"Saturn, the lord of subterranean places, Neptune, who governs strange spiritual enemies, and malignant Uranus, rule this night."*

Barrett stepped to the center of the room, where he could see the double windows that overlooked the Lachepaillet Walk. He saw a monstrous shape peering at him as, perched on the sill, it clutched the window-bars and slowly wrenched them apart.

The walls had become obscured with dense, vibrant mist banks, so that only in the center of the room was any light left. The incandescent lamps were now a dull, somber red that vainly sought to filter through the surging haze.

The creature's feet identified it as the monster of the moat.

Barrett saw now what had torn Louise's throat and drunk her blood, then taken three long strides and —

It had spread its membranous bat-wings and soared into the moonlight, and thence to whatever unknown hell had sent it forth. The face was anthropoid, but malignant, beyond the bestial wrath of any honest ape. The body was hybrid, neither reptilian nor simian: a blasphemy and an outrage whose hideously confused anatomy was all the more abhorrent in its mingling of hair and scales.

The feet were almost human at the heel, but branched into three claw-like toes, joined by webs. Beast it was, yet bird, and reptile. The hands were similarly formed, with arms long enough to accommodate the broad sweep of the membranous wings.

Barrett knew that the creature had no thought for him. He knew that he could then and there stride safe and harmless through the ever-thickening mist banks, past the somber, vengeful forms that leered out of the haze, and pass on, unmolested. The beast ignored him. It advanced with a slow, fluent, serpentine motion that was entirely out of accord with its grotesque, awkward bulk. It paused, ready to spring forward and rend Yvonne's throat, mutilate her as it had her sister.

The Basque maid, alarmed by Yvonne's single shriek of mortal terror, came running in, stared in incredulous horror. Then she screamed and collapsed on the threshold.

As the monster lunged toward Yvonne, who was para-lyzed by the apparition, Barrett seized a heavy chair and lashed out, shattering it across the simian skull. The beast recoiled, sank back to its haunches, shook its head as though bewildered.

Barrett stood for an instant regarding the fragments that remained in his grasp. Then in a flare of rage born of terror and outraged reason, he charged, driving the splintered stumps full into the monster's face.

The assault was vain. He had disconcerted the beast more than he had shaken it. It lashed out with arms that reached almost to its ankles, and enfolded Barrett with its shroud of membranous wings. It screeched and hissed in inarticulate fury. Its long carnivorous teeth sought his throat, even as Barrett, beyond terror or reason, evaded the fangs and sought to throttle the beast, and tear it to pieces with his bare hands.

It was a mad dream of combat in a steaming, prehistoric jungle. The reptilian exhalation of the monster, its squeak-ing, gibbering wrath and the stifling embrace of its wings, drove Barrett to an insane rage. The thing was strong, but not beyond the strength of human wrath spurred to frenzy; and the very horror of its presence stirred up reserves of destructive fury whose force was dimly echoed in Barrett's ears as he heard the splintering of furniture that crashed and fell into fragments as he and the monster rolled and leaped, broke, and closed in again, seeking each other's throat.

And yet for all his rage-inspired strength and agility, Barrett vainly sought to rend that tough, scaly body which yielded instead of tearing or breaking as he applied in suc-cession, one after another savage trick of wrestling, and murderous holds practiced by Japanese experts. Though, it could not quite overcome Barrett, it resisted the full flame of his fury. Its endurance was unflagging, and its counter attacks fresh and vigorous as from the start. It seemed to gain strength from Barrett's blood, which streamed from a score of cuts and scratches and long, ragged furrows gouged by its teeth.

Barrett's strength at last was consumed by the futility of his rage. As in a confused dream, his mind began double-tracking: one half still a vortex of flaming wrath, the other impersonally pondering on d'Artois's astrological observations. He knew that this division of consciousness heralded the end of his resistance; and exerting an ultimate, despairing effort, sought to sink his teeth into the monster's throat. But the mists blackened, and the enemy evaded him. His arms clutched a void of abysmal coldness shot with burning flashes of scarlet and orange and dazzling, metallic blue. Then it seemed that he was falling swiftly through unbounded space . . . and as from a great distance he heard a long drawn wail of uttermost terror.

III.

The Savor of Blood

WHEN BARRETT finally regained consciousness he saw that the lights were bright again. D'Artois, kneeling at his side, was sponging his wounds.

". . . all in the approach," a calm, deep voice was saying. "Your friend — though God alone knows how — withstood the beast by pure force of will to slay. But that was misguided effort."

Barrett with a sudden effort propped himself up on his elbow to confront the person who so lightly disposed of that nightmare battle with that monster from an unknown hell; but his strength was unequal to his curiosity, and he sank back to the floor.

D'Artois helped him to his feet. Barrett, still dazed, for a moment had assumed that d'Artois's presence left victory to be taken for granted; but a second glance at his friend's grim features and despair haunted eyes told him the truth.

"Where is she?" he demanded, stubbornly resisting his fears. "Good Lord, did it —"

And then Barrett saw d'Artois's companion, Sidi Abdurrahman. Despite the freshness of the occultist's bronzed skin, he seemed incredibly ancient. Barrett's first impression was that some solemn Assyrian colossus had come to life. The neatly trimmed, square-cut beard added to the resemblance; only the tall miter was lacking. For an instant Barrett's despair subsided; and then he remembered that d'Artois had failed.

"Where is she?" he repeated. "We can't stand here, idle."

"We do not know — yet," replied the *Chêla*, unperturbed by Barrett's impatient outburst. "But there are ways of finding out. First, be so good as to clear the floor."

Barrett shot a dubious glance at d'Artois. His friend's answering nod was reassuring. And while they cleared away the wreckage of the furniture, Sidi Abdurrahman laid off a circle which he subdivided into seven sectors, and about which he drew a concentric circle.

"As I was saying a few moments ago," resumed the occultist, "fighting that monster was misdirected effort. We must find its master; for even though we destroyed the beast, body and soul, he would create —"

"*Soul?*" exclaimed Barrett. "That —"

"Yes. We are confronted by the recrudescence of an ancient evil that began among the Black Magicians of Atlantis. It is written in the occult records: *The Atlanteans had become magicians who created monsters with the strength of the brute and the cunning of the savage; and these they ensouled with the most malignant of elementals, who became guards and messengers, the terrible symbols of the power of the Kings of Darkness.*

"*To bind these dread beings more closely to their service, they offered them sacrifices of slain animals and slain men. Fifty thousand years passed: and then the Dragons of Wisdom sent a doom forth from Holy Shamballah.*"

"Is that creature fifty thousand years old?" wondered Barrett.

The *Chêla* smiled and shook his head.

"That is only the time during which the Black Masters were at the height of their power. They were destroyed something like 850,000 years ago when the word went forth from Shamballah. And as it was done then, so must we do now: make the slave betray the master," continued Sidi Abdurrahman as he drew a seven-pointed star in the innermost circle.

"We will bribe and drug that monster with blood. It shall find its doom in the very evil by which it has lived all these ages; it cannot resist the bait; and instead of warning its master, it will lead us to him."

"For a Mohammedan," whispered Barrett as the *Chêla* reached for a small copper bowl which he had brought with him, "he certainly is unorthodox."

"Mordieu! Who said he was a Moslem?" countered d'Artois. "His name signifies nothing. He gets his knowledge from study of occult records which are the fountainhead of learning, and transcend race and religion."

Sidi Abdurrahman set the bowl at the center of the circles; then he cast into it the contents of a small packet: a fine, bluish powder.

That done, he drew a dagger, saying, "This will be its last drink of blood! And it cannot refuse the bait; for such is the law of its kind."

But before the keen blade touched the vein of the *Chêla's* forearm, Barrett interposed.

"Let me in on this," he said, thrusting forward his own arm.

"No. I have an old debt to pay. One contracted in a former life, by a former failure. Just is the Wheel, and unswerving and this is my debt."

With the evening's earlier madness, Barrett found the occultist's reference to a previous incarnation entirely rational. He stepped back as the blade bit, and the old man's blood spurted redly into the copper bowl.

When the bowl was filled to the brim, d'Artois stepped forward and with a handkerchief and lead pencil devised a tourniquet to check the flow.

They watched the occultist bow ceremonially to the cardinal points of the compass, and make ritual gestures. They heard him intone, *"The hour has struck, and the black night is ready . . . let their destiny be accomplished. . . ."*

And then Barrett could no longer understand the *Chêla's* utterance. The sonorous, majestic intonation was in a tongue so foreign and archaic that it seemed not even remotely related to any speech of mankind.

They stood, poised and expectant, watching the copper bowl and the blood that glowed like a monstrous carbuncle. They became aware of another presence in the room. A grayish vapor finally coalesced above the red surface; and then as Sidi Abdurrahman's great voice thundered the ultimate, triumphant syllables of that age-old occult chant, the materialization became complete.

Barrett started in sudden alarm as he recognized at the center of the circle the same beast which had so nearly overcome him; but it was now translucent and unsubstantial, a phantom replica of the living horror. It knelt submissively, wings folded over its back as though it were a bird of prey subdued and garbed in the mockery of human form; and as with bestial eagerness it lapped up the bowl of blood, its body seemed to become more dense. A musty, reptilian stench pervaded the room.

When the bowl was empty, Sidi Abdurrahman's arm flashed out in a commanding gesture. The monster shrank as from the touch of red hot iron, then stepped from the circle.

D'Artois slipped an automatic pistol into Barrett's hand. The cold metal reminded him that at least a shred of reality remained.

"There will be men, later," d'Artois explained. Then, anticipating Barrett's question: "When this is over, I will tell you the answer — if we survive."

The grotesque procession filed down the hall and to the deserted rue Lachepaillet. The monster shambled down the street and at the end of some fifty yards, crossed toward the parapet, then stepped into a narrow doorway. They followed it down a steep, rubbish-littered stairway that led to a vaulted chamber which, by the beam of d'Artois's flashlight, Barrett recognized as a long untenanted dungeon; and then, on its hands and knees, the apparition crept through a low archway. It emerged on the bottom of the moat.

"Ah . . . this is not entirely a surprise," muttered d'Artois as he noted the direction taken by their spectral guide. "And we'll soon see whether Don José is its master."

After passing Porte d'Espagne, they ascended the steep bank of the moat, and thence toward the somber grove at the Spring of St. Léon, where their spectral guide turned toward a casemate which was barely visible in the shadow of a solitary, gigantic tree.

Sidi Abdurrahman halted at the entrance of the casemate. His majestic features were tense; and the fixity of his gaze betokened the concentration whereby he maintained his control of the monster. The occultist gestured toward the passageway which led straight into the heart of the knoll that rose from the level of the clearing.

"Part of Vauban's fortifications?" wondered Barrett, as by the beam of d'Artois's flashlight they stepped into the darkness.

"For a distance, yes," agreed d'Artois. "But before we are through, we will enter a place which neither Vauban nor any other honest engineer ever built."

Although the apparition was faintly luminous in the darkness, Barrett was certain that the *Chêla* followed it by some sense other than the five which normal humanity has.

"How did he call that thing out of thin air?" whispered Barrett, to whom the entire uncanny proceeding seemed like the fantasy of a nightmare.

"He provided it with a body, very much as a spiritualistic medium furnishes the substance for a materialization," explained d'Artois. "Its visible form is made up of part of the etheric double which every living creature has. And in order to maintain the form that the creature is using, Sidi Abdurrahman is exerting a tremendous effort, and drawing on an incredible reserve of psychic and physical energy. Few can endure the strain of lending too much vital force: which accounts for the eventual collapse of most spiritualist mediums.

"The force that animates this materialization of the monster is the elemental spirit that ensouled the body of the beast that killed Louise. This which we now see is not its physical body; and thus, being bound in an artificially created etheric form, the elemental cannot warn its master of our approach — ah . . . we're getting somewhere!"

The passageway had opened into what seemed to be a squad room for that portion of the outer defenses of the citadel. Sidi Abdurrahman and his guide had passed through an opening which pierced the further wall of the chamber.

"This is where Vauban's work ends," muttered d'Artois. "Beyond — God alone knows!"

The opening had been roughly cut through the masonry. Beyond it was a low tunnel whose spade-marked walls showed that it had been recently dug. At the end of a dozen paces it terminated at the upper landing of a staircase which was not the work of any military engineer. It had been relieved of the earth which had buried it for uncounted ages — brought to light again by the black master who had sent death stalking in the moonlight.

An aura of incalculable antiquity oppressed them as they stepped to the threshold of the blackness below.

Flight succeeded flight, until they arrived in a vaulted passage whose walls were buttressed with pilasters of masonry whose prodigious bulk dwarfed the mighty columns of Karnack.

"Good Lord!" whispered Barrett, awed by the monumental architecture. "It looks as though we've gone beyond time and reason and —"

"Mon ami," countered d'Artois grimly, "the evening is young. Listen —"

Far ahead of them, out of the age-old darkness, came the muttering of drums and the wailing of pipes. Sidi Abdurrahman halted, gestured.

"He will stay here to hold the messenger," explained d'Artois. *"Allons!"*

As they advanced along the passage they heard chanting, and the antiphonal responses of a ritual. And finally, as they rounded a turn, the corridor opened into a vault which was pervaded by a vibrant bluish glow.

The dome, supported by colossal pillars, swelled high above those who flitted to and fro in the satanic twilight of great glowing orbs whose quivering radiance was beclouded by fumes that rose stiflingly sweet from tall censer-tripods. They were warped and gnarled, those subterranean dwellers, long-armed, hairy survivors of a race that had vanished aeons before man in his present form appeared.

One among them, however, was tall and towering, and resplendent in a robe that flamed and coruscated as though woven of gems; and on his head he wore a conical miter of beaten silver. At his gesture the drumming and piping subsided and the acolytes ranged themselves on each side of an arch that pierced the further extremity of the vault. The arch was veiled by a heavy damask drape of crimson shot with gold.

"The master of the show," whispered d'Artois. And then, as the tall, resplendent leader turned: "And I was right — *Don José!*"

The dabbler in forbidden arts had finally descended to become high priest of those subterranean beast-men. Barrett shuddered as he thought of what their food might be, since they did not appear by daylight to eat of what grew beneath the sun. He wondered whether they had always lived in those archaic vaults, or whether they had but recently been revived from suspended animation —

And then the crimson drapes parted like flames torn by the breath of some nether hell. Barrett knew then that Sidi Abdurrahman had guided them well.

In the niche exposed by the parting of the gold-shot curtains was a lotus blossom carved of rock that glistened with the glassy luster of lacquer-ware. In the heart of the black lotus sat Yvonne, eyes veiled by her long lashes, arms crossed on her breast, head slightly inclined. Her fine features had the tranquility of the drugged, or of the quiet dead.

Barrett's hand flashed to his pistol butt as he gathered himself to spring from the concealing shadows; but d'Artois restrained him.

"They will cut us to pieces with their knives," whispered the old man. "This calls for strategy."

The odds were twenty to one. Though they emptied their pistols and extra clips, the survivors could still overwhelm them; and the enemy had to be exterminated if Yvonne were to be taken from that satanic vault.

"Then let's go back and get reinforcements," suggested Barrett.

D'Artois shook his head.

"Maybe, maybe not. Better see what this show signifies. We might not be able to return in time to —"

"What's that — over there?" demanded Barrett. "Good Lord! Did it get away from Sidi Abdurrahman?"

He indicated something that stirred in the shadow of a pillar at the right of the altar; and then he saw that despite its similarity to the beast which had overcome him, it was distinctly another creature.

"A new monster about to be ensouled by an elemental, to be a companion to the one that killed Louise," explained d'Artois. "And Yvonne is here to provide the blood offering — remember Sidi Abdurrahman's remarks?"

"Let's go out blazing!" growled Barrett; but again d'Artois restrained him.

"Not yet," murmured d'Artois. "We have to get her out of here."

But despite the calmness of his voice, his features were pale, and perspiration cropped out on his forehead as in desperation he searched his brain for some device to accomplish the impossible. Sidi Abdurrahman, holding the first monster helpless, was out of the question as an ally; but now, if ever, they needed that great occultist's aid.

"He won't fail us," d'Artois said. "And we'll see our moment. . . ."

Two acolytes were advancing toward the altar. One had a bowl of burnished copper, the other, a long-bladed knife. And as they took their posts, Don José began chanting.

"Bal-Taratan, come forth! Bal-Karadîn, come forth! From the blackness and from Avichi, Dark Lords, come forth!"

The braying and bellowing of strange wind instruments and the savage thunder of drums was bestial as the sluggish shape that crouched whimpering by the altar, awaiting the elemental that was to emerge from Avichi, the eighth and nethermost hell.

"God . . . that's awful," muttered Barrett as he watched the weaving gestures of Don José and his acolytes.

Brass clanged. The deep, hoarse, booming blasts of horns shook the vault. Mists were writhing like phantom serpents basking in the rays of a phantom sun that revived them from the chill of night.

"Bal-Taratan! Bal-Karadîn! I open the Gateway! I mark the Path!" intoned Don José, his voice rich and clear above that lustful bellowing and the sharp *clack-clack* of pebbles rattled in a yellowed skull. The acolytes, gesturing now like automatons, stared glassily, unaware of the shapes that were becoming visible.

"Bal-Taratan! Bring him forth! Bal-Karadîn! Bring him forth! I have a house for him! And for him I have food! Ia Bal-Taratan! Ia Bal-Karadîn!"

And as Don José paused at the enunciation of the names

of the Lords of the Eighth Hell, the acolytes hissed a phrase that was a dying, evil echo of those dread words.

"A feast of blood! A drink of blood!"

The acolytes responded, "Yea, the fumes of blood! The fumes, and the savor!"

The mist was now thicker, and its coldness had become folds of reptilian foulness. D'Artois and Barrett crouched in the angle of the pilaster, stricken by the sorcery of that evil chant. The terrific blasting of that awful rhythm had numbed and paralyzed body and mind.

"Yea, the fume of blood, and its savor!" thundered the chorus.

They were weaving a red symphony. Blood . . . blood . . . red mists shot with streaks of blackness that coruscated, and blackness that flamed! There was a stirring and chirping and twittering, and the flapping as of monstrous wings beating the upper air of the vault.

D'Artois's cheeks were gray, and Barrett's face was distorted from the acute physical misery induced by that terrific reiteration and weaving of words. His teeth were clenched, and sweat poured from his brow.

The words of the chant now became strange syllables whose fusion and blending gave a meaning that transcended language, striking into the very souls of the two who crouched in the shadows, binding them with a hideous fascination.

The bowl was ready. And the knife was rising. . . .

IV.

The Lords of Fire

A SOLEMN COMMAND came from the chaos of sound: "Bring him forth, Bal-Taratan! Bal-Karadîn!"

Don José's voice was the final assault to pierce the veil, and open the Gateway for the elemental that was to possess that hideous body; but it served still another purpose. D'Artois flinched from the anguish of the impact; the shock wrenched into life his numbed muscles, his stupefied brain; and his wrath, suddenly released, sent his hand flashing to his holster —

"*Smack-smack-smack!*" The acolyte with the knife pitched forward. The one who held the bowl dropped to the flags.

"*Gardez-vous!*" shouted d'Artois, with his left hand jerking Barrett to his feet. "Pick them off! Steady, now!"

The ranks of the acolytes wavered before the deadly fire, broke in panic.

"Missed him!" growled Barrett, as Don José flattened behind a pedestal and a bullet ricocheted, whining into the shadows.

The enemy reformed and charged, knives advanced. They flashed forward like serpents, darting and zigzagging, hunched forward in a crouch.

Some jerked suddenly upward as a slug pitched them end for end.

Others, riddled, charged on, to collapse within a pace of their mark.

But many lived.

"Give me a clip!"

"*Fini!*" snapped d'Artois. "Take a knife —

His pistol for another instant chattered like a machine gun; then came a sudden silence. The enemy paused, wondering; then they understood, and closed in.

Hoarse breathing, and the *slip-slip* of bare feet that wove in and out, devil-dancers darting back and forth with flickering blades.

"Too many," gasped Barrett, during a breathing space when the fury of their concerted assault drove the enemy back in momentary panic. "Get us   yet — get that — get José —"

D'Artois, master swordsman, might with his uncanny skill bore through the press and close in with the high priest. No other resource remained.

But the voice of Don José urged his beast-men to the attack, and the overwhelming wave surged resistlessly forward.

"Back!" yelled d'Artois. "Before they surround us. Into the niche. *Ca!*"

Even as he spoke, he flashed forward — then back, and on

guard again, blade dripping afresh, hand ready to strike again, slash through some weak spot in the dense line.

Another command from Don José. The attack withdrew, and he advanced to parley.

"Ah . . . d'Artois," he said, "since steel will not dislodge you, let us try —"

Suddenly his dark eyes became fixed, and his hands made rhythmic gestures. D'Artois and Barrett, caught off guard by the unaccountable action of their empty-handed enemy, faltered for an instant, perplexed. Despite the wrath of battle, their instincts for a moment restrained their attack on an unarmed man.

D'Artois was the first to recover.

"Rush him!" he cried, leaping forward. But he had waited too long.

Flames began lapping up from the paving in a crescent that imprisoned d'Artois and Barrett in its semicircle. The fires slowly converged, inch by inch, hungry blue flame relentlessly advancing.

"Hold your breath and dive through!"

"No!" shouted d'Artois, seizing Barrett by the shoulder. "It'll burn us to cinders. *Elemental fires!*"

Barrett did not understand; but he read the desperation in d'Artois's eyes.

"Resist his will. Fight his thought! If you fear, you are lost!"

"What do you mean —"

"Do as I say or you're lost — she's lost!"

Barrett was dismayed by that uncanny, marching flame. Above his wavering crest burned the fixed, malignant eyes of Don José. The madness of that awful night had reached its climax when blue flames were exhaled by solid flagging. But when he saw that d'Artois's gaze was fixed, and his features composed, he gained courage.

"I defy your will and your power with my will and my force!" he heard d'Artois tensely whispering. The low murmur became rhythmic as drumbeats, and inexorable as fate. And Barrett began to repeat d'Artois's words, halfheartedly at first, then confidently.

"I defy your will with my will, your power with my power!" he repeated.

Suddenly he felt a strange thrill of triumph surge up from within him; and for an instant the psychic concussion of the liberated force, shook him, and his dry eyes blinded as he blinked, caught a sobbing breath, and repeated, "I defy you, my will against your will. . . ."

He saw that the flames no longer advanced. The intolerable heat scorched and singed, but no longer increased.

The flames retreated — only by the breadth of a finger — but they retreated, beaten back by will that fought will.

And then Barrett faltered, cracking under the terrific strain.

"Can't make it . . . I'm done in!"

They heard a cry of triumph from beyond the wall of flame. Don José knew that his victims were helpless, and stood waiting for the fires to close in. D'Artois and Barrett exchanged despairing glances.

"Try it!" muttered Barrett. "It'll roast us anyway —"

D'Artois nodded, and his fingers closed on the haft of his red knife, but his occult knowledge assured him that the blade would fuse from the terrific heat.

Don José's exultation, however, was checked as a mighty voice thundered from the passageway, *"my will against your will, and my power against your power!"*

It was awful in its richness and volume. Sidi Abdurrahman was chanting as he advanced, solemn, prodigious-seeming as a descending doom — a colossus of power stalking across the Border.

"I have returned to accomplish where once I failed. You escaped me, ages ago, when the Dragons of Wisdom proclaimed the black night of doom for lost Atlantis. I failed, but in the many lives I have lived since then, I have gained *power against your power, and will against your will!"*

Don José made a gesture. Then he found his voice, and uttered a command. The flames wavered as he spoke, then surged high as his followers clustered about him. They resisted the *Chêla's* awful will — but in vain. The tips of the crescent of fire drew from the wall. Don José had lost command of the weapon he had devised; it lived on by the force that the *Chêla* concentrated. Flight was futile; space is non-existent in occult combat. And the beast-men and their chief made their last desperate resistance as the flaming crescent reversed its curvature, enfolding them in its terrific embrace.

There was no outcry — only a hissing and crackling that endured but an instant. Then came the dreadful stench of searing flesh as flame, hungrier than any earthly fire, lapped with deadly swiftness, roaring, as winds lashing monstrous cliffs. A column of awful radiance burned for a moment with adamantine brilliance.

When their dazzled eyes had become accustomed to the ensuing dimness, d'Artois and Barrett emerged from their niche and strode over the blistering tiles. They were careful not to look at the spot where the flames had centered.

Sidi Abdurrahman's august features were still transfigured, but the power was leaving him. It was only with an effort that he kept his feet as, smiling wanly, he made a gesture of benediction.

"This is the end of an old feud that started many lives ago. I was not ready for this meeting — but to save her — and you — I spoke. The Occult Masters sought to help — did help —"

He gasped, caught his breath, and with difficulty resumed, "they warned me — I could not endure the test — since I could not — receive all the force they were sending. But I could not decline —"

D'Artois caught the *Chêla* as he collapsed. The silence for a moment was unbroken save for the bestial whimperings of the wounded who had dropped short of the vortex of flame.

"We can do nothing for Sidi Abdurrahman," said d'Artois. "Get Yvonne — quick! Before we all go mad!"

As THE SUN rose, Yvonne, revived from the drugs of the satanic ritual and quite unharmed, heard d'Artois's narrative. Barrett, bandaged and smarting from his wounds, answered her weary smile, then turned to his friend:

"Pierre, I'm still stumped by a few things."

"Only a few?" countered the old man with a flash of good-humored irony that for a moment struggled through the somber memory of death's double thrust at a lovely girl and a great-hearted occultist.

"Where did he get that awful body for the elemental spirit?"

"The crypts beneath the city," said d'Artois, "have spawned strange broods. Monstrous hybrids, perhaps archaic survivals of lost Shâlmali, revived from suspended animation by Don José. But that is an occult rather than a scientific problem."

"After all," said Barrett, "the final riddle is, why did anyone with Don José's talents dabble in such ghastly studies? What motive —"

"He was following the tradition of the Black Brotherhood," replied d'Artois. "He was moved by the lust for power given by the services of elementals. He needed familiar spirits to help him further his pursuit of dark arts. Blood alone would bind them to his will; and you know to what lengths he went."

Yvonne shuddered at the evening's memories, then interposed, "But why did your friend's heroism end fatally?"

"At the best, I can only guess," admitted d'Artois. "Despite his great learning, he was only a *Chêla*, not a full initiate. Thus he could not endure the forces which he called forth, and he knew that he could not. Yet he accepted the challenge.

"He created a psychic explosion whose repercussion literally blasted him to pieces. Not his physical body, but his vital forces, which were unable to withstand the strain of mastering that elemental fire."

D'Artois paused. The silence was acute; and for a moment it seemed that they felt the presence of Sidi Abdurrahman. Finally Barrett spoke.

"He mentioned other lives —"

"According to the traditions of his order," resumed d'Artois, "he believes in reincarnation. And it seems that in some former existence he failed in his duty, so that in the lives that followed, he sought to redeem himself.

"He stood there in the vault, holding the captured elemental a prisoner. He was oblivious to his surroundings; but when Don José called the fires down on us, the psychic impact aroused Sidi Abdurrahman and brought to his consciousness the presence of an age-old enemy of all mankind.

"But whatever the reason and however science may try to explain it, we owe our survival to Sidi Abdurrahman."

D'Artois cleared his throat, rose, stepped to the door.

"I am an old man," he said, "and vengeance leaves me weary. Let me therefore leave you in good hands while I rout out *Monsieur le Préfet*. I will have him dynamite the entrance of that accursed vault, so that no matter how ominous the stars may be, there will be no more archaic survivals coming forth in search of victims."

And Barrett, regarding Yvonne Marigny, knew that when grief had received its due, untroubled moonlight on the Lachepaillet Wall would make the Gray Sphinx of the Pyrenees more alluring than before.

WHO KILLED GILBERT FOSTER?

The Missing Manuscript

Raymond LANDON drove Eloise Foster's tan roadster down the dimly lit New Orleans street and stopped in front of her uncle's palm-shrouded mansion. As he eased his rangy, broad-shouldered frame out of the little car, Landon somewhat bitterly reflected that it was quite a come-down for a soldier of fortune, late of the army of Ibn Saud, to be translating Arabic manuscripts and running errands for a crack-brained old professor.

Of course the job had its compensations — for example, Eloise. But now that Landon had finally gotten her to the point of attending a *Vieux Carré* party with him, damned if old Foster didn't have to send a telephone message over from the Hotel Roosevelt, where he was to address a gathering of archeologists, asking Landon to run out to the house and fetch the manuscript, which the professor had absent-mindedly left behind.

Why hadn't Bert Collins, the professor's secretary, reminded his employer of the manuscript? That was *his* job, not Landon's. And why hadn't the old buzzard sent Collins after it, instead of him?

Meanwhile, the sappy blond Collins was probably at that moment hanging around Eloise. He might, in fact, have engineered the whole performance, just so as to break Landon's monopoly. Not such a sap, Collins, after all!

Landon shrugged and glanced up at the unlit house, bulking large in the shadows. The street was deserted. It might have been midnight or early morning, rather than slightly past ten.

Landon shuddered. He had not been in New Orleans

long enough to accustom himself to the musty, somber old residential quarters of the city. Then he swung open the creaking cast-iron gate, wound his way along the stone-paved path between swaying broad-leaved plantains and clusters of rustling bamboos flanked by tall palms and white-blossomed magnolias, and mounted the steps to the broad *piazza*. He applied Eloise's key to the massive door.

The door swung, noiselessly back, almost as though aided by some unseen hand. Landon groped a moment, found and snapped the switch. The ancient Napoleonic chandelier, with its scores of glass prisms, blazed to life.

The mahogany newel post and balusters gleamed dully as he soundlessly ascended the richly carpeted stairs. The thick, velvety silence made him unconsciously tiptoe.

At the top of the stairs he stumbled. The baluster creaked as he caught it for support, but the sound was swallowed by the stillness of the house.

He crossed the hall, opened the door to the library and jabbed the switch.

Instinctively his gray eyes swept around the room. The three desks — his and Collins's and the professor's — littered with papers as they had left them when they had knocked off work that afternoon; but the chromium plated circular door of the little wall safe stood ajar! Landon, side-stepping the central desk, bounded toward the safe. But he halted abruptly, in mid-stride.

Professor Foster, in full evening dress, lay sprawled grotesquely on his back, his eyes staring sightlessly upward, his mouth open and distorted, his arms out-flung, his fingers clawed, and the carved handle of an Oriental dagger protruding from a red splotch in the middle of the left side of his starched shirt front.

Robbery and murder!

Landon's first reaction was sheer horror. His next was pity for Eloise. Then he began to attempt to reconstruct the crime.

For several weeks, Professor Foster had been bargaining with Alcide Dumaine, a local dealer in antiques, for the purchase of Shah Ismail's prayer rug from one of Dumaine's unnamed clients. Finally the price of twenty-five thousand dollars had almost been agreed upon, and the professor that very day had sent Collins, his secretary, down to his safe-deposit box at the Hibemia Bank to get and sell Liberty bonds to that amount. The proceeds had been put in the wall safe. Professor Foster alone knew the combination.

Someone who knew that the purchase price of the rug was in the wall safe had either tricked or forced the old professor into opening the safe. That the dagger was one of those which formed a collection of antique weapons on the tapestried wall of the room indicated that the murder had been unpremeditated.

Suddenly Landon thought of his own situation. Lord, what a jam!

He was a stranger in New Orleans. Foster had picked him up on one of his archaeological expeditions to the Arabian desert. Who would vouch for him? Who would believe that he hadn't robbed and murdered his employer?

A frame-up from the start! Landon understood now the phone call from the bell captain at the Roosevelt, telling Landon that his employer wanted him to rush out to the house and fetch the missing lecture manuscript!

Wrath wiped the dismay from his features. His lips straightened into a thin grim line, and his eyes became cold as sword-points. The only way to clear himself was to stay and cut the web of treachery which, centering about Shah Ismail's prayer rug, had brought death to Gilbert Foster.

Landon glanced about the spacious library. He saw a hundred-dollar note lying near Foster's desk, and stooped to pick up the loot the murderer had dropped. It was new, and must have come from the packets that had been in the safe. Landon's move was an instinctive impulse to salvage the property of his employer; but he restrained it, remembering that nothing must be touched.

His senses sharpened, now that the shock of discovery had subsided, he distinctly felt a menacing living presence in the room, and heard a faint rustle, as of the stirring of the window drapes or wall hangings. He wheeled around, but before he could complete the turn, a vase crashed against his head with a devastating impact that drove him flat to the floor. His fingers dug into the nap of the Feraghan carpet, as he sought by sheer force of will to recover and grapple with the enemy. Blinded and dizzy, he rose to a crouch and lashed out. But as his hands closed on his adversary's wrists, a second blow drove home. Landon pitched forward, his brain a globe of roaring fire. Despite his lingering vestige of consciousness, he could not force his nerveless limbs to act.

As he lay inert, Landon felt the trickle of blood from his scalp. He heard, as from a great distance, the distinct note of a doorbell — someone ringing for admittance. Landon tried to cry out, but only a gasp resulted. Again the insistent jangle of the doorbell.

"Hell!" exclaimed a frantic voice nearby. Footsteps rushing across the room — the click of a window latch — the sound of the window being hurriedly raised.

Then the painfully distinct *tick-tick-tick* of the electric clock as it marked off the seconds during which the murderer was making his escape through the window, down the tree outside and across the lawn.

Through the window, from far away, the shrill cry of a police siren tore into his consciousness. The piercing note was repeated, came nearer. That whipped him to desperation. He regained his feet. He tottered dizzily, snatched a decanter of brandy from a tabouret, and took a deep draught. That helped. He shook himself and squared his shoulders.

"Knocked me cold, then turned in the alarm to make sure I'd take the rap!" he muttered. He gingerly felt of his blood-matted hair. "With these wounds on my scalp and the signs of struggle about the library, it's a clear case against me. I'll get 'em all right — but I can't do any detective work from a police cell!"

The gritting of brakes, the tramp of feet, and the sharp commands, as the police patrol drew up, told him that his chance of escape was slender. Retreat by way of the lower floor was impossible. Concealment in some corner of the mansion would be equally futile. The police were already pounding at the door.

When in Doubt, Attack!

The trap, however, was not complete. The open window and the limbs of a magnolia promised at least a momentary refuge. Landon leaped from the sill and plunged into the shelter of the dark, waxen leaves.

"Give 'er hell!" commanded a voice in the shadows of the

garden below. There was a grunt of men moving in unison, a crash of splintering wood, and the tinkle of glass. Landon judged, from the prompt forcing of the door, that whoever had turned in the alarm had rendered a lurid report of what a dangerous character he was.

The entire police squad, however, did not pour into the house. Landon heard the order to surround the building. A second squad car disgorged its quota. He saw dark forms in plain clothes, caught the gleam of badges on uniforms.

"Horse, foot, and artillery!" he muttered bitterly. "Lucky I wasn't knocked out completely!"

For a moment he hoped that the police would overlook his place of concealment; and then he remembered the betraying window. He wondered why his assailant had elected it as an exit, instead of the front door; then he remembered the insistent ringing of the doorbell, which he had heard just before the murderer had departed.

Landon peered into the darkness, seeking to estimate the distance to the low roof of the garage. If he could reach it undetected, he could clear the high, spike-tipped cast-iron fence and perhaps elude pursuit.

That plan, however, died at birth.

"He went out through here!" boomed a voice, as the burly form of a police sergeant appeared in the brightly lighted window of the murder room. "Oh, Duval! McCarthy!"

Voices from the ground answered the hail. Two uniformed patrolmen were directly beneath Landon, looking up into the light that streamed from the window.

"See where his tracks lead," came the order from the sergeant, "and be careful you don't gum up his footprints."

Footprints! The very thing! Landon settled back less tense on his perch in the tree, for there would, of course, be the footprints of the man who had preceded him out the window. The police would follow those prints and leave him alone.

But his joy was short lived.

"There he is — up there!" shouted the police sergeant, pointing out the window toward the tree. "Look out! He may be armed!" The sergeant stepped back out of sight.

The two cops below circled the tree, staring stupidly upward into the leafy darkness.

Landon, his head by now fairly cleared of the savage slug-
ging he had received, poised himself, ready to take the
aggressive. His desperate position warranted a desperate
device. He jumped.

His descent was so swift that the rustle of leaves and the
snapping of twigs did not warn the police below. The impact
drove one officer flat and breathless to the ground, groaning and gasping. Landon scrambled to his feet just a split
second before the other officer gathered his wits. The
advantage, though trifling, was sufficient. Landon ducked
the sweeping night stick; and as the cop's hand flashed for
his pistol, Landon's fist shot out and connected with the
point of the policeman's jaw. But the cop, although out
on his feet, yanked the trigger with his last convulsive
twitch.

The blast attracted the pack. The cop on whom Landon
had crashed regained his breath and bellowed the alarm as
he struggled to his feet.

Landon dashed across the grounds, but despite his start,
the enemy gained on him. For a moment he was screened
by a cluster of plantains, but as he emerged from their shelter, jets of flame stabbed the darkness behind him, and
the crackle of pistol fire accented the roaring confusion.
Landon zigzagged, weaving in and out among the shrubbery, taking cover as he ran toward the comer of the estate.
He was gaining, for the pursuit, in order to fire more accu-
rately, had halted, certain now of capturing him either dead
or alive.

The cast-iron picket fence which checked Landon's flight
was too high and too hazardous to risk vaulting. Scaling it
deliberately was not to be considered, he would be too distinct a target silhouetted against the dimly lit street beyond.
As he hesitated, a bullet sifted through the shrubbery at the
foot of the fence and seared his ribs.

He was cornered. Then he saw a way out. The stalk of an
exceptionally tall, sturdy plantain would give him the necessary elevation. He leaped and swarmed up. A volley spat-
tered through the broad leaves. Then the police dashed forward, withholding their fire, certain now of an easy capture.

The stalk swayed perilously, bent the wrong way — then
dipped back toward the spiked fence.

Landon's headlong dive took him clear of the sidewalk. He landed on soft earth between paving and curb, rolled into the shelter of a tree, then recovered and sprinted down the street. A few seconds had been gained. The plantain stalk had collapsed under the concerted assault of the patrolmen. It was no longer available as a ladder. They had to double back to the gate.

Landon turned and ran down a private driveway that led to an adjacent estate, cleared the stone wall, worked his way toward the next street.

As he emerged he saw a cab parked at the corner.

"Down Saint Charles!" he commanded, and thrust a dollar bill into the driver's hand. "Illinois Central Hospital. Emergency case!"

This would fit in with the police sirens, and justify Landon's haste. The Yellow took off with a leap and nosed into the traffic. But Landon knew that by now radio squads would be combing the city. Whoever had turned in the alarm had undoubtedly given out an accurate and detailed description of him — for the frame-up must have been carefully planned.

As the cab rounded the turn toward the hospital, Landon slipped to the curbing. During his brief ride he had wiped the blood and dirt from his hands and face; but his bedraggled evening clothes made him conspicuous.

Off came his dinner coat, vest and black bow tie, to be rolled up and stuffed under his arm — and, at the first opportunity, to be dropped into a wastepaper can by the curb. His shirt was too far gone to betray its style; and the piping on his dark trousers would not be noticeable. He strode swiftly down South Rampart Street, mingling with the Saturday night crowd of drunks, derelicts, and ragamuffins, both white and black.

In the first pawnshop, he bought a cap and a clean shirt, and haggled just long enough to seem in character. A block closer to Canal Street he purchased a cheap linen suit and a string tie. The next shop equipped him with a razor, soap and brush. He put on the cap and the tie, slipped the shaving things into his pants pocket, and carried the suit and shirt.

The going was perilous. Audacity alone could serve him.

Every radio that blared from the lunch counters and soft drink parlors reminded him that the short-wave sets were picking up police calls that must be on the air; but he dared not hurry. With his bundle under his arm, he sauntered along, pausing to peer into shop windows.

The trickle of blood from his left side would again make him conspicuous. Some rooming house on the other side of Canal Street, however, would afford a temporary haven in which to staunch the seepage — the wound was hardly more than a scratch — clean up, and plan his campaign.

Attempting to leave New Orleans would be fatal. The ferries across the river, the railroad stations, and the highways would all be guarded. The city was his only refuge. And while he was the hunted now, he would have to turn hunter to vindicate himself.

An hour later he emerged from a cheap lodging house, his appearance completely altered. He wore a colored shirt and a linen suit. His old shirt he had torn into strips and used to bandage his side. And instead of removing his pointed black mustache, which had been his most conspicuously identifying feature, he had trimmed it to a couple of Hitler-like patches just beneath the nose, thus avoiding the obvious device of the fugitive. Finally, he had trimmed and narrowed his eyebrows.

He had stuffed wads of paper into his shoes, and had experimented with them until he had finally developed a slightly limping gait which, while not eccentric, was different from his natural stride and carriage.

As Landon strolled through the French Quarter, he favored various ash cans with bits of his discarded apparel. The entire lot in one place would attract attention. His smile was grim and bitter as he paused at a building from whose arched windows came music and laughter and the tinkle of glass. A party — the one from which he had been called by a fake message scarcely more than an hour ago. The party where Eloise still awaited his return — perhaps just beginning to wonder at his delay.

Or was she? Perhaps she had forgotten him. Or perhaps she and Collins were in the angle of the patio, where the fountain's silver veil screened out the artificial moon-glow. Then he realized that he had other matters to worry about.

This was no time for him to be mooning around the *Vieux Carré*.

So he hurried back to Canal Street, bought a second-hand suitcase, and took a taxi to a cheap hotel, where he registered under a name which matched the initials on the suitcase.

He turned in at once. Thus far he had no plans for taking up the trail of his enemies. That could await the morrow, when his head was clearer. What he needed now was rest.

Landon, Public Enemy!

THE SUNDAY *Picayune* and *Telegram* gave Landon an amount of space which would have been flattering, except for the contents. His photograph, reproduced from passports the police had found in luggage in his apartment, occupied the central position on the front page of both sheets. The headlines were lurid.

PUBLIC ENEMY NUMBER ONE read the *Telegram*. Landon carried the paper over to the mirror and compared the passport picture and the printed description with his present appearance.

The same clean-cut, bronzed features, the same keen gray eyes, stared back at him from the mirror, but the Hitler mustache and trimmed eyebrows gave such a different cast to the rest of his face, that no one but a very intimate friend would suspect his identity. The picture in the papers was at best a caricature. It would mislead, rather than help the police.

Satisfied on that score, Landon sat down on the bed and carefully studied the press accounts.

The stories in both papers were substantially the same. Raymond Landon, linguist and soldier of fortune, had robbed and murdered the employer who had befriended him. Then, with the same daring and vigor which had marked his cavalry operations against bandits of the Arabian desert, while in the service of Ibn Saud, Captain Landon had fought his way through the cordon of police who had surprised him at his crime.

The anonymous tip on which the police had acted was ascribed to an accomplice of Landon's, with whom he had probably quarreled over the division of the twenty-five thousand dollars in loot.

The press report went on to say that the victim, Professor Gilbert Foster, had just completed delivering an address on Arabia to a convention of the American Society of Archaeologists at the Hotel Roosevelt, when he had been called to the telephone. Thereupon he had left the hotel in considerable haste and obvious agitation.

The next paragraph mentioned Alcide Dumaine! The dealer in antiques admitted having phoned Professor Foster at the Roosevelt, to tell him that the owner of Shah Ismail's prayer rug had at last agreed to accept twenty-five thousand dollars for it. Foster had readily enough consented to leave the convention, and had made an appointment to meet Dumaine at once at Foster's home.

When Dumaine had reached the place, he had noticed Miss Foster's car standing at the curb. Though the house was lit, no one answered his persistent ringing. And then the police had arrived, arresting him as he stood on the gallery with the prayer rug under his arm.

A telegram from Biloxi, signed by Chris Panopoulos, and instructing Dumaine to sell the rug, confirmed the story. Dumaine had not been detained by the police. They had nothing on him.

"A perfect alibi," muttered Landon to himself. He frowned and shook his head. "Maybe, and maybe not. If it is on the level, it explains why the killer left by the window. But I'll bet Dumaine knows more than he's telling. His story is too damn good! Particularly from a sleek number like him."

Turning the page, Landon saw what was captioned as a picture of Shah Ismail's historic prayer rug. But even allowing for hasty press photography, it bore not the slightest resemblance to the rug which Alcide Dumaine had been trying to sell to Professor Foster.

"Something's all wet!" Landon said to the emptiness of his hotel room. "Dumaine gave the police a substitute to photograph. Why?"

Here was a clue to work on! Flimsy, but yet a clue. Landon continued his reading.

The police had interviewed the dead man's niece, Eloise Foster, and his private secretary, Bertram Collins, and had obtained the story of the long negotiations between the professor and Dumaine for the purchase of the prayer rug. They even told of the afternoon when, as a final bluff to shake Dumaine from his demands, Professor Foster and the man who was later to be his murderer — Landon grimaced at that — had held the precious rug by its silken fringe, while Collins, operating the professor's miniature movie camera, had shot a reel of color films to record the matchless hues and luster of the antique fabric.

"Since I'm not going to pay such an outlandish price, I'll at least have a reel to illustrate some of my lectures," the professor had explained to the puzzled dealer. Dumaine had been so visibly disconcerted by the bluff that he began to weaken in his demands. A few days later Foster ordered Collins to sell the liberty bonds, so as to be ready for a showdown.

And then Landon's eye caught an item which caused him to jump off the bed with a whoop. Eloise was quoted as saying, "I know he didn't do it. I'd trust him anywhere."

So he had one friend! With the whole town against him, Eloise still had faith.

Jamming his hat on his head, he left the hotel and walked briskly up town. Every telephone booth that he passed invited him to call Eloise and tell her how he appreciated her quoted remark.

"May be a trap," he warned himself. "That interview may be faked just to get me to phone her."

He passed several booths.

"But if she's really for me, she can dig into things and help me catch the real murderer — Hell, she *can't* believe I'm guilty!"

Thus he finally justified his foolhardiness in stepping into a cigar store and calling the Foster residence. It was really the sound of her voice, rather than her aid, that he desired.

"I've seen dozens of 'em hooked this way, but here goes!"

He held his nostrils pinched between thumb and forefinger, to disguise his voice; but this precaution proved needless. It was Eloise herself who lifted the receiver.

"Listen carefully," he cautioned her, "and don't mention my name."

He caught her gasp of amazement, heard her say, "They've left. Oh, isn't it just dreadful —"

"Hop a cab," Landon interrupted, "and meet me at the Magazine Street entrance of Audubon Park. Right away. And wait for me to speak first."

He hung up, before she could protest or question him.

Landon boarded a Magazine Street car. The park would be crowded on a Sunday, and his altered appearance should protect him against any but close observers. Alighting at the first stop past the entrance of the park, he mingled with the crowd.

Presently he saw Eloise emerge, on foot, from the tree-shaded coolness of Exposition Boulevard. She was wearing a dark blue suit, with white linen cuffs and collar.

"All clear," said Landon softly as she approached.

She started, looked up furtively, and then stepped back from him, her eyes wide with suspicion.

"Why, Eloise!" he began.

She laughed nervously, then smiled.

"I would never have known you," she said. "That is — you *are* Ray Landon, aren't you?"

"Of course I am."

"You look so changed. Your face is entirely different. You've done something to your mustache and — and your eyebrows, haven't you? And even your walk is different."

"Very observant, Eloise." Then, noticing the drawn expression of her piquant face, the tightness of her lips, and the dark shadows beneath her eyes, he exclaimed, "Why, you poor kid! Here I am thinking of nothing but my own predicament. I know what it means to you, dear, but there is nothing I can say."

"It's awfully good of you to think of me, Ray," she said, her fingers closing on his arm. Landon's heart leaped at her acceptance of the endearment that had cropped out, but his expression of solicitude did not change.

"Never mind me," she continued. "We two have a job on our hands. But you shouldn't have taken such a terrible risk, meeting me —"

"No more risk here than anywhere else," he countered,

feigning assurance which he by no means felt. "Let's sit near the merry-go-round — so much racket no one will overhear us."

Under cover of the blatant music, Landon outlined his suspicions. "Dumaine undoubtedly had something to do with it, and yet all that I have to go on is that he gave the police the wrong rug to photograph."

"But what good would that do him," asked Eloise, "since we have the colored movie which you and Uncle Gilbert took?"

"That's so. Where is it now?"

"At home. The police ran it through a projector down at headquarters, and then gave it back to me."

"Well," Landon continued, "if Dumaine's story is true, he couldn't have committed the crime himself. But one of his 'clients' may have. You remember how, all through the bargaining, Dumaine insisted on cash. He wouldn't even take a certified check."

"My uncle thought that that might be because the rug had been stolen or smuggled into the country; but it looks otherwise now."

"Exactly," Landon agreed. "I don't believe that shifty-eyed faker ever intended to sell the rug. He held out until he knew that your uncle had the money actually on hand. Then gave the signal for the robbery."

"And stood guard at the door, while his accomplice was inside," Eloise suggested.

"Mmmm — hardly," Landon decided. "The mur— robbery was committed before I entered, and yet Dumaine was not there when I arrived."

"But without Dumaine and the rug present, how was Uncle Gilbert induced to open the safe?"

"Who else had the combination?"

"Only Uncle Gilbert. He didn't even have a memorandum — just kept the numbers in his head."

"Nobody! Not even you — nor Bert Collins," Landon pondered. Then, abruptly, "Where was Collins last night?"

"You don't suspect him, do you?"

"No, of course not. Not that drink of water! But I'd like to know where he was last night."

Eloise eyed him narrowly. "Why, Ray! He was at the same party that you and I attended."

"And took you home, I suppose, when I failed to show up," Landon grumbled.

Eloise placed her hand on his arm, and looked up into his face. "Of course not!" she said indignantly. "Bert had one of the *Vieux Carré* crowd in tow. A dizzy blonde. He paid no attention to me all evening. I waited and waited for you, and then — then the police came." Her voice broke.

"Poor dear," commiserated Landon, patting her hand. "Suppose you get the police to investigate Bert Collins. Find out who he has been running around with lately. That woman he was with last night may have been in Dumaine's employ. She may have fed Collins a few drinks too many, then taken his keys and slipped them out to Dumaine."

But Eloise shook her head. "Bert was perfectly sober, and the girl herself was too lit to have pulled a stunt like that," she said.

"Well," Landon persisted, "they may have lifted the keys off him earlier in the week and made duplicates. Returned them before he missed them. You get the police to check up on him. In the meantime, I'm going to work on Dumaine. If he's in on this, I think I can crack him wide open."

"How?"

"It's a wild shot." Landon shook his head and grinned. "A combination of bluff and burglary."

"*Burglary!* Oh, Ray!" Eloise cried.

"Right," said Landon. "In my position, a bit of breaking and entering is only a trifle. And now you'd better run along, before we push our luck too far."

"But please, Ray, don't take the risk!" she pleaded. "Better lie low and wait for the police to turn up some clue."

"We'll see," he said noncommittally.

Eloise shook her head, pressed his hand, made a gesture of farewell, and mingled with the crowd. Landon watched her lithe figure blend and disappear in the confusion of shifting color; then he strode rapidly toward the street-car line.

*   *   *

The Congress of Crooks

THAT AFTERNOON Landon reconnoitered the block in which Alcide Dumaine's antique shop was located. An alley led to the rear, and here at night one would be quite unobserved; but the heavy steel fire doors and window-shutters made some other approach preferable.

The Sparta Hotel, next door to Dumaine's establishment, was the answer. But, as he needed to purchase certain supplies, and as the day was Sunday and the stores were not open, Landon was forced to wait until the following day for the next step.

Sunday evening he took in a movie — no danger of being identified in the darkness of the picture house. When the show was over, he decided to take a long walk to work off the nervousness caused by enforced inaction. And because he intended to keep to the more poorly lighted streets, he slipped the pads of paper out of his shoes.

He wandered aimlessly until he suddenly realized that a homing instinct had led him to Eloise's somber mansion. He paused on the opposite side of the street, and leaning back against the fence, stared across at the big house, which loomed black and curiously ominous amid palms and magnolias.

Scarcely twenty-four hours ago he had stared at that same house, with feelings of instinctive dread, while a murder was being committed inside. And tonight —

A dark figure came skulking down the opposite sidewalk and halted at the Foster gate. Then, very gently, the prowler swung the gate open and slipped inside. The black shadows of the shrubbery swallowed him.

Eloise was in that house! Landon dashed across the street, slipped quietly through the half-open entrance, and then stealthily followed the winding path through plantains and bamboo clumps to the front door.

No sign of the intruder. Landon tip-toed across the gallery and jabbed the push-button. He waited, back half turned to the door, alertly scanning all possible approaches.

The door swung silently open. Landon wheeled. The Fosters's Negro butler, startled by his sudden appearance, stared at him without recognition.

"Quick!" snapped Landon. "Where is Miss Eloise?"

The Negro turned slate gray. He recoiled a pace, his eyes widening to black-centered white globes.

"Mistah Landon!" he exclaimed. "Ah — Ah —"

A woman's scream shrilled from the upper reaches of the house. Thrusting the stupefied Negro aside, Landon bounded up the thickly carpeted stairs.

There were lights in the library. A man gruffly commanded, "Shut up, you little fool, and give me that film! It won't do you any good to holler for help. If anyone does come, I'll drill 'em!"

Landon bounded into the library.

Eloise stood just beyond the central desk, a flat tin container clasped in her hands. Across the desk from her was a swarthy man of about Landon's own build, threatening her with a .45 caliber automatic.

Landon charged. The swarthy man wheeled and jerked a shot. The blast shook the house, but Landon, ducking, flung himself at the intruder's legs. The flying tackle was good, but as they fell, his quarry smacked Landon's head with his pistol. The blow grazed his head, cutting, rather than stunning. Landon snatched the man's wrist before he could strike again.

Two more shots, as the intruder strove to force his weapon into line. Landon wrenched fiercely and the automatic clattered to the floor, but the gunner jerked free, clutched Landon's throat with both hands. Landon's fists smashed home, but the throttling grip closed tighter.

Breathing was impossible. Landon's blows became weaker. The room swam in a red haze, through which he could hear as from a great distance the voice of Eloise crying, "Ray! Ray! Hang on!"

She swooped in, hammering the intruder about the head with the tin film box. He ducked and squirmed, then loosened one hand to ward off the blows. That gave Landon his chance to break away. He staggered to his feet — only to be seized from behind by two strong arms passing around him and pinioning his own arms to his side.

The imprisoning hands were black. "Ah done got him, Miss Ellie," said a familiar voice in his ear.

Meanwhile the swarthy raider had regained his feet,

seized Eloise and held her as he scanned the floor for his missing gat.

"You fool, Isaac!" cried Eloise. "That's Ray! Let him go!"

Landon jerked away from the dismayed Negro and charged back into action. But the prowler flung Eloise between them, blocking Landon's rush. Before he could swing clear of her, the enemy's fist caught him on the point of the chin. That piled him into a corner — but within reach of the missing automatic! He seized the weapon, blinked, staggered to his feet. The raider, meanwhile, had snatched the tin film box from Eloise and was diving for the window.

Landon snapped the gun into line and fired, but his head was still swimming and his hand wavered. He missed. Gritting his teeth, he forced himself to fire deliberately. That was as bad — the target won by a hair, clearing the sill a split instant ahead of the blast.

Landon rushed to the window. A dark shape was streaking through the shadows and foliage. Landon's head was now clear, but gloom and a swiftly moving target were too much for three deliberate, closely spaced shots — then the slide locked open. The gun was empty. The fleeing intruder dodged into the shadows of the bushes which lined the lawn.

Landon, cursing wrathfully, turned from the window just in time to catch Eloise as she tottered and swayed dizzily. For an instant she clung to him, then opened her eyes and drew out of his arms.

"I'm all right," she said, with forced steadiness. "But you, Ray?"

"Oke now," he said lightly. "Well, they got the color film!"

"And that answers your question of this afternoon as to what good it would do them to give a fake picture to the newspapers, with this film still in our hands," the girl added.

"Also it ties Alcide Dumaine all the closer to this mess," Landon said. "He gave the fake picture to the press, so he must have sent this thug to rob you. Lucky I happened to be walking by."

"*Happened?*" she teased.

Before he could reply, an approaching police siren cut in on their conversation. Despite brick walls and muffling vegetation, the shots had been heard.

"Oh — they'll find you here!" gasped Eloise.

"Tell them I've escaped, and send them hunting me." Landon, though tense, was unperturbed. "Here you, Isaac!" The Negro servant was still standing open-mouthed in the doorway. "Tell the police that Mr. Landon is upstairs fighting with Miss Eloise. Just that, and not another word. Now scram!"

"Yassah, yassah!" Isaac hastened to the head of the stairs.

"Come," said the girl, leading Landon across the hall and opening a door. "Hide in here — and give me the gun."

It was a spare bedroom. Landon hurriedly surveyed the room, opened the window, gauged the distance to the ground, and noted a wisteria trellis which ran up beside the window. Then he closed the door to just a crack, and sat behind it, in darkness.

The doorbell jangled. Isaac flung open the front door.

"Yassah, yassah," Landon heard him say. "Mistah Landon done been fightin' wiv Miss Ellie in de liberry."

A gruff command, the thudding of feet as the police charged up the stairway.

"Oh, I'm so glad you came!" Eloise gasped out, meeting them at the top. "Landon was here. I was terribly frightened. He demanded the film which showed the prayer rug. He pulled a gun on me, but I wouldn't give up the film. He tried to grab it — it was lying on the desk here, before I snatched it up. Isaac helped me. The gun went off a couple of times. I got the gun, but he got the film and escaped through the window."

"There were more than two shots heard," one of the policemen asserted suspiciously.

"Yes," Eloise readily admitted. "I fired at him as he was going out the window, and again as he was running across the lawn. I — I guess I'm not a very good shot."

"Neither were we, the first time we tangled with Landon," grinned the sergeant.

Then he turned to question Isaac. Landon, listening from cover, wiped the sweat from his forehead and crouched, ready for action, as the Negro answered; but his replies were a masterpiece of incoherence and confusion.

"Very good, Isaac," Landon whispered, relaxing as the sergeant finally cut him short.

Then they tramped down the stairs and slammed the front door.

Landon emerged from his hiding place. "Great work, darling." Then, catching her arm: "Now we can have a few words to ourselves."

But Eloise shook her head. "Better leave right away, they may come back. Isaac will show you out the back way. And please, Ray, don't go robbing Dumaine. You may get caught."

"It's our best bet, Eloise," he insisted. "Tonight's performance convinces me all the more that he is in on all this."

Then he pressed her hand, and followed the waiting Negro.

The next day Ray Landon kept to his room, going out only to purchase, one at a time, a glass-cutter, a coil of stout clotheslines, a flashlight, and — from a toy store — a set of rubber-tipped arrows.

The newspapers featured his daring raid on the Foster mansion and the theft of the color film, but contained no information Landon could use.

Late that afternoon, packing his newly acquired belongings into his suitcase, he walked over to the Hotel Sparta and engaged a room for the evening.

He had no difficulty in justifying his demand for a room whose windows opened directly on the flat roof of Dumaine's store. "So I can check out in a hurry, if her boy friend follows us," he explained, with a wink at the hotel clerk, and paid three dollars in advance for the one-dollar room. "And if anyone asks for me, remember I'm not in."

He registered with a name which obviously bore no relation to the initials on his suitcase. The clerk, noting the discrepancy, winked, grinned knowingly, and pocketed the over-payment.

From the window of his new room, Landon carefully studied the roof of Dumaine's store, noted the location and the construction of the skylight, and took into account the obstructions that might hamper him in the dark.

That done, he crossed over to Exchange Alley, where the bartenders are too busy to note individuals. His supper was a sandwich and one of the big beers that make the place popular — and crowded.

From observing Professor Foster's dealings with Alcide Dumaine during the prayer rug negotiations, Landon knew that the little Frenchman dined late, and usually stayed in his store until dinner time. Accordingly, after his own meal, Landon phoned Dumaine.

He dropped his nickel, and a moment later recognized the antique dealer's perceptible French accent.

"Nice work last night, Dumaine," said Landon. "You know who this is — uh-huh. Don't blat my name out that way! When do we split that dough you picked off on Saturday?"

Dumaine's startled exclamation contained enough alarm to prove that the random shot had not missed. He had mistaken Landon for Chris Panopoulos, the "client" who had wired from Biloxi.

"Don't stall!" he snapped, driving home his advantage. "You call up the boys and tell 'em to meet us at the store tonight."

Landon hung up. Dumaine's alarm was a fair assurance that, whether or not he was holding out on his allies, he would take the course of an innocent man. He would call together "the boys" — whoever they were — and try to convince them that he was on the up and up.

There was one flaw in Landon's strategy, but he had not overlooked it.

"Panopoulos may show up or run into some of 'the boys,' and may deny that he phoned Dumaine to arrange the meeting. But he and the boys are likely to suspect that Dumaine lied about the call so as to slip something over on them. And Dumaine may suspect that Panopoulos *did* make the call, and lied out of it so as to cast suspicion on him, on Dumaine. And if they get excited enough in their wrangling, someone will spill something."

Landon waited near the entrance to Dumaine's establishment until, shortly after dark, he saw the little Frenchman hurry out for his evening meal. Landon at once returned to the Sparta, grinned at the clerk, and ascended the two flights to his room. Then, emerging from a window, he dropped to the flat roof and set to work with his cutter. The skylight was not of reinforced glass, so his work was easier.

First he moistened with his tongue the sucker-end of an

arrow and pressed it against the surface of one of the panes until it stuck by vacuum. Then he cut a small circle around it, tapped the piece lightly until it broke loose, and lifted it out. Thrusting his left hand through the hole and applying his palm to the under surface of the pane, he cut out another piece. Finally an entire pane had been removed, leaving an opening large enough to admit his body.

Placing his piece of gas pipe athwart the hole, he doubled the clothesline around it and lowered himself into the black depths. Then, separating the two reaches of the rope, he pulled down on one and gradually eased up on the other, ending with a jerk and a let-go, which spun the pipe off the skylight and brought it and the rope to his feet.

Nothing now to indicate that anyone had entered, except the open pane, and that would not show against the overcast sky.

Landon snapped his flashlight and swept it around the room. The entire second floor was a dusty, somber confusion of antique furniture, genuine and synthetic.

Right beneath the skylight was the clearest place in the whole loft. Here was a modern desk, strewn with papers; a telephone set, several chairs, and a large double-doored safe. Evidently it was Dumaine's "office," although open to the rest of the storeroom. Nearby stood a huge walnut wardrobe — a perfect observation post from which to watch the congress of crooks.

Landon then explored further among the helter-skelter collection of museum pieces. Two flights of stairs, boarded in, led down from this story. Landon tried the one to the rear and found that it ended at the ground level, in a pair of heavy steel fire-doors, secured by a massive hinged bar that dropped into sockets. He tried the bar and found that the door easily opened. Beyond it was an alley.

Landon then returned to the second-floor storeroom and took cover, leaving the wardrobe door open perhaps a quarter of an inch. After waiting about fifteen minutes, he heard a key slipping into the lock of the front door. A wall switch clicked, snapping on a cluster of lights well past the middle of the shop. Furtive footsteps echoed in the front stairway, and then a short, stocky man stepped into the room.

It was Dumaine. By the dim illumination, Landon could

see that the shabby little Frenchman was worried. He paced the length of the central aisle that roughly divided the tangled confusion of furniture, statuary, *bric-a-brac*, large cloisonné vases, and great curved earthenware jars in which olives had been shipped from Spain years ago. He finally seated himself, shifting uneasily in his chair, and from time to time glanced nervously around the storeroom.

A few minutes later there was a heavy pounding on the street door. Dumaine started apprehensively, then rose and hurried down the stairs to admit the unfortunate visitors.

Conversation began almost immediately, and continued as the three men tramped up the stairs, but Landon could catch only fragments.

Muttered cross fire of query and accusation; then, a strangely familiar gruff voice: "Shut up, Schwartz! I'll handle this!"

A flash of Dumaine's rapid fire sputter, ending with, "*Mordieu!* But it is jus' as I have told you!"

The gruff voice again: "Skip that tripe, Alcide. We was complimenting you on bumping off the old guy so nice, and pinning it on Landon!"

They reached the top of the stairs and crossed the room to the office space. And then the watcher in the wardrobe saw that the gruff-voiced speaker was the tall, swarthy raider Landon had grappled with in the library of the Foster home the evening before. His companion was a. short, heavy man with a close-cropped bullet head: Schwartz who, despite having been silenced a moment ago, resumed: "Alcide, you should divide up the loot right now, even if you did shoot the professor."

"He *stabbed* him," corrected the tall dark man. His grin was a wolfish flash of ivory and gold. "Anyhow, Alcide, you did a good job. But it's pretty smart not to try and run out on us."

Dumaine gestured toward several chairs near his desk. His guests eyed them, decided that the antiques would support their weight, and seated themselves.

"Listen, Pichetti," protested Dumaine, becoming more and more uneasy, "I don't know what you and Schwartz mean, asking me why I killed Foster."

"Never mind that bunk!" growled the tall dark man,

glancing significantly at Schwartz. "Get down to business! Whatever Panopoulos told you goes for us. And you might as well cough up — he sent us to get you straightened out."

"Didn't I prove to the police that I *couldn't* have killed Foster?" Dumaine desperately challenged.

Schwartz chuckled faintly, and winked. "Nice work, ain't it? Instead of stallin' around until we faked the holdup, he shot Foster, and now we have both dough and rug. Only — he should not try to hold out."

"I tell you, Schwartz, he *stabbed* him," snarled Pichetti. "Get your story straight. You'd be a hell of a witness in a police round-up!"

"But, gentlemen," reiterated the little Frenchman, "I swear by the —"

A flash of lightning illuminated the skylight overhead, and the windows at each end of the loft. It was followed by a crash of thunder which blotted out Dumaine's words.

"— anything of the kind," he persisted. "And you may as well give up the idea of trying to blackmail me. I have not the money. Take the rug, and leave me alone."

"Yeah, leave you alone with the dough!" snarled Pichetti, his lips curling back in a gold-filled leer. "If you didn't get it, who the hell did?"

"And that phony picture in the paper —" Schwartz objected.

"You *know* why I handed the reporters a rug from my own stock," explained Dumaine. "Someone might have recognized the real one, and then we'd all be in a jam with the customs authorities."

"Customs authorities, hell!" snarled Pichetti. "You mean Barloff's gang would land on us for hijacking the rug *they* smuggled into the country. And what good did it do us to have the papers print the wrong one, while those phony pictures with the colored film are still loose?"

"I thought — I hoped —" Dumaine began nervously.

"That we wouldn't read the papers?" Pichetti cut in.

"Landon," interposed Schwartz, *"he* has the film."

"Landon hasn't got it anymore than he killed Foster," Pichetti asserted. "I got it. And that wasn't Landon at Fosters's last night at all. It was one of Barloff's men I socked hell out of!"

That was a bombshell!

"For the luvva —" gasped Schwartz. "Are you sure?"

Dumaine shivered, seemed to shrink perceptibly, and said nothing. Pichetti gloated wolfishly.

There came another flash of lightning, followed by a long rumbling roar of distant thunder.

"Well, Dumaine," snapped Pichetti, "we want our cut, so we can haul out before Barloff makes a nuisance of himself."

"But gentlemen —"

Pichetti whipped out a gun from beneath his left arm pit. "I said we want our cut!"

Dumaine made a despairing gesture and tremblingly suggested, "Let's open the safe. I'll show you I have no money. And you can take the rug right now."

Schwartz nodded approvingly, as Dumaine slowly rose from his chair. Then suddenly his expression changed from approval to mild surprise. He tilted back his bullet head, stared incredulously above him, then held out his hand palm up.

"Rain!" he exclaimed. "From the skylight! It's open!"

A large drop splashed on Dumaine's desk. Then another, and another. Schwartz blinked as one caught him in the eye, and pushed his chair out of range of the downpour.

Pichetti jumped to his feet, yanked a flashlight out of his pocket, and played it on the ceiling above.

"Hell!" he exclaimed. "One big pane's out. And no glass on the floor. Been that way long?"

Dumaine despairingly shook his head. "Maybe Barloff is here right now!" he muttered.

This was Landon's chance! Catch them flat-footed, before they began the inevitable search for an eavesdropper.

He flung the doors of the wardrobe apart and flashed forward in a low, swift lunge that connected as Pichetti half turned toward his place of concealment. Landon's fingers closed about Pichetti's wrist, throwing the pistol out of line. The shot, going wild, shattered a mirror; and as they plunged headlong into a group of Sheraton chairs, Pichetti's automatic clattered to the floor.

Pichetti, dazed by the shock and the pain of his wrenched

wrist, was for the moment out of action; but before Landon could snatch the pistol, Schwartz, remarkably swift for one of his stocky build, drew his own weapon, whirled, and fired as Landon flattened to the floor. The tongue of flame singed Landon's hair. Pichetti, recovering, struggled forward and across Landon to reach his own automatic. Schwartz, not daring to risk a second shot for fear of hitting his ally, swung at Landon with the butt of his weapon.

The surprise attack had gone sour; and the uproar would soon bring the police.

Schwartz's pistol crashed home, but Landon, jerking his head, evaded the full force of the blow. Though shaken, he twisted, jack-knifed, and shot his feet upward, catching Schwartz in the pit of the stomach and sending him crashing against Dumaine's desk. In that instant's respite, Landon snatched Pichetti's pistol, smacked him across the head with it, and whirled in time to confront Schwartz, who, groggy but determined, was struggling to his feet. He still gripped his clubbed pistol by the barrel; but before be could shift the weapon to fire, Landon's boot lashed out, catching him on the jaw. Lights out! Then, with the two thugs temporarily out of the battle, Landon covered Dumaine with Pichetti's pistol.

"Open that safe!"

Landon, taking his coil of clothesline from the wardrobe, followed Dumaine. At the best he had but little time — yet if the safe did contain the loot, it would be worth the risk.

"Hurry, Dumaine! If the police pick me up, I'll tell them an earful about your peddling stolen property!"

Dumaine seemed relieved, rather than worried at Landon's demands. The combination was simple, and he made no attempt to fumble. The doors swung open. Landon slipped Pichetti's pistol into his pocket, pushed Dumaine to a chair, trussed him up, and then investigated the contents of the safe.

Shah Ismail's prayer rug, which Landon recognized in spite of its being compactly bundled, lay on the bottom of the safe. Pulling it out and setting it to one side, he began his search through the confusion of pigeon-holes and drawer compartments. The scream of a siren told him that the police were on the way from the third precinct, only a few blocks distant.

Landon swiftly cleared a few more pigeonholes.

Again the siren blast. He dared not risk another instant seeking the loot that would clear him. He snatched the ill-omened prayer rug and dashed down the rear stairs. Swinging the hinged bar from its socket, he pulled open the heavy steel door and stepped into the alley. The brief tropical shower had stopped. From beyond the low roof of the store, Landon heard the scream of brakes and police pounding for admittance. It would be but a matter of seconds before they forced the front door, and at any moment part of the squad might cover the mouth of the alley.

A six-foot wall directly across the alley offered the safest escape. Landon heaved his bundle over the barrier and gathered himself for a leap upward to catch its crest.

"Steady, there!" said a low voice at his side. "And keep your trap closed!"

The muzzle of a pistol prodded Landon's ribs, and a heavy hand caught his shoulder. . . .

Criminal's Alley

WELL, THE POLICE had him at last. No use to risk certain death with that gun in his ribs. Better go along meekly, and watch alertly for a break.

"Straight ahead!" An arm reached past Landon. A latch clicked. A doorway right beside Dumaine's opened in the darkness, and his captor pushed him through and closed the door.

They were now in an angle of the courtyard of the building which adjoined Dumaine's store. A moment later the iron exit of Dumaine, Inc., clanged open, and the police came charging out into the alley.

"Better come along quietly, if you don't want the cops to get you," whispered his captor.

So he was not in the hands of the law after all!

"What the hell's all this about?" he whispered back.

"Wait and see," countered the other, with an ominous chuckle. He took the pistol from Landon's pocket. "And don't try any monkey work. Walk straight ahead now."

Landon advanced through the darkness of a narrow passageway and emerged onto the street in front of Dumaine's establishment. A car was waiting at the curbing, just behind the squad car of the raiding officers. A dark, stocky man, with cap pulled low over his eyes, sat alertly at the wheel.

"Get in!" commanded Landon's captor.

Landon, as he complied, wondered whether in escaping the law he had made a profitable exchange. He had only to shout to the driver of the police car ahead in order to find out, but he decided not to take the chance. He turned and sized up his captor, a heavy-jawed, swarthy giant with graying hair. This might be the Barloff Dumaine's allies feared. But his features were not Slavic. Perhaps —

"Careful of that pistol, Panopoulos," hazarded Landon as the car started out into the traffic. "And what's all the fuss about?"

The Greek started at mention of his name and prodded Landon with the muzzle of his automatic. He studied his prisoner intently from beneath thick black eyebrows, then said, "When Dumaine phoned me tonight and asked why I hung up so quick, I had the hunch someone was pulling a fast one. So I tell the boys okay to come see him, just like he ask — and here I find you, just like I think."

The Greek, instead of blatting out that he hadn't phoned Dumaine, had planned to trap whoever had impersonated him!

"You punks ought to know when we got you beaten," continued Panopoulos. "Barloff might as well forget that rug. You birds'll never get it."

Landon laughed. "Is that so?" he mocked. "Well, now, it happens that I have got it."

"*What?*" Panopoulos sat bolt upright, and regarded Landon sharply. Then he addressed the driver: "Jake, pull up to the curb when we come to the next street light. I want to get a good look at this guy."

"Here's a flashlight, Chris," suggested the man at the wheel, passing it back. Panopoulos snapped it on, and scrutinized Landon's face. Then, "Say, what you think we got here?"

"Barloff?"

"Hell, no! Nobody I ever seen. Say, punk, who *are* you?"

"Maybe he's the guy who bumped off the professor," suggested the driver, without looking back.

"I think you're right, Jake," said Panopoulos. "He don't look at all like his picture, but he's tall and dark and about the right age, and he jumps when you say he kill Foster. Yes, I think you're right."

"You've got me wrong, Chris," said Landon lightly.

"I got you dead to right, you mean. Jake, turn around. We'll take him to the police."

"And lose the rug?" Landon asked calmly. "No. I don't think you want to do that."

"I don't believe you got the rug."

"No? Well, skip it for the present. Do you want my testimony about tonight's hold-up added to Dumaine's against Pichetti and Schwartz? And furthermore, I can prove that it was Pichetti who stole the color film from Miss Foster last night. And she'll back me up in the identification. I guess that will pin the murder of Professor Foster on Pichetti, all right."

Landon's arguments did not make any impression at all upon the huge Greek. But the driver was worried.

"Chris," he said, "turning him in might play hell with the boys. Why not take him to our room, so we can study on it awhile before we do anything?"

"All right," agreed Panopoulos after a moment's reflection.

Jake turned into a side street, then cut down an alley, where he parked. It opened into a court. Landon was piloted toward a doorway, and thence up two flights of stairs to a furnished room.

"Tie him up," commanded Panopoulos, "and gag him."

A few minutes of well applied effort left Landon securely lashed to a chair.

"Now we get a cup of coffee and study on this."

So saying, Panopoulos and Jake left. Landon began to realize how weak his bluff had been. His captors might conclude that Pichetti and Schwartz, held on charges pressed by Dumaine, could — by proper bargaining with the police — be released in exchange for the surrender of Landon. That would be too tough!

He heard footsteps in the hall, a murmur of conversation,

and the sound of a key slipping into the latch. Panopoulos and Jake stepped into the room.

"Untie his feet."

Jake did so.

"It's a long drive out to the Rigolets," objected Panopoulos, as Jake boosted Landon upright. "Isn't there some place just as good — and closer?"

That implied something worse than being turned over to the police. The Rigolets, which drains Lake Ponchartrain into the Gulf of Mexico, was something like ninety feet deep in spots. Anyone properly weighted would sink into the bottomless mud beneath those black waters.

"But I still don't see why we gotta croak this guy," Jake protested, "even if he is one of Barloff's outfit — which I think he ain't. Don't get us anywhere, does it?"

"Do I have to go into all that again?" demanded Panopoulos.

"But how the hell you going to get the boys outa the can?" Jake's perplexity was evident. "Dumaine will say they made him open the safe. Then had a fight and beat each other up. No matter how much they squawk, they can't touch *him* — he's a business man — and with that skylight out, and everything, they're framed for burglars."

Why was Jake arguing for Landon's life? And then, in a flash, Landon understood. Jake, a small-time gangster, looked up to soldier-of-fortune Ray Landon, the daring murderer who had made a monkey of the police. It was the admiration of an apprentice for a master craftsman.

"But, Jake, I tell you this fellow will spill the beans!"

"Chris, how the hell can he spill any beans?

Afraid he'll make it worse for Pichetti and Schwartz?"

Panopoulos shook his head and chuckled. "No, he'd make it better for them — his story would get them loose! Right now they're just where I want them. If Dumaine killed Foster and got the money, I won't have to split with them if they're in the jug. And if Dumaine didn't get the money, they'll think that I did, and be coming after me. Leave 'em in the jug."

"But this guy says he's got the rug."

Panopoulos sniffed contemptuously. "Where's he got it? He didn't have it coming out of Dumaine's."

"Hell!" muttered Jake sadly, giving in at last. "But he's one great guy."

And Landon, gagged, bound, but with his feet untied, faced his captors. He would be dead in a few minutes, so what did it matter if he overheard their plans?

He glanced past them to the door of the room. It was not latched — stood slightly ajar. He felt a slight current of air, noted that the door was slowly, almost imperceptibly swinging open.

The Greek's pistol, covering Landon, had shifted slightly out of line. When the draft opened the door enough, he'd lunge forward, butt the Greek in the stomach, and make a break! Landon tensed, ready for the leap.

Meanwhile Panopoulos was saying, "We'll take the money and the rug off Dumaine and sell it in New York. Get forty grand, perhaps. Why not? I've got Pichetti and Schwartz just where I want them."

"Oh, yeah? Leave us in the can, eh?" snarled a gruff voice. The door swung all the way open. On the threshold stood Pichetti, gun in hand.

Panopoulos fired as he whirled, but Pichetti's shot was a split-second early. He charged into the room, followed by Schwartz. Jake, flinging himself aside, returned their fire.

Landon dropped flat to the floor. Panopoulos, riddled with lead, kept his feet. His .45 drowned the sharply barking .38's. Schwartz dropped, blasted into a corner. Panopoulos sagged to the floor.

"Drop it, punk, and get on your feet!" snapped Pichetti turning to Jake, who had taken cover in the angle of the mantelpiece. The deck was cleared — but you can't be chief without at least one henchman.

Now Panopoulos, mortally wounded, was forcing his pistol into line. Landon held his breath, fascinated by that grim, vengeful courage.

Pichetti sensed his peril — but too late. The Greek's heavy slug pitched him end-for-end against the wall. Bull's-eye! And then Panopoulos slumped face down, finished.

A police whistle shrilled outside the house. Landon, hands tied, struggled to his feet in a desperate effort to leave by the back way before the police came in from the front. Then he saw Jake crawling toward him, with gun in hand.

Troubles Pile Up

"STEADY, FELLOW! I'll cut you loose."

Jake drew a knife. As the blade passed between Landon's wrists, there was a pounding at the back entrance, two flights down. No escape that way. Landon snatched a pistol from the floor. Jake paused to latch the door of the room. "Out this way!" Jake stepped through a window to a balcony that ran along the side of the rooming house. From there they swung across to the gallery of the adjoining building, entered the house and descended to the ground level. Then a swift dash across a court, and down an alley opening into a side-street.

Jake reeled, recovered. He coughed and wiped a red froth from his lips.

"How much lead did you stop?" demanded Landon, catching his ally by the arm. "I'm still wondering why you turned me loose —"

Jake grinned and shrugged. "Chris is dead, and his gang is all shot. You're worth teaming up with."

He staggered again. Landon saw that quick action was imperative.

"Come on. I think I know where you can hide out." Then, as he hailed a cruising taxi. "Do you know any doctor in town?"

Jake shook his head. "I'll get turned in sure as hell when the doc reports gunshot wounds."

"Where are you hit?"

Jake indicated his side. Some blood oozed out of his mouth and trickled down his chin.

"Can't merely paint you with iodine and mark you duty," Landon muttered. Then, to the driver, "Uptown, buddy. I'll tell you when to stop."

Jake regarded him inquiringly, his face drawn and gray.

"Only chance," said Landon, "but I think it'll work."

Landon's plan was dangerous, but he saw that Jake needed immediate attention. Changing cabs would avail them little; they would eventually be tracked to their destination.

"Cover this bird," he whispered. "And see that he doesn't

pull any fast work. I'm going to phone a friend who'll hide us. Then I'll get a doctor, blindfold him, and poke a gun to his ribs."

"Gosh, you got your guts!" muttered Jake admiringly.

Landon, though disheveled, was not conspicuous as he stepped into a drug store. He called the Foster, house. Eloise answered.

"Careful what you say," he cautioned. "Hop into your car, park on Saint Andrew, just off Prytania Street. I'll hail you from a cab."

Landon instructed the driver to circle the block he had designated to Eloise. They had not made more than three trips when he recognized Eloise's roadster, parked on a side-street. She herself was standing on Prytania.

"Clever girl!" said Landon to himself, as he instructed the cab driver to draw up by the curb. "He won't even notice her car."

He stepped from the taxi. Eloise came running up.

"Oh!" she exclaimed in dismay. "What ever in the world have you been doing — your face is a sight!"

"I've got a wounded comrade," he whispered. "Take him to the house, and I'll rustle up a doctor."

"Haven't you enough grief of your own?" she protested hysterically.

Landon returned to the cab.

"Jake?"

No answer. Jake was slumped in a comer. He muttered hoarsely, made a feeble gesture of protest as Landon sought to lift him from the seat.

"Never mind me, I'm through. Get the hell out!" He coughed, shuddered, and then Landon recognized the wheeze and rattle in his throat. Death had cancelled the debt.

Landon backed out of the cab and handed the driver a bill.

"Straight down the street!" he said. "Don't stop, and don't look back. If you don't want to die of lead poisoning, be damn sure there was one — get me? — *one* man who hailed you. And stick to it. One crack out of you —" Landon regarded the driver intently, then concluded in a tone that matched the steel gray glitter of his eyes, "I've got your number and I'll remember it. So give me a chance to give *you* a break. Beat it!"

He watched the tail-light disappear down Prytania Street, then turned to Eloise. "I didn't know he was hit that bad or I'd not have pulled you into this. But he saved my hide, and —"

"I know. But let's move on, before that cab driver gets over his fright."

As they drove by a long round-about way to Eloise's home, Landon outlined his encounter at Dumaine's and his escape from Panopoulos.

"It's all such a dog fight that you can draw almost any conclusion you want," he summarized. "When Dumaine called your uncle from the convention, under the pretext of selling him the rug, the stage must have been set for a faked robbery, to get possession of both rug and cash. But someone, working almost on a split-second schedule, beat them to it — and, for good measure, framed me."

"That looks like the fine hand of Panopoulos," suggested Eloise.

Landon shook his head. "I don't think so," he said thoughtfully. "Panopoulos seemed to think that Dumaine has the money. But I'm quite sure that neither of them has. And now the Greek's gang is blotted out."

"There goes your chance of clearing yourself," sighed Eloise. "You'd better fade out of here. I — I can join you somewhere later, after it all blows over."

"Do you mean that?" he said.

She averted her gaze, and nodded.

"Then I'm going to stick right here in New Orleans till I clear myself."

"But how can you solve it, if everyone is dead?"

"Everyone except Dumaine," he corrected. "And somebody named Barloff, from whom Panopoulos stole the rug." He told her how Panopoulos had mistaken him for one of the Barloff gang.

There was no chance that they had been followed. Landon accompanied Eloise into the somber old mansion.

"Where do we go from here?" Eloise said.

"To the library."

Hand in hand they ascended the broad stairs.

"Eloise," he said, "we've got to figure out who got your

uncle to open the safe, and then prove it. Who else would have had the combination?"

Eloise sighed wearily. "Nobody. Uncle Gilbert opened the safe often during the bargaining, but never while Dumaine was here, so he couldn't have noted it. He'd not have had any reason to until after Bert Collins sold the Liberty Bonds for uncle."

"By the way," wondered Landon, "where has Bert been ever since Saturday?"

"He's kept away from here," said the girl.

"He'd better! Did you have the police check up on his whereabouts for the last week or so?"

"Yes. But he not only gave a straightforward account of himself, but also still has the keys — showed them to the police."

"He might have lent them to someone," Landon hopefully suggested.

"At least not on the night of the — the robbery," said Eloise, with a little catch in her voice, "for that girl he was with at the party had her hooks on him all evening. Anyway, why worry about keys, with that magnolia tree standing right there within easy reach of the window?"

"That's right," Landon agreed. "And say! That magnolia gives me another idea. Someone, posted in that tree with a pair of field glasses, could have watched your uncle and gotten the combination! I'll see how far away I can read the numbers with my naked eyes."

He backed slowly toward the window.

"Look out!" she warned.

Landon wheeled and reached in his pocket for his gun. He tripped on the fringe of the rug and crashed against the front of one of the desks.

"Oh, I'm so sorry! I was trying to warn you not to bump into that desk."

Landon ruefully eyed the front of the desk as he regained his feet; but he suddenly dropped to his knees before it.

"That's odd!" he muttered, frowning. "I never saw that before."

He indicated a place in the back of the desk a few inches above the floor, where a round plug about the size of a quarter-dollar, and stained to match the color of the wood, had been pushed in slightly.

He pushed the plug. It slipped through, leaving a small round hole slanting downward and into the large double drawer on the right of the desk. He jerked the front of the drawer. It came off, leaving the rest still in place. He pulled out the remainder of the drawer.

"What on earth are you doing?" said Eloise.

"Frankly, I don't know," Landon replied. "It's just odd — and it's certainly no accident, this freshly drilled hole."

"Oh, by the way," Eloise broke into his pondering, "I told the police about your getting that call from the bell captain at the Roosevelt, saying that Uncle Gilbert wanted you to hurry home and get the manuscript of his lecture. But the bell captain and all the bellhops deny having sent any such message."

"Which proves that that call was framed. Well, let's not get led off on a tangent. I'll get out into the tree and see how the safe looks from there. You stand in front of it, to represent your uncle."

"I'm too small," she objected. "You stand in front of the safe, and I'll take your picture with Uncle's Cine-Kodak from inside the window, but from the direction of the tree, while you pretend to be opening the safe."

"By Jove!" he exclaimed. "That's how they did it. Your uncle himself suggested the method. His bluff. Shooting a reel of film, and declaring that, even if he didn't buy the rug, he'd at least have a color-picture of it. And that got to Panopoulos, or to Barloff, whoever he is. A man in the magnolia tree could have photographed your uncle opening the safe, could have done it weeks ago. The film could have been enlarged where it showed the end of each spin of the dial. Let's try it."

Eloise brought her uncle's movie camera, and placed it on one of the desks, pointing, toward the wall safe.

"Now you twirl the dials," she said. "No need for me to get out into the tree. All we want to find out is whether the numbers will register on the film. This camera will work by electric light."

"Oke. Shoot!" He spun the dial of the safe. Then, "Go ahead and run the camera."

"I am," she replied. "Can't you hear the motor?"

He shook his head, and continued to operate the safe. Finally she snapped the control.

"But," she objected, "it will be about five days before we can get this reel back from the finisher."

"No," said Landon. "I'll take it to my room, cut off a two-foot strip, and develop it just like Kodak film, by hand. I can get a developing set in a drug store. Then in the morning, if we're on the right track, I'll dope out some means of getting the company to check their records. There can't have been so very many motion picture reels developed for New Orleans customers during the last few weeks."

He removed the exposed reel from the camera and thrust it into his pocket.

"And now I must hurry along," he said. "Among other things, I'm going back to get the prayer rug from the alley near Dumaine's store."

"Why?"

"Give it back to Dumaine. Then tip off the police to keep an eye on him, to see who goes after it."

"Good night — dear. And do be careful."

She let him out through the back door, near the garage. From the rear drive he stealthily approached the street. All clear — until he reached the sidewalk.

A man emerged from behind a nearby tree. Landon wheeled, reaching for his pistol, but a heavy hand caught his shoulder from behind. A voice rasped in his ear, "Hold it, brother!"

And the one approaching from the front disclosed a silver shield gleaming in the glow of distant street lights.

"We rather figured we'd find you here, Landon," he said. "Come along with us to Headquarters."

Out of the Frying Pan

Ray Landon meekly submitted to arrest. His two captors led him to a waiting car, parked in the next block. There they searched him thoroughly, and removed his gun and the reel of film.

"Ah!" one of them exclaimed. "The missing color film of the prayer rug! I figured it hadn't been stolen."

"That's one on you!" chuckled Landon. "It's unexposed film. Take a look if you don't believe me!"

They handcuffed Landon, boosted him into the car and started off. He slumped down in his seat, trying to devise a line of argument to persuade the police to investigate his flimsy clues.

Suddenly he sat erect. "This is a hell of a way to go to police headquarters!"

"Police! We're taking you to Barloff!"

Landon settled back against the cushions of the car. He concealed his elation. Nothing could be better than meeting the one man who was the key to the tangle. That is, if Landon survived the encounter.

"So this is Captain Landon!" sneered one of his captors. "The police must be saps to call you a hard guy!"

Landon ignored the gibe.

"Better blindfold him," suggested the other. "We're getting near."

They bandaged his eyes; and long before the car crunched to a halt in a graveled driveway, Landon had lost all sense of direction.

His captors dragged him from the car, prodded him up five steps, across a broad gallery, and down a hallway. There they halted. A soft voice purred, "The master will receive the guests here in the library."

Something odd about that voice. Though not familiar, its subtle overtones awoke lurking memories.

Landon's two guards hustled him ahead, then swung right.

"At your pleasure," one of them respectfully announced.

"Remove the blindfold." A second purring voice, and with that same subtle, lurking ghost of familiarity.

Landon blinked at the sudden glare of light. He stood in an ornately furnished drawing-room, confronting a portly man in full evening dress. His face was dark and grim as his black eyes; his nose was a commanding beak. A small gardenia blossomed on one lapel.

"Well, Captain Landon!" he purred, stroking his short black beard. "This is a pleasure!"

Barloff — his allies were Russian, but he obviously was an Arab. Then it clicked: Shah Ismail's rug must have been smuggled out of Persia and across Russia; and this self-styled Barloff tallied closely with descriptions of a bandit whose doings were a byword from Cairo to Turkistan.

"*W'aleikum as-salaam wa barakat 'ul-lahi, ya skaykh!*" Landon greeted in Arabic. Then, grinning amiably, "Barloff — but this is as good as any of the names mentioned when the King of Iraq put a price on your head. So you're a rug dealer now, eh?"

Barloff started, and his lips tightened; then they relaxed in a smile and he replied in Arabic, "Captain, perhaps we two can trade?"

"You might," countered Landon, wondering at the implied proposition, "release my hands."

The Arab murmured an order, and as his Russian henchmen unlocked the handcuffs, he continued, "I am certain you did not kill Foster. I've heard as much of you as you have of me. Captain Landon would not kill a benefactor. And since you could easily leave New Orleans, you must be staying to try and clear yourself."

Landon nodded. Things were coming his way.

"Neither did *we* kill Foster. We want Shah Ismail's rug. Help us get it and we will help clear you. Allah will make it easy for you."

Maybe Allah would, but Landon temporized: "How should I know where it is? Ask Dumaine."

"Dumaine, before he died —" Barloff paused to let his smile drive the words home — "said you took it. That rings true."

Little doubt how Dumaine died — or why!

"Too bad, Barloff. That spoils my best chance of clearing myself."

"I have information that would help."

"Maybe." Landon was on thin ice. Dodging Dumaine's fate would require slick work. "Anyhow, I hid the rug."

"Where?"

"We'll get to that," evaded Landon. "Your frankness about Dumaine hints that you'll make it darn sure I'll never be talkative."

Barloff laughed and gestured reassuringly.

"My careless remark, even if made to the whole world,

wouldn't hurt me. And once I get the rug, I'll be gone before you could get anyone to listen to you. Clearing yourself will leave you little time to worry about Dumaine's — ah — mishap, one might call it."

"Reasonable," agreed Landon. Which it was; reasonable. But still — it did have fishhooks. "Let's go, then. I'll play. But give me the roll of film."

"Very well. Vassili, handcuff him again, while I change my clothes. And stuff the film into his pocket. You can see it hasn't been developed."

Barloff presently returned, wearing an inconspicuous business suit. Landon, again blindfolded, was led out to the car.

After a few minutes' drive the blindfold was removed. They were entering the downtown New Orleans. It was now around midnight, and the streets were nearly deserted.

Landon directed them toward Dumaine's place. The car halted at the end of the alley.

"Ivan, you sit in the car and watch this end of the alley," Barloff commanded. "Vassili, you go on ahead of us to guard the other end. Yakushev, you come with us. And, by the way, Captain, better go ahead of us. And be careful. No false moves."

As Vassili ran on ahead, Landon, Barloff and Yakushev entered the dark depths of the alley.

"And now where is the prayer rug?" Barloff said.

"I'll show you," Landon replied. Barloff's eagerness to *know*, instead of waiting to see, renewed Landon's suspicion that the deal was to be one-sided. While Barloff scarcely needed resort to treachery, he might decide to play safe. And Landon saw his chance to beat him to it.

Instead of heading to where the rug was hidden, he led the captors toward the doorway through which Panopoulos had taken him earlier in the evening — this same evening, though it seemed weeks rather than hours ago.

"It's in here," he lied. "Just a second — I'll drag it out."

"Where?" That same eager reiteration.

"Get the key so you can turn me loose," temporized Landon, "when I hand you the rug. This neighborhood is tricky, and if we have to run for it, I want my hands clear. We can meet later, where you can give me the evidence I need —"

"Hmmm . . . cautious," murmured Barloff. Then, after getting the key from Yakushev, he added, "And that reminds me. Just to be sure you'll be discreet, I'll mail the evidence to Miss Foster."

Barloff's show of counter-caution almost masked his play to lull Landon's suspicions — almost, but not quite.

Landon opened the door. Barloff followed, closing it after him. The locality was dangerous, and if the police were on the prowl, the closed door would help.

Landon advanced across the courtyard, and into the passageway through which Panopoulos had led him to the street. Barloff's gun prodded his back.

With his manacled hands, Landon groped slowly along the walls of the passageway.

"Here! Feel in here!"

Barloff eagerly pressed forward. His pistol-muzzle shifted. This was the moment for which Landon had been waiting. He wheeled, knocking the barrel out of line, and driving one knee up to Barloff's groin, and followed through with both shackled fists sinking him in the stomach.

Pay-day! The Arab collapsed, paralyzed. His gun clattered to the flagstones.

Landon retrieved the gun, then fished in Barloff's pockets and found the key. He held it in his teeth, and in a moment unlocked the manacles. That done, he snapped them on Barloff, so as to fasten him to an iron window-grating.

Barloff, though breathing, was still too weak to groan.

One end of the passageway led to the street, and safety. The other was guarded by Yakushev. Beyond him was the wall over which Landon had thrown the bundled up prayer rug earlier in the evening. He retraced his steps. Must get the rug. It was evidence.

As he stepped from the courtyard to the alley, he turned and over his shoulder remarked, as if to someone just following, "Well, Barloff, I hope you're satisfied, now that you have the rug."

Yakushev exclaimed and crowded close. Landon's pistol checked him.

"Not a yeep, or I'll plug you," he warned, taking the Russian's gun. But instead of pocketing the weapon, he smacked Yakushev across the head with it.

Then he crossed the narrow alley, pocketed both guns and bounded up, to catch the crest of the wall with his hands. And then Vassili, at the further end of the alley, sensed trouble. As Landon pulled himself to the top of the wall, a shot rang behind him. A slug jerked through his coat, raking his back. Another blast — but he dropped from the barrier as lead whizzed past and ricocheted from a wall beyond. Recovering from the impact, Landon groped in an angle of the courtyard. He found a bundle, seized it, and struggled to his feet.

Landon was concealed by dense gloom; but someone, clearing the wall he'd just scaled, was silhouetted against the sky-glow. Someone else was running down the alley. Vassili and Ivan! In their position, they had nerve to spare, chasing Landon!

He snapped his pistol into line. *Smack!* A yell, and the head disappeared. Pursuit was checked, but the heat was on now!

Landon turned and groped his way toward the house that enclosed the court. In the darkness he found a door. It was locked. Feeling along the face of the building, he found a window — open. He stealthily cleared the still.

He was in a perfumed silence. A decidedly feminine sweetness burdened the air. But not a sound. Bundle under his arm, Landon picked his way, his free hand feeling ahead of him for unseen obstacles. Once out of the house, he had a chance.

Another pace . . . and another . . . some *Vieux Carré* beauty did go for *Nuit Amou-reuse* in a large way! Thank God she was out — or was she?

A chair blocked him. He turned, but a shoe threw him off balance — and something low and soft, catching his chin at the wrong instant, completed the job. He pitched forward, landing on a low bed. A shrill scream, and someone slight, energetic and feminine writhed clear of him.

Landon flung himself backward. Landing afoul of the chair, he crashed to the floor. A light snapped on. He scrambled to his feet — but not in time.

"Don't move, or I'll shoot!"

A tiny pearl-handled Luger stared him in the face. Behind the unwavering weapon was an extremely pretty olive-skinned girl, clad in a smart blue robe of Russian design.

When Danger Pursues

LANDON swallowed his admiration and his heart at one gulp. Something had to be done in a hurry. "That gun makes me nervous," he began, making a good effort at an engaging smile. "I lost my keys and —"

But before he could get as far as reminding her that burglars don't *enter* with baggage, she snapped, "Drop that bundle, and reach for the ceiling!"

"Absolutely," agreed Landon. "And speaking of bundles —"

But instead of dropping it, be flung the rug at her pistol-hand. The Luger crackled, but before she could jerk a second shot. Landon had closed in and wrenched it from her grasp.

"Sorry, darling." he apologized, as he retrieved his bundle, "but I'm in an awful hurry!"

Her violet eyes narrowed, and she nodded knowingly.

"Why didn't you say so?" she asked, smiling amiably. "I heard the shooting out there and — but if you're in a jam, better hide here. They'll never imagine —"

"Thanks a lot." She was right, but her sweetness was a bit overdone — like her perfume. With significant abstraction he fingered Barloff's pistol as he added, "Better stay right where you are — you look perfectly lovely that way — while I check out. Be seeing you sometime later."

"That's a promise!" she smiled. "And don't forget the address."

The sudden intentness of her eyes contradicted her lips. She must have recognized him and was hoping to trap him, later.

"Not a yeep out of you," he warned.

Pistol leveled, Landon backed toward the door. The encounter, though brief, had cost precious seconds. The screech of brakes, the pounding on doors, and the uproar of voices in the alley told him that the police had arrived. Flashlight beams crisscrossed the courtyard he had just left.

The door behind Landon was locked.

"Where's the key?" he snapped.

"Try and find it!" the girl challenged, laughing maliciously.

"Suit yourself!" retorted Landon. "If I have to stay and shoot it out, you're going into that clothes closet with me, and —"

He advanced a pace, shifting his pistol to his left, and reaching out with his right. That settled her. She cried out and gestured toward the dresser.

There was her key. But as Landon snatched it, two uniformed figures dropped into the court. He lost an instant snapping off the lights. A yell from without: a command to halt.

Landon sprayed the window with lead. The machine-gun rattle would make them keep their heads down as they advanced. During the scant seconds he won, Landon unlocked the brunette beauty's door. She was shrieking to the whole *Vieux Carré*. A pistol blast, the smack of lead, and a yard of plaster clattered to the floor as Landon bounded to the hallway. Slugs riddled the panel; but he paused, locking the door from the outside. The barrier would gain him the time he had lost.

As he reached the rear gallery, he heard a rumble of gruff voices, accented with feminine hysteria. Then a pounding, and the creak of wrenching door-panels. But that faded as he scaled a low wall and dropped into an adjoining court. The occupants of the building he had left had either ducked for cover, or were heading for the main disturbance.

He finally emerged on Bourbon Street and headed uptown. He reached his hotel, once more in the clear — for a while.

The first thing that he did was to shave off the rest of his mustache. Enough people had now seen him with it, even in its changed form, so that it would no longer serve as a disguise.

His bullet-creased back was becoming annoying. But with the aid of two mirrors, he determined that the wound was superficial — a dab of iodine and an awkward bit of bandaging settled it. But, tired though he was, he had to develop the film.

He ventured out again, picked up an amateur developing kit at an all-night drug store, and, on the way, mailed the prayer rug to Eloise. To keep it in his hotel room would add to his risks. Thin and of silk, it folded readily; he guessed the weight, and twenty-four-hour service at the main post office provided stamps.

When he finally turned in for a few hours' sleep, his fingers were stained with chemicals and his head was swimming. But the developed film demonstrated that a clear picture could be taken at night with the professor's movie camera — clear enough so that the combination of the safe could be seen with a glass.

Landon slept late the next morning. Around ten o'clock, he came down for breakfast. And since the absence of his mustache might be noticed if he ate where he had been seen recently, he went to a small arm-chair restaurant a short distance from the hotel. He'd need a new hideout, quickly!

On the way he bought a morning *Picayune* and spread it out and read it as he had his breakfast.

The front page was good: "Captain Landon overpowers Alcide Dumaine and two customers —" Customers, eh? So that's what Dumaine called the two gunmen of Panopoulos? No wonder the police let them go!

"— and escapes police with customary daring. Soldier of fortune kills three accomplices —" Accomplices! Two of 'em were customers a minute ago!

"— in desperate gun-battle in rooming house, quarreling over division of the loot.

"Fourth victim dies while escaping in taxicab." Poor Jake!

"Landon later returns and murders Dumaine in cold blood." Barloff's work!

"Then holds up Glenn Thomas, a cotton buyer from New York —" Couldn't Barloff think up a better alias than that?

"Wounds Thomas's chauffeur in the head, but not seriously." Too bad about that not seriously part!

"Escapes through house of Jeannette Levaseur, cabaret dancer. Blocks police with fusillade while fleeing from her bedroom. The Levaseur woman is being held in jail on suspicion. She denies knowing Landon." Landon grinned reminiscently.

Then his grin faded as he saw, pictured on the page in front of him, the steel-trap features of John Healy, Chief of Detectives, and read his promise:

"Landon, dead or alive, within twenty-four hours!"

His eyes strayed from Healy's picture to that of the alluring Jeannette Levaseur. Eloise must already have read the account. And the reporters of course would feature the dancer and his midnight call. Murder was one thing, but to be branded as a friend of the notorious Levaseur woman —!

He hurriedly gulped his coffee, paid his check, and headed for a telephone booth. Healy or no Healy, he *had* to speak to Eloise.

Eloise herself answered the phone.

"Darling, this is Ray," he said. "I never saw that woman before I escaped last night."

"Silly!" she laughed. "Of course you didn't! But who killed Dumaine?"

"Tell you later. I've got to skip out before they trace this call. *Our experiment is okay.*"

He hung up and hurried from the restaurant, glancing both ways as he emerged. In one direction were two policemen, talking together on a corner. And from the other direction came the one man in all New Orleans whom Landon most feared to meet, the one man who knew him intimately enough to recognize him in spite of his trimmed eyebrows and absent mustache: Bert Collins, private secretary to the late Professor Foster.

But Collins hadn't yet seen him, so Landon ducked across the street. Glancing back, he saw that Collins was following him, but still apparently unaware of his identity. Landon ducked back into a doorway.

Once inside, he looked about him. The room was crowded with men, mostly standing up. Along one side of the room was a large blackboard, on which a clerk standing on a stool was chalking figures: "20 1/8, 20 1/4, 20 1/2."

This was the stock-brokerage office of Bennett & Keene.

Landon seated himself in an inconspicuous corner and pretended to be studying an investment bulletin. Neither

Collins nor the police would think to look for him here. The hangers-on, either actual traders or tapeworms, would be too much interested in the market to have any thoughts for trifles like murder.

And then came a familiar voice, low, but clear above the clatter of the teletype and the orders snapped into the battery of hand-sets on the desks of the customers' men: "Buy Fourth Liberty Loan — ten one-thousands and a five hundred.

"Yes, at market."

Landon froze against the leather upholstery of his chair. Bert Collins was speaking. Landon dared not even risk a glance; nor was a glance necessary to assure him that fate stood at the nearby desk.

"Just take a seat," the customers' man was saying. "We'll have a confirmation for you in a minute, Mr. Collins."

Of course Collins might walk into the reference room to wait, but the seats right beside Landon would be the most handy. Landon felt the perspiration cropping out on his forehead and trickling down his cheeks. Bennett & Keene's, of all places — with half a dozen other houses that Collins could have picked!

So this was why Collins had seemed to follow him across the street — Collins had been bound for the very doorway into which Landon had ducked to avoid him. What beastly luck!

Landon drew a deep breath, clenched his fists, tried to relax, to control himself, to assure himself that Collins would not expect to find him watching a quotation board.

Someone was taking the next seat. In spite of himself, Landon could not resist the temptation to glance up at his neighbor. He felt eyes boring into him. Then he saw the man get up again and go toward the reference room. The tall slouching form and the gray suit were familiar. Collins had undoubtedly recognized him, and was now on his way to the telephone to call police headquarters.

"I can beat that," was Landon's thought. "Just as he clears the door —" Landon rose slowly from his seat. There was plenty of time.

And then he saw that he had jumped at conclusions. The man in the gray suit had not been Collins. Collins himself was now standing directly before him. Their eyes met!

The consternation on Collins's pale features, and the expression of his blue eyes, left no doubt that he was terrified at confronting such a desperate killer face to face.

For an age-long instant both men stared. Landon recovered first, but before his fist could drive home it was too late.

"It's Landon!" shrieked Collins. "Stop him!" Landon's fist connected like the smack of a baseball bat; but Collins, recoiling in mortal terror even before the blow started, missed its full force. Even as he crashed backward into a chair, he repeated his outcry.

That precipitated a panic.

Landon charged into a knot of customers that blocked the narrow hall. Those nearest him gave way. Some dropped to the floor to avoid the burst of pistol fire which they expected. Those in the rear crowded forward, valiantly yelling to the others to seize Landon. He knew that he could reach the door in a few seconds. Those whom he could not hurdle he could knock down; but Gravier Street, the heart of the financial district, had hair-trigger nerves. At any moment bank guards, armed with sawed-off shotguns, would be in the street. Policemen would come dashing up.

A final rush, and Landon reached the sidewalk. Clear — but which way? There was an alley across the street, but Landon had no idea of what lay at its further end. He glanced swiftly, right, left, trying to see a way of escape.

A traffic officer was at that moment racking his motorcycle at the curbing to Landon's right front.

"What the hell's up?" he demanded, as he turned from his machine. Cries of "Landon! Landon!" came from the crowd that surged out of the brokerage house in the wake of the fleeing man.

No time for parley or strategy. Landon saw the officer's querying expression harden into grim recognition. But as the cop reached toward his holster, Landon charged, striking the officer's wrist. An instant after that paralyzing slice checked the draw, Landon's fist crashed home against the officer's jaw.

The impact sent the patrolman spinning to the gutter, his pistol clattering on the paving. Landon swung into the seat of the motorcycle, kicked the starting pedal, and roared off down the street. There were still a few seconds to spare before the pursuit could be organized and directed, but the odds were against him. A police department motorcycle ridden by a bare-headed civilian is harder to conceal than a carnival parade. A traffic officer hailed him as he sizzled past the first intersection, then blew his whistle.

Landon jammed on his brakes, whipped around the left of a street car, and charged through the cross traffic.

Dryades Street and its slums seemed the best refuge. There were alleys and crazily constructed buildings which concealed mazes of backyards. And then he saw Dryades Market looming up.

Landon snapped his fingers.

"Better yet!"

He ran the red betrayer into an alley, where he abandoned it, emerged on a parallel street, doubled back around the block, entered the long public market, and mingled with the crowd of shoppers. No one connected the noise of pursuit with this apparently casual arrival. He purchased an armful of vegetables, a bag of bananas, and several coconuts. The load, supported on his left forearm, afforded a partial screen of celery and turnip tops. He quite naturally cocked his head to one side to keep his purchases from falling; and with his free hand he held a banana, which he ate as he strolled up Dryades Street, paralleling Saint Charles, through slums within a stone's throw of the main drive of New Orleans.

His thoughts, sharpened by his recent narrow escape, began to assemble the contradictory fragments of evidence that pointed to the slayer of Professor Foster. Thus far, he had been dodging too much lead for thought.

Foster had not been forced by the thief to open the safe. On the contrary, the thief had obtained the combination by photography, had opened the safe himself, *had been surprised by the professor's unexpected return,* and had killed in self-defense. This eliminated Dumaine: the professor was returning to meet the dealer. It let out Chris Panopoulos and his thugs. They would have been in touch with Dumaine's movements, unless the Frenchman had staged the robbery — and that likewise was out. Barloff was the only remaining suspect — but how hang it on him?

Landon suddenly halted. The pieces clicked.

He glanced about. No pursuit in sight. He was in front of a cheap clothing store.

Entering, he asked, "Can you fix me up with a hat?"

The proprietor could, and quickly did.

"You keep these vegetables for me — I'll be back later."

With his new hat pulled down over his eyes, he strode briskly and resolutely to the Foster mansion.

Eloise admitted him, her dark eyes dismayed.

"Oh, Ray, what in the world do you mean coming here in broad daylight? I tried to tell you, but you hung up. The police know that you met me last night. That cab driver's story in the paper was faked, to trap you. Get away from here —"

"You don't know the half of it!" he retorted with a wry smile. "Collins recognized me at Bennett & Keene's stock exchange a few minutes ago. Let's go up to the library, and I'll tell you all about it."

On the way up the stairs, he briefly sketched his clash with Barloff, and his run in with Collins only a few minutes ago.

Eloise sighed and sank into a chair. "You simply must get out of town, Ray! Don't stay here another moment!"

"Nothing doing. I'm playing a hunch."

"Collins will surely lead the police —" She stopped. A car drew up before the house. Eloise parted the window drapes. "They're here now! Hide in that little storeroom, and when they enter you can —"

"No go," said Landon, stepping to another window. "The whole place is surrounded. Plainclothes and uniformed cops."

Another car pulled up to the curbing. A riot squad with sawed-off shotguns emerged. Landon regarded Eloise with a grim smile.

"Can't make it. Dozens of 'em, and they mean *dead or alive*. Pay day, darling!"

"I know where you can hide. They'll never think of looking in the —"

But before Eloise could name the corner that would afford a refuge, they heard footsteps in the hallway.

Eloise screamed. Landon whirled. Four plainclothesmen, with drawn pistols, stood in the entrance of the library. At their head was John Healy, the Chief of Detectives who had promised to take Landon, dead or alive, within twenty-four hours.

"Stand fast, Landon, and hoist 'em! Way up!" Healy's voice was calm, but the fierce gleam in his steel-blue eyes and the unwavering muzzle of his service thirty-eight told Landon that the gray-haired veteran was more formidable than a whole squad of his subordinates.

"Oh, all right," agreed Landon. Then, with an amiable grin, "Mighty glad you brought Mr. Collins along."

In the background Landon saw Professor Foster's secretary. It must have been his keys that had enabled the police to make their silent entry.

"Put the irons on him," snapped Healy. "I'll keep him covered. And watch your step!"

"If you have some extra handcuffs," said Landon, as the steel clicked about his wrists, "put 'em on Bert Collins."

"Come along, and cut out the bull!" growled one of the coppers, prodding him with the muzzle of his pistol, but Healy's eyes gleamed with sudden interest.

"What's that?" he demanded.

"I'm telling you who killed Professor Foster," answered Landon. "Shall I prove it to you now, or after you've let him go?"

Eloise regarded Collins with dark eyes narrowed and glittering. Healy turned to the secretary and sized him up.

"Wait a minute! Let's listen to this!" he said.

"Ridiculous!" protested Collins. "He's crazy. I was at the same party as Miss Foster until after midnight, and I can prove it by —"

"Your lady friend was so pie-eyed that she wouldn't know whether you left her alone for two minutes or twenty," retorted Landon. "Or long enough to kill Foster, shag me, and call the police. It's only a short taxi ride from here."

Collins started; then, after a perceptible pause during which he vacillated between derision and dignified denial, he countered, "Preposterous! Who saw me leave the party? And why should I have killed my employer?"

"Because you'd embezzled a bunch of his Liberty Bonds," said Landon. "There had been fifty thousand in bonds in Professor Foster's box in the bank. The professor never visited the box himself — always sent you. You stole — and sold — exactly ten thousand five hundred, I think, Bert."

Collins paled at Landon's mention of so exact a figure.

Landon continued, turning to Healy, "When the twenty-five thousand dollars was placed in the professor's wall safe, to buy the prayer rug, Collins saw his chance to make a theft which would not be traced to him. He intended to use part of the stolen money to replace his earlier speculations, and still be nearly fifteen thousand to the good. *He did use part of the stolen money that way this morning!*"

Collins swallowed, licked his lips. He dropped his eyes to avoid Eloise's accusing eyes. But Healy looked incredulous.

"You and Collins may have been in cahoots," he suggested. "How about it? Can you prove your story?"

"He can't." But Collins's protest was a prayer.

"Hell I can't!" retorted Landon. "You were buying bonds at Bennett & Keene's this morning — to replace your theft before the estate was settled. Where'd you get the ten thousand five hundred dollars to pay for them?"

"Spit it out, Collins," growled Healy. "Either Landon is nutty, or you've got plenty to explain. Why were you so anxious to have us catch Landon?"

"Open Foster's safe deposit box at the bank," said Landon. "That'll prove it."

"Look into it, O'Toole," directed Healy. "Right now!"

"I took the bonds," admitted Collins, seeing the futility of denial. "But I didn't kill him. And yon can't — I didn't leave the party, I tell you!"

"Shut up!" barked Healy. "If you'd steal, you'd kill. Never mind the bank right now, O'Toole. Take charge of this bird."

Steel closed about Collins's wrists.

"But I didn't kill him! He didn't catch me opening the safe. I couldn't open it. He never gave me the combination."

"He's right," Eloise reluctantly admitted, as Healy caught her eye.

"So of course he'd have given it to me, a comparative stranger?" was Landon's ironic retort.

"But you could have asked him to open it on some pretext, and then stabbed him!" cried Collins, regaining his courage.

"No fingerprints were found on the dial," countered Landon. Then, as Healy nodded, he continued, *"If Foster had opened his own safe, would either he or the person that killed him have wiped Foster's prints off?"*

"Bull's-eye!" exclaimed Healy. "Someone that knew the combination to open that box — and you, Collins —"

"But I didn't know the combination, I tell you!"

"Oh, yes, you did," contradicted Landon, his face grim, his eyes hard and relentless. "You made a movie of the professor when he opened the safe, and you read the numbers from the film. Eloise, get the camera. Sergeant, pull out the big drawer of that desk."

The front of the drawer came away in the officer's hand.

"Now pull out the rest of the drawer." The officer did so.

"See that plugged-up hole in the back? This camera" — Landon took the Cine-Kodak from Eloise — "isn't cranked. It runs by clockwork, and by jerking a string tied to the release Collins could have made the film without anyone's noticing that he was operating a camera concealed in the desk."

"How about it, Collins?" demanded Healy.

"Suppose there is a hole in that desk?" Collins's face was white. His voice cracked as he desperately denied Landon's assertions. Then, a sudden, triumphant gleam in his eyes, he said: "Find the film! That'll prove his point!"

Healy gritted his teeth. Collins's ready defiance proved that there must have been such a film — and that it must also have been destroyed.

"Too bad," he muttered. "Take 'em both along."

"Too bad hell!" countered Landon cheerfully. "I found a piece of the film. He forgot to burn all of it. It's in my left coat pocket. Somebody get it."

Healy reached into Landon's pocket and produced about a foot of miniature movie film. Collins slumped into a chair. He exhaled a long sigh.

Healy snatched the scrap of film from Landon's fingers.

"Quick! Give me that reading glass!" Then, as he peered at

the film: "You could get those numbers if you enlarged it enough on a screen."

He whirled toward Collins, who was staring dully at the mocking, silvery-gleaming safe, and thrust the scrap of film under his nose.

"Come clean!" he barked. "Thought you burned it all, eh? D'ya want to confess now, or" — Healy's heavy hand clutched him by the shoulder — "do I have to take it out of you at headquarters?"

Collins shrank from the scrap of film as though it were a living serpent. His muttered reply was scarcely articulate.

"I was sure he — everyone would be away. But he came back and caught me opening the safe. I killed him, but I didn't intend — in the beginning —"

"And then you phoned Whitman's party and got me to come to the house, to take the rap?" demanded Landon.

Collins nodded, muttered, "Yes."

"Take him away," commanded Healy. "Landon, you're still under arrest, until I can check up on the rest of your doings."

Healy removed Landon's handcuffs, phoned headquarters, then listened to Landon's account of the intricate mesh of treachery and counter-treachery that had been connected with Shah Ismail's prayer rug.

When Landon concluded, the gray-haired detective put his hand on his firm chin, pursed up his lips and narrowed his eyes thoughtfully.

"Hm!" he said. "And no wonder! Shah Ismail's prayer rug, is it? Faith, and it's *Satan's* prayer rug I call it. We have a request in at Headquarters right now to send it to the Persian *chargé d'affaires* at Washington, for return to his country. It's a national relic and sacred to an important sect of Moslems. No wonder it caused all this trouble!

"But where did you find that little piece of film? How would a smart fellow like Collins be that careless and leave it lying around?"

Landon glanced at Eloise and grinned. "I didn't find it. Miss Foster and I *made* it."

"*What?*"

"Sure. Look closely. That's me in front of the safe. Miss Foster shot it last night to find out whether you could really get the combination that way. I noticed the plug in the desk, but didn't connect it up in my mind with the camera until about half an hour ago. It had never occurred to me to bluff the case. But when Collins fairly asked for it, I finally tumbled. This piece is a negative, but Collins didn't notice that. And luckily, it caught fire while I was drying it, so that he thought it was a piece which he himself hadn't completely burned. He was too scared just now to be observant."

"But why didn't you bring the film to Headquarters?" demanded Healy. "Your story would —"

"If I had come to Headquarters, I'd have gotten a hunk of rubber hose over the bean, and the papers would have said, *'The police are momentarily expecting a confession.'* Furthermore, I didn't get the embezzlement slant until I heard Collins *buying* bonds instead of *selling* them. And it wasn't until after I'd stolen that motorcycle and made my escape and calmed down again that it occurred to me that the pictures had been taken through the hole in the desk. That made things click."

"But just the same," objected Healy, "you shouldn't have shot at those cops last night, and socked that motor cop this morning. He might have shot you. You took an awful chance making that useless getaway."

"So did Bert Collins," grinned Landon. "And as soon as you get out of here, I'm going to take a much longer chance."

As he spoke, his eyes shifted and he regarded Eloise inquiringly.

"If you never take any worse risks," she said, "you'll live a long time."

www.ingramcontent.com/pod-product-compliance
Lightning Source LLC
Chambersburg PA
CBHW030526020726
47494CB00004B/1250